ⓂORIGINALS

NEW WRITING FROM
BRITAIN'S OLDEST PUBLISHER

This is the second year of JM Originals,
a list from John Murray.
It is a home for fresh and distinctive new writing;
for books that provoke and entertain.

Marlow's Landing

Toby Vieira

JM ORIGINALS

First published in Great Britain in 2016 by JM Originals
An imprint of John Murray (Publishers)
An Hachette UK Company

2

© Toby Vieira 2016

A CIP catalogue record for this title is available from the British Library

Trade Paperback ISBN 978-1-47363-317-9
Ebook ISBN 978-1-47363-318-6

Typeset in Sabon MT by Palimpsest Book Production Ltd,
Falkirk, Stirlingshire

Printed and bound by CPI Group (UK) Ltd, Croydon, CRO 4YY

John Murray policy is to use papers that are natural, renewable
and recyclable products and made from wood grown in sustainable
forests. The logging and manufacturing processes are expected to
conform to the environmental regulations of the country of origin.

John Murray (Publishers)
Carmelite House
50 Victoria Embankment
London EC4Y 0DZ

www.johnmurray.co.uk

'You are so subtle, Marlow.'
'Who? I?'

Он не любит Москву?

Introductions

Call this a river.

Nothing stirs, nothing lurks beneath its dead grey surface. The tourist barges plod up and down: the Vice-Admiral Golubtsov; the Academician Berdichevsky.

Goldhaven knows about rivers. Real rivers, rivers that gurgle and gush and kill. Rivers bearing riches. Rivers that will snap at you, rivers with things stuck in their murky alluvium.

You had to be insane to go diving in it, or desperate, or both. Goldhaven was neither, and still he had jumped at the chance to put on the patchy old wetsuit, ripped and snapped at, one of its legs disconcertingly missing. Ouais il a pas eu de chance celui-là, the rig operator had said with a shrug when

Goldhaven asked. The rig was moored right in the middle of the river, it might have been the Kasaï, or perhaps it was the Tchikapa, or maybe the Charï, they're all the same really, fierce and teeming and alive. What do I do now, Goldhaven had asked. You go head first and you point the nozzle, the rig operator said. OK, Goldhaven said, and he did. Goodness knows what the rig operator made of him, he probably thought him a suicidal nut, no one in their right mind would go and brave this camouflage-coloured broth, no one apart from a few teenagers from the village round the next bend in the river, and they had no choice. But what did Goldhaven care. Goldhaven was not afraid. Goldhaven is never afraid. Goldhaven dived in, holding his breath, with nothing more than the ragged old wetsuit and a leaky mask.

How was that, Goldhaven asked when he was back on the wobbly planks of the rig, the thick plastic hose jerking down into the water, the pumps belching, the gruel of rocks and sand splattering into a trommel out aft. Impeccable, the rig operator said.

Goldhaven stripped off the patchy old Neoprene, stood in the blazing equatorial sun in his boxer shorts, his wet hair glistening like a big black pearl. Well, Goldhaven said, in English, It sure is the craziest form of mining known to man. The rig operator grinned and nodded. He did not understand a word.

4

Et maintenant on va déjeuner, Goldhaven said, and jumped overboard, cutting back in a smooth fast crawl to the chalky riverbank where his driver was filleting the largest African snook ever caught in this stretch of the river, slicing it up into little white sashimi rectangles, laying a little folding table with white linen, the engine of Goldhaven's Land Rover running on to power the cooler for the Montrachet—

But this, call this a river?

It's there, but that's about the only meaningful thing you can say about it. It's colourless, reflects nothing, contained by concrete embankments, flanked by freeways. Goldhaven is bored out of his wits. He's tapping the side of the bottle, pink, Cuvée Rosé, Laurent Perrier, they add a zero to the street value when charging it to your room tab here, but who cares. Goldhaven's favourite colour is pink. The Russians are not smiling. Five, in black leather jackets and gabardine trousers, looking out past Goldhaven at the river as they drink his champagne, the city, grey specks and ash-coloured turrets. Pink, Goldhaven says, and takes out a pen. Like this, he says, drawing on a napkin. A double triangle, one on top of the other, upside down. Pink, Goldhaven says, and again he taps the bottle with his pen, and then he draws a dollar sign. Bolshoi, he says, and the Russians are not looking. Bolshoi dollar. Another bottle sir, the waitress says. Pretty, blonde, petite, heavily made-up, purple fingernails. Goldhaven thinks she's been staring at him ever since he arrived. It's true that nothing becomes Goldhaven like north light. In profile, by the great curved window of the bourse, three storeys high, or here in the lobby of the Tretyakov Grand, cleft chin shaded by nascent stubble, his hair a lustrous carbon, his scar a romantic brass rubbing against the pale hue of his skin. But after seven measures of Khlebnoye Vino and too much overpriced champagne, who can tell.

Goldhaven came out here on the midday plane from Brussels on a scrap of hearsay. There's a geezer in Novaya Zemlya, deals with security in the processing plant. He's noticed some odd hues on the washing racks, some funny business in the sorting room. An additional container locked into the glove-box; boxes taken away outside the official dispatch slots; some new pieces of hardware in the compound car park, too fancy for a company salary. The geezer has a friend who comes to Antwerp on some tendering business. The friend has too many beers and starts chatting. And it does not take long for your average bit of Antwerp chit-chat to reach Goldhaven's ears. The kind of chit-chat that will prompt Goldhaven to speed down the motorway to Brussels and elbow his way onto the next plane to Moscow. Some intermediary who claims he has a line to the folks in Novaya Zemlya has arranged to meet Goldhaven in the lobby. Goldhaven is playing it by ear. Goldhaven does not speak Russian. The Russians ask for cigars, start puffing on log-sized Cubans. You know how to get some interesting stones, huh, Goldhaven says. The geezers drink and puff. One of them says something in Russian, the others laugh. You got stones, Goldhaven tries. The geezers drink and puff. Bolshoi dollar, Goldhaven says, again, one last try. Fuck, Goldhaven says, looking out at the river. The Russians laugh, get up. Let's go, one of them says, in English. The tab goes on Goldhaven's room. They march Goldhaven out to a black Dodge truck with gilded exhausts. Through the smoggy twilight they ride for an hour, maybe two, maybe three. There's a Russian rapster on full volume on the car stereo, and the men are punching the air to the beat. Somewhere in the suburbs, crumbling concrete slabs covered in garish neon hoardings as far as the eye can see, the truck takes a sudden swerve into an underground car park. Goldhaven is taken to a lift, up a dozen floors, maybe more, in through an armoured door.

The apartment is empty but for an old metal desk in the centre of the living room. A man in a dark suit sits behind the desk. Money, is all he says, pointing at the desk. I'd like to see the goods, Goldhaven says. First money, the man says. This runs counter to any buying etiquette Goldhaven can remember, but it does not look like he has much choice. He takes a bundle of crisp dollar bills from his pocket and drops them on the table. Nothing was said about numbers or transactions, so here is one hundred and fifty grand for starters. The man in the suit takes a scrap of paper from his briefcase, unwraps it carelessly. Two pale carbuncles, probably two carats each or thereabouts, tumble onto the scratched grey tabletop. Colour-wise, it is hard to tell from where Goldhaven is standing, though the stones seem to have a champagne twinkle of sorts. Goldhaven bends over, gets his loupe out. Instantly, the Russians are upon him, snatch the loupe away, have Goldhaven in an armlock. Whoawhoawhoa guys, Goldhaven tries as cordially as is possible in the circumstances. You buy we sell, the man with the suit says drily. And with that, Goldhaven is hustled out of the empty apartment, ushered down to the carpark and into the Dodge truck with the gilded exhausts. Goldhaven is dropped off on the quayside near the Pushkin Museum. He walks back to the hotel in a rage. In his hotel room, Goldhaven has a closer look at the goods. Even under the feeble bulb of the desk lamp, he can tell instantly he has been had. The stones are natural enough, but they are about as pink as a lump of charcoal: under a crude coating of pinkish-purple resin, the stones are a dirty khaki colour and awash with inclusions.

Goldhaven yanks open the mini-bar, crashes out on the bed.

At two in the morning, there is a knock on the door. Two suits and two uniforms. Goldhaven barely has the time to put his trousers on. Come with us, they say. The night receptionist looks away as Goldhaven is hustled out of the hotel and bundled into a grey Volga. A silent drive across town, somewhere downriver from the towers of the University. At length the car turns into a compound somewhere in the outer suburbs. Guards with sub-machine guns stand bored and shivering in the early morning chill. There is a flat concrete building at the centre, surrounded by a park and lit up by a blaze of floodlights. In a windowless meeting room with filing cabinets around the walls, a stocky man with a crewcut is waiting for Goldhaven. Have seat, he says, in passable English. We hope you enjoy stay in Russian Federation. You are here on business, yes, Mr Goldhaven. I'm a tourist, Goldhaven says. Of course you are tourist, the man says. We understand you undertake certain business activities, Mr Goldhaven. I am not sure I know what you are talking about, Goldhaven says. I am sure you know what I talk about, Mr Goldhaven. Or perhaps you want to call British consul. Or French consul? You are hard man to pin down, Mr Goldhaven. The man passes an old bakelite telephone across the table with a theatrical flourish. Goldhaven, who certainly does not want to call any consul, shrugs indifferently. So what exactly is this about, he says. Violation of foreign currency legislation, or what.

The stout man picks up the phone. One of the suits who picked Goldhaven up from his hotel room arrives with a brown envelope. What is this, Mr Goldhaven? They are the stones Goldhaven bought from the Russian conmen. Lousy lumps, full of dirt, worst buy of my life, Goldhaven is tempted to say, but thinks better of it. Uh, don't think I've ever seen those before, he says. Mr Goldhaven, do you know what is penalty in Russian Federation for unlicensed acquisition of unpolished gemstones? You could take very long holiday in very cold part of our country. Now, this – the stout man points to the paltry stones on the table – is not Russian goods. This is very, how do you say, poor impression of beautiful goods our country produces. Where do you think this is from? Goldhaven shrugs his shoulders. No idea. He has a pretty good idea they are from Mbuji-Mayi, but why would he share his hunch with these people. Exactly, says the the stout man. Congolese, and not even nice ones. You would not look at this if offered to you in the bourse. So to pay one-hundred and fifty thousand is, how do you say, a bit over the odd, Mr Goldhaven? Goldhaven says nothing, but he can see it coming. The Russians would not have brought him out here simply to read him his rights over a few carats of Congolese boart. Now you would not have come here from Antwerp for that, would you, the stout man says. And you do not come all the way here to meet Russian woman, Mr Goldhaven, did you. We know you like Flemish woman more than any other. Except African woman, maybe—

Goldhaven wasn't expecting this. The stout man picks up the phone. Would you like coffee, Mr Goldhaven? He puts the phone down. There is something you want, and it is not Russian woman. So we have supposition, shall we say, you want something else, something we want also. I think you have good idea what I mean.

Right now, the only thing Goldhaven wants is to get out and on a plane home. OK, he says, what do you want me to do. The stout man opens a file on the table. You are very gifted at finding stones, Mr Goldhaven, are you not. You have big, shall we say, reputation. So you will find pink stones, real stones. And you will find persons selling stones. You will find leak in the pipeline.

Goldhaven knows he is in no position to negotiate. Uh-huh, he says.

One month from now, you come back to Moscow. You stay in the Tretyakov. And you will have some stones. Big. Nice colour. Very pink. And names. The stout man gets up, signalling that Goldhaven is free to go. Goldhaven shrugs, and walks out, along the empty boulevards. Goldhaven has no intention of honouring his promise to the Russians. Goldhaven honours his contracts, as long as they are genuine. Goldhaven is no con. But what's the contractual value of an ambiguous and non-binding Uh-huh, uttered under duress. Bugger-all. There's no way Goldhaven is going back to Moscow. Far too cold; the girls snotty and expensive; the cops too well-informed.

Goldhaven has hurtled down the motorway and across the German border. There are times when Goldhaven feels more at ease after crossing a border. A month has passed since Moscow. Goldhaven has stopped in Dusseldorf, hit a bar off the Koenigsallee. Black velvet, tall girls in strapless cocktail dresses. Slick square-jawed guys with shaven torsos behind the bar. Eighties music, shiny suits and deep décolletés in the soft upholstered twilight. No one will recognize Goldhaven here. Goldhaven squats on a barstool, orders scotch, gin, brandy, pours all three together, downs them in a single gulp. He is alone, tonight, though chances are he will not finish the night alone. Hell no. Goldhaven has come here to forget, for now. Na, a girl with a snake tattoo and black lipstick says. Hey, Goldhaven says. You come from far, the girl asks. Well, Goldhaven says. I've been here, and I've been there. Drink? Sure, she says. A Rhinegold. Rhine what, Goldhaven says. You're not from here, ha, the girl says. Liquorice liquor and gin. What do you do, she asks. Hoho, Goldhaven says. Easy now, easy now. I'm just a guy in a bar, having a drink. Trying to get over some bad shit. A woman, the girl says. Well yeah, Goldhaven says, you're pretty smart, huh. I can tell, the girl says. She was very close to you, ja? Yeah, Goldhaven says. Real close. She was pretty special, huh. Yeah, Goldhaven says. You know, when you think you got something real special, you think it's gonna last, and then someone comes along, takes it all away, you know? Yeah, she says. Guys, huh? Yeah, Goldhaven says. Guys. You ever been to Africa? What do you mean, Africa, she says. Ever seen an African sunset, Goldhaven says. Heard the lovebirds chattering in the branches at dusk. Watched the crocodiles watching you from the riverbank. Crocodiles, she says. See this, Goldhaven says, and shows the scar on his face. Crocodile did that, Goldhaven says. Mensch, she says, awesome, and moves her barstool closer to Goldhaven's.

There's a momentary hush in the bar. The music seems to fade for a split second; the lights dim in the batting of an eyelid. A cold gust whips in from the street. A stout shadow of a man, bullet-shaped, a long black leather jacket over combat trousers, has stepped through the door, preceded by a boom of bad vibrations.

He sits down on a barstool next to Goldhaven. We talk, he says, not looking at anyone. But first we drink. Ginger ale and vodka. Ginger ale? The barman thinks he must have misheard. Ginger ale, the man says again, and the barman almost trips over in his rush to the fridge. Ah, ah, thirty euros bitte, the barman stammers. The man shrugs. He pays, he says, pointing at Goldhaven. What? Goldhaven has not paid much attention to the man in the long leather jacket. A nutter, or a bit of a joker, he thinks. He's joking, Goldhaven says to the barman. The man puts his hand on Goldhaven's shoulder, and it feels like Goldhaven's collarbone is being fed into a stonecrusher.

I pay, Goldhaven says. Fuck. Goldhaven takes a closer look at the man. Age indeterminate, broad nose slightly out of joint. Head almost shaved, a scar running from just below his eye to his upper lip, longer and etched more precisely than Goldhaven's. No tattoos. Ex-army, or ex-con. Or a copper. Something like that. A large steel pilot's watch with Cyrillic lettering on its blue and silver face. Oh man. Goldhaven feels a spasm in his stomach.

The bullet-shaped shadow of a man reaches inside his jacket, pulls out an envelope. He puts the envelope on the counter. Look, he says. Goldhaven picks up the envelope. The girl with the snake tattoo shifts uneasily on her stool. Goldhaven opens the envelope. There is a single photograph inside, black and white. A mugshot of Goldhaven, a little dated. Goldhaven wearing a pith helmet, by a river, palm trees and smiling natives in the background.

I find you, the man says, and pours the ginger ale down his throat, followed by a quickfire shot of vodka.

Who are you? Goldhaven says.

No, the man says, his voice cold and dispassionate as a vending machine. You don't ask questions. Zog Shikzahl ask questions. The man's accent is sour, lugubrious and Cyrillic.

Zog Shikzahl, huh. Goldhaven has never heard the name before. It sounds like a joke, but Goldhaven is sure it is not.

Zog Shikzahl asks for another ginger ale and vodka, drinks in silence. Goldhaven turns to the girl with the snake tattoo, but she has slipped away. Goldhaven's skeletons have caught up with him. And Goldhaven will not finish the night alone. But now he wishes he could.

We go, Zog Shikzahl says at long last. Goldhaven rues the sixty euros he has blown on ginger ale and vodka. He thinks of the night he could have had with the girl with the snake tattoo. He rues the two hundred clicks on the motorway. Zog Shikzahl lays his hand on Goldhaven's shoulder, and it drills a spasm into Goldhaven's left side. Where to, Goldhaven says. I ask, Zog Shikzahl says. He gets up, walks out, Goldhaven in tow, preceded by a wedge of worse vibes now than even before. Scheisse, was war'n das, the attendant kouroi mutter, and the girls, no shrinking violets either, press up against the walls in terror.

You drive, Zog Shikzahl says and walks close behind Goldhaven. There is a large bulge in the pocket of his leather jacket, and Goldhaven is not taking any chances. Key, Zog Shikzahl says. Goldhaven hands over his keys. In, Zog Shikzahl says. Goldhaven gets behind the wheel of his black beemer. Zog Shikzahl closes the door, aims a sharp focussed kick at the lock, gets in on the passenger side. Drive, Zog Shikzahl says. Goldhaven drives. Down the Koenigsallee. Down to the river, down to the Rhine. Past tedious meadows and sleeping cows. Up a concrete ramp. Onto a sliproad. But, Goldhaven says. Oh shit, Goldhaven says, and slows down.

No swearing in presence of Zog Shikzahl, Zog Shikzahl says. Drive, Zog Shikzahl says.

Goldhaven drives on, knocks over traffic cones, crashes through a wooden barrier, scrunches over a pile of gravel. Baustelle, the sign says. What the fuck does that mean, Goldhaven asks. No swearing in presence of Zog Shikzahl, Zog Shikzahl says, and lays his leaden hand on Goldhaven's shoulder. Goldhaven keeps driving, drives right on up the bridge. There is a sudden lurch, the nose of the car drops, a painful grating sound, the flash of sparks in the night. Stop, Zog Shikzahl says, calm, bored. Goldhaven hits the brakes. The airbag punches Goldhaven in the face. The car alarm comes on, blaring out into the still night.

An oily black surface passing way down below the car, occasional ripples in the scant moonlight. The Rhine. Another bridge fragment, ahead, across the river. The car sits balanced on the frazzled edge. Goldhaven tries to open his door, finds that it is jammed. Zog Shikzahl's kick. The man must be wearing steel-capped boots. Now we talk, Zog Shikzahl says and takes out a flickknife. You fucking psychopath, Goldhaven says under his breath. Zog Shikzahl puts his hand on Goldhaven's shoulder. The pain is like the sudden surge of an electric drill on full hammer setting. Zog Shikzahl pokes his flickknife at the airbag. It pops like a balloon. You have job, Zog Shikzahl says. You give word. No idea what you're talking about, Goldhaven says. Zog Shikzahl takes out a big felt-tip pen and starts writing in giant characters on the inside of Goldhaven's windscreen. Дурак. Dumbo, dumbo idyot, Zog Shikzahl says. You go to Moscow. You go in deep trouble. You make very angry very important people with much money. You promise you come back with good. Durak. Where you got good? Good?

Goldhaven doesn't get it. Good, he says, I don't know about good. Zog Shikzahl rubs two fingers together. Uh-huh, Goldhaven thinks, the goods. I got ripped off, he says, not my fault. Nothing to do with me. Durak and all that, yeah.

Zog Shikzahl gets out of the car, slams the door shut. Phew, Goldhaven thinks, and rues the write-off of his beemer. But then the car starts to shudder and move. Goldhaven looks in the rearview mirror, sees the cold expressionless face of Zog Shikzahl, his arms stretched out, pushing the back end of the beemer. The car starts to see-saw gently.

One

Up the River

I

If it wasn't for Goldhaven, I'd still be counting beans for the Indians behind their shop on Hoveniersstraat. A cosy commute from Mechelen to Antwerpen Centraal, nothing to write home about, but the pay was decent enough—

And then Goldhaven walks into the picture. Just my luck. I was babysitting for the Indians, taking a couple of Angolans out for dinner, and who's sitting at the next table but Goldhaven, his slicked-back hair shining like glazed Zirconium, his white shirt unbuttoned down to the wiry black fleece on his chest. He's dining some Flemish Barbie type but, soon as he sees the Angolans, he gets up and comes over all chummy, next thing you know he's going Saúde with the Angolans, Barbie's getting jumpy and throwing noxious glances, but Goldhaven knows a goldmine when he sees one, and *boy* would he like to get up close and cosy with these Angolans and their big shiny marbles.

Now, anyone tells the Indians someone's chatting up their Angolan connection, most of all a notorious renegade like Goldhaven, and I'll be on the next ferryboat back to Hull. But Goldhaven's not about to overplay his hand. He's managed to swap cards and arranged for the Angolans to drop in on his offices the next day. With that, Goldhaven's back at his table, sweet-talking Barbie, getting her in the mood; and I've had a slap on the back and a Keep it Up, Kid.

Next time I see Goldhaven, I'm over at the bourse with the Indians. Goldhaven's just loitering about the tables, on the lookout for some easy trade, and when the Indians go upstairs, briefly, with the client, Goldhaven sidles up like an old friend, all smiles. Ever thought what it would be like to get your hands on a big pink stone, he asks, be the first to see it, to feel it?

I leave Mechelen in a hurry. Too much of a hurry. I barely have time to kiss Kaat goodbye. We make love in a rush, in a night that's too short, alarm going off at five, thunder rolling on and off in the distance. Kaat does not come. A short sweaty night.

What exactly is this about, Kaat says. You know,

I say, business. You never travel, Kaat says in her blunt Flemish way, you're just an accountant. The Indians want me to check out the audit trail for some stuff, some complicated stuff. They don't trust the people down there. But you of all people, Kaat says. You wouldn't even know where to find it on the map, this St Andrew's, Kaat says, staring at the ceiling. It's on the coast, I say. The Caribbean. Beaches, rum. Calypso in the sun. I think.

Kaat does not like the sound of that.

Calypso in the sun. You bet. Skimpy bikinis in turquoise lagoons. Hot fun in the summertime. Bugger-all. Kaat need not have worried. The closest you get to the sea in St Andrew's is the backside of the sea-wall. There's no beach. Hundreds of miles of coastline, and not a single beach. Lumps of concrete piled up against hurricanes and floods. And the sea itself, about as turquoise here as a concrete barrier along the Antwerp–Brussels motorway. Mingle, Goldhaven had said, blend in. Be a tourist. What does Goldhaven know. There are no tourists in St Andrew's. The only people on the plane in from Miami were immigrants on home leave, grannies with bulging bagfuls of Hershey bars and DVDs, little girls all dolled up in beauty-pageant princess kitsch, and young guys, wannabe toughs with mirror shades and badly cut leather jackets back from driving airport cabs in Queens or stacking shelves in downtown Philadelphia.

They looked at me, unfeelingly, as one might at a lost sparrow flying up and down a supermarket aisle. Kaat need not have worried.

I hate broccoli, always have done, sight of it makes me want to throw up, and here I am, like a fly getting its nose pushed in the broccoli pie. Nothing but broccoli as far as the eye can see, green bump after green bump, and sometimes a stream snaking, milky-tea brown, going nowhere. And all of a sudden, the plane banks and goes into a stomach-churning dive. Cayata, the pilot says, pointing down with a grimace, and the broccoli morphs into trees, silly green spears just standing around, waiting for nothing, with not even a breeze to move them.

Cayata is a loose smattering of shacks by a bend in the river. You can get here in a couple of hours by renting an Islander at Willaerts Field back in Hopeton, the capital, on the coast, or you can come up here by boat, and goodness knows how long that'll take you, or whether you'd even make it.

It's been raining. The red soil has the springy feel of marshmallow pie. The smell's not good. There's all sorts of winged mischief in the air. By the patchy track leading from the airstrip to the first few houses, rubbish piles up in messy little mounds. From down here on the ground, the forest doesn't look one bit like broccoli. More like sticks planted randomly in the ground with torn green rags thrown on top.

Among the dozen or so huts that make up Cayata, I need to find the one that accommodates a certain Jocelynho, or Juscelinho, or the like – Goldhaven wasn't sure. But Goldhaven told me to find Jocelynho, and mention his name. From then on, it should be a simple in-and-out job. Jocelynho has the stone, and all I need to do is take it back to Hopeton and out of the country.

It takes some asking around to find Jocelynho's hut. Most of the locals shrug, suspiciously, looking up from their rickety tables, on which the tools of the trade are set out. The scales. The lamp. The sieves. They're Lebanese, mostly, round here, and keep themselves to themselves. Jocelynho, an old man sitting on a trunk by the river says at long last. Try dem dere hut, and he points to a stilted shack on the edge of the settlement, gnawed at by the soupy darkness of the jungle.

The stairs are shaky; there's a stained old tablecloth with tulips and windmills in the doorframe for a curtain. Up in the corner, a TV set is blaring out some Brazilian plantation soap. Where's Jocelynho? In a patchy armchair, a teenage girl lounges, olive-skinned, black-haired. Jocelynho's daughter? His mistress? Little droplets of sweat have formed on her forehead. A packet of doxycycline lies in her lap, carelessly torn open. Sitting at the only table in the room, by the open window, a little boy is playing with a set of grading sieves. Hi, I say, I'm looking for Jocelynho. The girl does not move. Staring immobile at some spot in the middle of the room. The boy shrugs his shoulders. Não há, não sei, he says, and points vaguely to the window, the forest.

Beyond Cayata and Jocelynho's name, I have nothing. No Plan B, no contacts. Not even a proper map. I swear, noisily. The girl keeps staring, doesn't bat an eyelid. The little boy gets back to clanging his sieves together, gliding them over the dirty tablecloth like a bevy of luxury yachts.

There's nothing for it but to stay. I stomp back to the airfield, tell the pilot he can fly back to Hopeton.

I wasn't planning on this. The only place in Cayata that will put up visitors is the brothel. It doesn't have a sign. There's a couple of Brazilian girls sitting on the patio outside, and three chicken-coop cubicles inside, wood-framed, hung with patchy curtains. At nightfall, occasional clients start trundling in; and the patio in front of the shack turns into a social club of sorts. A handful of buyers; a miner or two, fresh from the bush. Jocelynho, I ask, Jocelynho? It turns out Jocelynho went upriver a couple of days ago, out buying. Upriver? Only one way up, one of the miners says, and no way back, haha. Keep going long enough and you'll get to Brazil. But by then you'll be dead, man. Haha. Still, with a bit of luck I might get a boat tomorrow: one of the buyers is going to a landing upriver, a place called Marlow's, or Marlowe's, and he's got some space in the canoe, if I'm willing to pay. I am.

Where you going, man, one of the punters asks me, later, as things get into full swing and I sit watching the hands of my watch, thinking about the very big pink stone. Upriver, I say. Marlow's. Shit man, he says, what you doin' yourself Marlow's for, ain't no good never come out of Marlow's. I'm a tourist, I say. Birds beasts waterfalls pretty flowers. Shit, you got yourself the wrong country man, he says. You wanna do Guyana. You wanna do Brazil. You don't wanna do this place, man. Ain't but one reason to come and do yourself this place, he says, and rubs his dirty thumb and index together. So you going to Marlow's, huh. Knew a man who go to Marlow's once, he a good man, he want to hit the big one. He never come back, man. So what happened, I ask.

No one know what happen in Marlow's, he says. They say Marlow's got the jinx. You pay me a thousand bucks, no way I'm going to Marlow's. Bad people in Marlow's. Bad things happen in Marlow's. You ask me what happen in Marlow's? I say there's a bad man in Marlow's, he take your body and your soul, he tear you to bits.

The punter lets out an eerie cackle. The flimsy door to one of the cubicles opens, one of the girls beckons.

You listen to me man. You want a good time, you go where I go now. You don't do yourself Marlow's, man. And with that, the punter is gone.

The shack shudders in the night with groans and thrusts. Do I love Kaat? I like Kaat's no-nonsense Flemish smile. I like Kaat's long Flemish legs. I don't like Kaat's no-nonsense parents, cement merchants in some hole up by the Dutch border, all swimming-pool showrooms and garden centres and gnomes. And I know they disapprove of me. Do I love Kaat? I almost proposed to Kaat, once, in a tacky hotel on the Normandy coast one Valentine's Day. I'd started looking at rings in the displays of the pile-'em-high merchants everyone in the industry tells you to avoid at any cost. I didn't, in the end. We fell out just as I was about to pop the question over a *trou normand*; had some petty argument over something I have long since forgotten, drove home in a rush, didn't see each other for weeks. At times, perhaps, it has felt like love. At times I have just been glad I could pick up the phone, stuck in my suburban Flemish rut. I like Kaat's legs, long and smooth.

That was before. The shack shudders, the curtains rise from time to time; clients stick their head into my cubicle, pause, curse in some strange Portuguese creole, glower at me.

I'm woken at dawn by a shrieking racket in the

green canopy outside. The boatman's name is Old Road. *Old Road?* Place where I was born, he says. And with that he's cast off from the wedge of sand that is Cayata's harbour. And then it's wilting green stalks and heat. The buyer sits stony-faced in the bow, his arms folded around a rubbed-down leather attaché case. I sit amidships, and Old Road brings up the rear with his coughing outboard. No one talks; the forest murmurs; occasionally the canoe will hit a bump under its keel, and Old Road will shout *cayman* with no other purpose than to scare his passengers. Some two hours into the sweltering morning, the river narrows; there's a makeshift dam of sticks and white sand, and dodgy earthworks by the starboard bank.

Uh, so, is this Marlow's, I venture. Marlow's, Old Road says, Marlow's long way up the river, man. I never seen *this* place before.

Up on the riverbank, a rough path has been cut into the sponge-green.

We gonna be long, I ask Old Road. Nobody knows, Old Road says. You know something? I don't know nothing, he says with a dark cackle. Old Road steers over to the riverbank and ties the boat to a tree. What's all this? I got to fish, he says. Fish? *Jaws*, he says with a chuckle, and throws a line into the olive-hued broth.

I get out and follow the path up into the green.

There is a clearing further in, or what might pass for a clearing here. Nothing's ever clear here, everything just grows, turns foul, sinks into the slime or is swallowed alive by the creeping chlorophyll. Huddled up against the bunched greens on one side, patches of canvas lean on rickety shafts. A rough table, old aluminium pans, bits of bedding, cans of *feijão verde*. A boxy old TV set. A generator. Whoever set up the camp left in a hurry. An old issue of Frowstein's Market Monitor. Opened on a feature on how to price fancies. *Fancies?* Maybe this was Jocelynho's camp? But then again, Brazilian diggers are a dozen a dime, this neck of the woods.

Across the white sands, the brown river gurgles and foams, steadily eroding the dam back into the flow of things. At this rate, there won't be anything left a month or two from now.

When Old Road hauls in his line, the sun is filtered through the canopies that line the river bank. Clouds of mosquitoes rise from the dirt-brown pallor of the river. All of a sudden, Old Road is looking worried. Move on man, he says, move on. We late. We push and shove the canoe across the makeshift dam.

2

Where am I, anyhow?

Somewhere on the Northern Seaboard. Somewhere just inside the outer edge of the board. Put a coin on the side of a table and give it a light shove with the side of your hand, that's how far in I am. Too far, and not far enough by far. The only map I have is full of white patches. There's no such thing as Cayata, on this map. The map is pasted into the back cover of a volume saying *Babbon's St Andrew's and the Maritime Territories* in quaint gold italic letters stamped on red cloth. It is not dated, but it looks old, and it is falling apart at the seams. Many of the pages are loose. Babbon's is the only travel guide I could find to these parts, in a second-hand bookshop off Grasmarkt in Antwerp. And half a paragraph in a Lonely Planet, which I did not buy. Don't bother going to St Andrew's, that one said. If you want fun in the sun, go to the real Caribbean, it said, go up North. Go to Trinidad. Go to Barbados. Don't go to St Andrew's. If you want wildlife and waterfalls, go to Guyana. If you want colonial cuteness, go to Georgetown. If you want rockets and pastis, go to Cayenne. Don't go to St Andrew's. St Andrew's is malaria and drive-by shootings and drugs. Don't go to St Andrew's. Some holiday. I'm on leave, officially. The Indians don't know a thing. If the Indians knew, they'd kill me. Or fire me there and then, at the very least. Who can blame them. If the company knew that the Indians employed someone moonlighting for Goldhaven, they'd make sure the Indians never got another trade.

Everybody knows that the company doesn't like Goldhaven. And everybody knows that Goldhaven doesn't like the company. After that encounter in the bourse, I met Goldhaven once more, in a bar by the waterfront. The kind of place where you'd expect to find Goldhaven, all hushed leather, baroque chandeliers, classy-looking girls, cocktails the price of a mid-range engagement ring. Not that I knew much about Goldhaven, then. Not that I know much about Goldhaven now. What does anyone know about Goldhaven? The usual gossip.

Goldhaven likes fish, preferably raw. Goldhaven

does not like meat. Goldhaven is not married. Goldhaven's favourite colour is pink, but that does not make him a sissy. Goldhaven knows how to handle a gun, but that does not make him a thug. Goldhaven has a heart, but like all his precious things, he keeps it locked away. And Goldhaven has a scar. Barely visible, a mere pink hint of a shadow across Goldhaven's lower jaw, as if he'd been freshly smacked by one of his women. The rumour is, he got it from a crocodile, sitting under a tree in the afternoon sun by the Sankuru river where he's set up camp for the night, reading some schmaltzy bit of airport dross to kill the time, waiting for one of his runners to come up and tell him about a stone, some rumour of a big stone, ready to jump in the Land Rover and bump over the dusty pistes for a day and a half to take a clay-stained handkerchief from a sucker in a torn T-shirt that says 'West Coast Champion's League'. And then he'd count the poor devil his dues in crisply pressed nouveaux zaïres – so many noughts, and the next day the sucker would be dead in a ditch anyway. So Goldhaven's sitting there, and he hears this pat-pat of little feet coming up just to his right and a little behind, four o'clock, thinks it's the runner. Except it's the crocodile, a real eight-foot stinker of a Nile crocodile, three-figure IQ and a tail the length and circumference of a racing yacht's boom. The croc's about to do his usual music-hall trick, sidle up all friendly and zoological to the length of white meat sitting there by the riverside, wink a little fraternal reptile wink, like, We're all brothers in this together, right, then with a single whiplash whack of his tail incapacitate his prey before dragging it, shhhlop, into the muddy brown waters of the Sankuru river and upstream to his larder. But Goldhaven's not about to sign off on a distinguished buying career and dodges out of the way before the croc has had a chance to execute his music-hall routine, only just catching the dragon sawed tail-end that snakes round the back of the tree and strikes Goldhaven from leeward in the subtlest swipe across his face. With blood seeping out of the crescent-shaped wound, Goldhaven rams the dime novel he's been reading up between the crocodile's jaws and with his bare fist lands a knock-out blow between its eyes. And with that, the croc, still unconscious, goes back into the Sankuru river, to become larder-fodder for one of his many cousins. Or so the story goes.

The scar was there, when I met Goldhaven in the bar; I had not noticed it in the bourse. Goldhaven had a chummy smile: knowing, complicit, understanding. He bought me one of the very expensive cocktails; it had a sliver of gold in it, I think, and left me feeling a little dizzy. Is it true, I asked, that your favourite colour is pink. My favourite colour,

Goldhaven said, used to be white. Now, he said. It's really quite straightforward. You take a holiday. No conflict of interest. If there's an issue with the Indians, I'll smooth it over. Why, I asked. Goldhaven's smile receded a little. Simple, he said. I don't have the time to go, myself. And I'm not everyone's flavour of the month, as you may have gathered. Some of the people down there may be a little unhappy at me barging in on their pipeline. So here's to a fresh face. Goldhaven ordered me another gold-streaked cocktail, and pushed an envelope across the table. Expenses, Goldhaven said. And a cut of the price when you bring back the stone. Goldhaven finished his drink. Not a fancy cocktail, just a very large whisky, neat. One more thing, he said. Be very discreet. Nothing declared, no forms. They're all thieves down there. Yes, but is it legal, I wanted to ask, but for Goldhaven the interview was over. Another knowing smile, a firm handshake. I finished my gold-streaked cocktail, and felt queasy. But Goldhaven was gone.

What does Babbon have to say about the part of the country Old Road is taking me to? Not much, since Old Road is heading into the heart of the biggest white patch on Babbon's map. Babbon, it turns out, never made it back from the white patch. Babbon died before he could finish his book. There is a quaint preface:

What little is known about the farther reaches of this northernmost expanse of the Amazon, we have learned from the last manuscript found upon the remains of Joshua Babbon, whose expedition to the spring of the Malakuzi in 1887 may have expanded our knowledge of this part of the forest by some considerable degree, but also implied Mr Babbon's own demise, as that of his companions and the loss of a not inconsiderable detail of native porters.

Whatever. I need to find Jocelynho and get the hell out of here.

Slow river, slick river, sick river. How much further to go, Old Road? Till we get there, man, says Old Road, and the dealer with his attaché case chuckles.

Another bend in the river, another crop of green stalks. Brown shapes below the milky dirt of the snaking stream. When night falls, Old Road ties up in a little lagoon. Disembarkation, gentlemen, he says. The buyer disappears in the undergrowth. Old Road stretches out in the wet sand and falls into a rough snore. And the caymans, Old Road, I say, what about the caymans? Old Road snores on. Above the river's tea-coloured surface, the winged legions are fuzzing into view. I stomp inland for a minute or two, kick the brush into a circular clearing, rig my net and bed down.

Night comes crashing in without a knock, just spreads its black-out sheets over the forest, and gives the crawling legions the thumbs-up. They come six-legged at first, with their shiny black and brown shields, antennae, humming wings glistening in the moonlight, tiny jaws bearing saws and scalpels and drills. And then they come eight-legged, bristling with hog-hair, the size of guinea-pigs, their eight-pack eyes sizing up the fresh cut of meat. I hear them parachuting out of unseen branches onto the taut trampoline of my net. They wrestle each other for a view to a kill; they hiss and they hum as they crawl, position themselves for the slightest let-up in the gauze that enshrouds me.

Around eleven, curled into an embryonic ball, dripping with grimy sweat, I fall into a nervous slumber. Brown-scaled, grey-fanged caymans catwalk across my dreams bearing sieves and sharpened spades, looking for the action. An ogre whose torn T-shirt says Juscelinho, or Jocelynho, is on the rampage in the broccoli fields, scattering stalks to the sickly warm winds, snapping Pipers and pirogues over his little finger.

A branch breaks somewhere in the forest. I sit up with a start, knock something hairy and tense off the top of my net and into the further reaches of darkness, where it bristles and hisses with venomous rage. Another twig creaks, closer at hand now. There is sniffing, panting, a big feline pang. Two pink diodes flare up above my bedstead. I pass out.

I dream of a grey city by another river, dull with a white glaze, circled by dead-eyed pigeons. Gothic towers barricade the horizon. Down in the huddle by Central Station, a lot of money is afoot. What am I doing here? Right, it's where the money is. I don't see it. I never get to see the goods. I stay in my back office. The Indians come and go, upstairs, in and out of their carpeted suites, the glitzy salons where they meet their high-end clients. Once a year, they all suit up in black tie and decamp to some big barge moored out in the Schelde, by the docks, kitted out for the night with red carpets and walkways and silver cutlery, and the industry has its annual ball. Have they ever offered me a ticket? It's been a while now that I've worked for the Indians. Not once have they invited me. The office empties, earlier than usual, there's a buzz in the air, wives in fancy gowns put their heads in the door, bow-ties are adjusted, knowing smiles exchanged. I've heard people brag, in the lift. They take you from the dockside to the barge in a courtesy launch, a Riva, all shiny brass and leather and wood. They bring the VIPs in by helicopter, landing on the roof of the barge, all lit up like a Christmas tree.

And there's a show. Models winched down onto the decks, bedecked with tiaras and necklaces and pendants. You can tell, I overheard one of the younger ones say once, a nephew perhaps or a second cousin's son, you can tell they're not ordinary girls, it's like they've got this presence, this thing, you know, like wow, makes your heart skip a beat when they brush past you, so close you could touch them.

And I go back to my office and my counting-machine. I've never been offered a ticket. I don't hang out with them. They have their haunts, I think. I imagine them in lush golf clubs along the coast where they meet up with the other Indian families to look at each other's Mercs and consult their astrologers about matches for their many sons and daughters and nephews and nieces, and plan weddings that cost as much as a very, very large stone. They wouldn't waste their breath on me. They keep themselves to themselves. They all keep themselves to themselves, the mineral dynasties, the gem kings, the Lebanese, the Israelis, the Chinese. And everyone, secretly, looks up to the company. You can tell the company men from a mile away. They have the neatest suits. The firmest handshakes. The most confident smiles. They keep a low profile, most of the time, but they know when to put on a show of force, and then they'll slip off again to their HQ in Nairobi, out of sight but never out of mind. Everyone wants to be a company man, really, deep down. I've never talked to them, and they'll never talk to me. Goldhaven's not one of them, though he knows them, and they know him. He'll never be one of them. I'll never be one of them. Perhaps that's why he chose me.

I circle the grey city with the dead-eyed pigeons. If they could see me now—

When I come to, the sun is filtered a mouldy shade of turquoise down to the forest floor. Clouds of green wingdings are swirling above puddles of green goo. My clothes are dripping wet. My arms are covered in itching little pink bumps. And my net has disappeared. Dammit. I get up, aching all over. There are people who would pay for this, to wallow with the bloody fauna and get bitten and trampled on. My dad would, if he had money to burn, and if he was alive; he made me stomp through sodden fields and over rainy bogs when I was ten, to see a bunch of herons squatting in a tree, or count the guillemots standing on some rocky pile, in the cold, pecking each other. It didn't do it for me, really. Yes but, I wanted to say. I felt sorry for the tree, spindly, black and leafless, which the herons had shat to death. And I felt sorry, in a way, for the guillemots, who would never be penguins.

My bag is where I left it, back by the river. Old

Road sits on a log, chewing some glutinous substance. The buyer sits in the canoe, clutching his case. So, er, what was that racket last night, I ask. Old Road shrugs his shoulders. Nobody know what them animal do in the night, he says. Nobody know. You leave well enough alone, man.

We continue upriver in silence. The mosquito bites on my arms swell into penny-sized pink platelets. Old Road gives the occasional chuckle when the canoe hits some unseen shape in the river and bucket-fuls of brown water slosh over the sides. Logs, maybe. Or something else.

I don't like the look of those logs, I say to no one in particular.

Old Road grunts. Only a fool in a boat be scared of a cayman, he says to no one in particular.

What do you mean, I say. Only a fool would not be scared of a cayman.

Only a fool be scared of a cayman in a boat, man, Old Road says again.

I don't know what you're talking about, I say. I'm not plunging my hand in this river.

Old Road spits in the ochre waves and mutters some ancient creole curse.

We chug along for an hour or two, and suddenly Old Road says, Cayman don't give shit about some piece of meat in a boat, man. Cayman he a smooth operator, he use his brains, he don't think with his jaws, man. You wanna know how cayman hunts, you listen to Old Road. Fuck you, man.

Old Road is silent for ten minutes or so. And then Old Road tells it how it is.

Cayman be a clever bastard, man. He sit down in the water like you sit in some hot tub in your fancy hotel in Hopeton, man. He sit, he float, he watch the world go by. He don't give shit about no boat, no man in a boat. He don't give shit about no tree-trunk floating down the river, man, he don't give shit about no fish swimming in the river. Cayman don't give shit about no dolphin jumpin' bout the water, man. Cayman know what he want. Cayman keep a good lookout, and all the while he be floatin' real quiet. You don't see cayman, but cayman sure see you, man. He know when you eat, when you sleep. He know when you go take a shit. He know who you talk to, he know how many stone you carry in them your pocket. He know your credit card number. And he sure know when you go wash in the river.

Old Road is interrupted by a flock of shrieking Froude's egrets rising in an explosion of white from the riverbank. There is a splash and a thrash in the water, then nothing.

And when cayman really know you, Old Road continues, he eat you.

We chug along in silence. The first body floats past around two in the afternoon.

3

Only suckers reply to ads in the classified section of *Accountancy Today*. Only suckers read *Accountancy Today*. Accountancy Today. Accountancy Tomorrow. And accountancy the day after that, and after that. Not if I can help it. Not if I get hold of the stone. An easy in-and-out job. No more accountancy, today or tomorrow. What you talkin about, Old Road says. I must have been talking to myself, lying back in the pirogue, in the heat, in the green stew, no longer wiping the streaming sweat off my face. Letting go. You wanna know who's in charge today, you talk to Old Road, he says. Old Road screws up his face and points at the muddy water.

I have never read *Accountancy Today*. I don't read,

if I can help it. Magazines, perhaps, the kind that don't have a lot of words in them. But I replied to that ad, just that once, and I got the job. I swapped one shade of grey for another. What do you know about the industry, one of the Indians asked me, the most junior cousin, or nephew, or the like, tasked with interviewing me when I came in on a cheap flight from Newcastle. Nothing, I said. Good, he said, we'll keep it that way. I thought that was it, but a week later I got a call. Antwerp, people said, the few who said anything, why the fuck do you want to go to Antwerp. Holland, they said, cheese and windmills and what not.

Antwerp, I said, is not in Holland. It's where the money is, I said, by way of an answer, quoting someone or something, I guess. And the money was good, or at least it looked good. Double what I got back home. And it looked sexy, somehow, the Indians' website, all sparkle and shine. No more going over the inventory declarations of the county council. I never could explain to people what I did, and who would have wanted to know. A pair of hands and eyes attached to a calculator with a silly paper roll. But it wasn't sexy, when I started with the Indians, in the end. An office like any other. A view across a dim courtyard, another office building on the other side, faces in ties. I cannot fathom what they do; but they seem to be having more fun than me. The Indians keep me here,

44

in their back office. I look at acronyms I do not understand and add up numbers, and that is that. I never get to see their stones up close, but once in a while, they will call me up to babysit a client. As a last resort of last resorts. I imagine the Indians busy at their never-ending weddings, eating sweet treacly things with silver foil, admiring wedding cakes the size of fountains, swaying to the drumbeat of a hundred beturbaned lackeys flown in for the occasion from Mumbai, or Gujarat, or Hyderabad, or wherever. They've never invited me to one of their weddings. They've never so much as invited me for a drink. They don't go for drinks. They do business, with each other mostly, and then I expect they go to their golf clubs, and each other's weddings, and then they're gone, off behind the walls and security cameras of their big houses in the southern suburbs, off to polish their Mercs and think about the next wedding. Oh no, I imagine them saying, we have the Angolans coming over, we can't let them down. Ah but, some bright spark will say, there's that accountant, and then a call will come through to my office, and a promise of a raise, and there goes my evening. And then Goldhaven waltzes into the picture.

The body is belly-up, but fresh enough not to be too bloated. Bearded, pink-skinned, eyes wide open. It has a tidy black spot on its left temple. Oh man, Old Road says, hauling the body in just long enough to take a closer look, then pushing it off into the khaki soup. This been real clean and close, Old Road says.

We cruise on for an hour or two up the river. The morning beats on my bare mosquito-eaten arms and bakes them a pink shade of scarlet. When we pull into the river bank, it is midday and there is not a sound above the green and brown. The animals have fled into the shade. Old Road ties the boat up on a pole by a small beach. There are shacks up by the trees. Another body lies face-down in the skin-coloured silt of the beach. So is this Marlow's, I ask. Old Road chuckles. You in a hurry man, you better take the express. This place called Li'l Nickery. Or some shit like 'at. Keep changin' name up here.

Under a corrugated iron roof, three Brazilian miners sit drinking gin, eyes dilated in anticipation of the next malaria attack. Packs of chloroquine are scattered on the table. Boa tarde, I say. A hollow-cheeked phantom of a man stalks past. The phantom is wearing a khaki shirt and knickerbockers and has a sergeant's stripes on his sleeve. The phantom sits down with the miners and takes a swig from the bottle of gin. One of the miners says something in Portuguese; the others laugh. The sergeant takes another swig from the bottle. Não percebe nada, the miner says with a grin, pointing at the sergeant. Them people bring nothing but trouble, the sergeant says to no one in particular. Used to be nothing but trees here. Them people and their money they bring bad manners and bad morals. We're good god-fearing people. Them people from over the border and their money and their stones and their drugs is nothing but trouble, man. One of the miners points to his head and says, Louco, or the like. The sergeant looks up at the mushy pastel sky and lets out a sudden dog-like yelp, then takes another swig from the bottle of gin. There is a solid black circle, the diameter of a pencil, on his left temple. Vinham a tarde, one of the Brazilians says. They come in the evening, the sergeant says to no one in particular, staring straight ahead. Just drop out of the trees. Wearing these strange rags, like aprons. All in tatters. Faces all painted in green. Hoods like you canna see their eyes. First thing they do is come up to the station. This big guy, he stick an AK in my face, tell me he want to see the officer in charge. I say he's talking to him, and ain't nobody but me for being in charge of. Say I take him down the buying office of Rorke & Co. So we go down to Rorke's, man says to open the safe. Soon as the safe door's open, he shove me down on the ground. Them bandits empty the safe there and then, right there, and ain't nothing I can do. I run, pull my gun, they start shooting. Whhooooahhh, the sergeant suddenly howls, wolflike. He takes a swig from the bottle and continues. I run, go for shelter over them there huts by the river. Bandits keep shooting. Damn bullet goes right through the hut. Slow it right down, man. But not enough. It's my skull that stops it, in and out, man. I shake my head and I feel a draught. The sergeant slaps the flat of his hand against his forehead, stands up and lets out a lion-like roar that has even the Brazilian miners choking on their gin. The sergeant sits down and stares at the bottle. When they is finished with Rorke's, them rascals move down the way and do the other buyers. Anyone don't want to hand over the goods or the money, bang! and straight in the river, man. An hour later, they out of here and not a stone left in town. Seem as though they heading upriver. Who know. Maybe they headin' for that place they call Marlow's. The sergeant gets up, brays like a wild ass, then walks off towards the river. The miners go on drinking gin. Have you seen Jocelynho, I ask, Sabe onde está o Jocelynho? O Jocelynho, one of the miners says, shrugs, and points upriver, vaguely.

I go back to the river. Old Road is sitting in the pirogue with a worried look on his grizzled face. The buyer has split. What's up, Old Road, I say. You wanna go to Marlow's, you better find some other fool. Marlow's no good this day, man. Why's that, Old Road, I say. We had a deal. The Boss don't give shit about no deal, Old Road says, casting a furtive look up at the ramshackle huts of Little Nickery. They say the Boss ain't happy. The Boss, I say. What boss. I'm your boss for the duration of this trip, remember. Old Road laughs. You be the Boss, I be the King Cayman, he says. You nobody, man. You a know-nothin' joke on stilts, man. You don't cross the Boss, Old Road says. Hey, I say. You keep saying that. So who is the Boss? You listen good, Old Road says. I tell you how it is. And then Old Road tells me how it is.

You don't cross the Boss. You don't mess with Macquarie. Ain't nothin' moves in the forest without Boss Macquarie givin' his noddin' to. You never think so, lookin' at the Boss. They say he lie in a hammock all day long. But he raise an eyebrow, you be sure there's gonna be one hell of a panic in the brush. The Boss lift a finger, everyone jumps. Jaguar and jackass, you be sure. The Boss lords it over all. And then he rakes in, man. All the chips, man, they end up on Macquarie's table.

Old Road pauses and looks at me. You nobody, man, next to the Boss. You got nothin' on the Boss. He old, so old. He older than them trees there, man. He been around when there nothin' but big cats here. He been around when there nothin' but big lizards out here eatin' each other. When nobody lay hand on them trees. He been here before the pork-knockers and the hookers. He been around when

nobody even dream of this Li'l Nickery shit. And
you know somethin', the Boss, he one of us. He ain't
your fancy struttin' piece of shine from town. The
Boss, he be a real piece of business, man, but he be
one of us. He talk just like me, man. He got skin
like you, man, but he talk like Old Road. He be a
pale brother, is what.

Old Road is grinning at me now. What do you
say to that, his grin is saying.

You know what they call Boss Macquarie, Old
Road says. No, I say. Mad Max Macquarie, Old Road
says. Master Macquarie. Max the Knife Macquarie.
You know where Boss Macquarie come from, Old
Road says. No, I say. Old Road leans over, his eyes
wide open, looks past me, points at something in
the distance, upriver. They say he come down one
day from the house of the gods. Old Road laughs.
But you don't wanna mess with the Boss. Any deal
go down this part of the woods, Boss Macquarie
gets his penny, man. He got his brethren all along
the river here. He got pork-knockers out there, calling
in every week. He got snitches in the landings up
and down the flow, man. You buy, you sell, you be
sure Boss Macquarie know before long. He got folks
on payroll all over. Old Road falls into a whisper,
looks up at the canopies hanging over the river. And
you know what, man. He got sentinels up the trees.
They got the eye on you. They hangin' up there,

countin' and stuff. They say they got nothin' but a machete and a quart of moonshine. You never see them, but they see you. And when you see them, you know you're headin' down the flow for good, man.

Old Road chuckles. Boss Macquarie, he got one on the man. Ain't no way the man gonna get to the Boss. The Boss take his dollar. Old Road points at the shacks of Little Nickery. Ain't nothing changing dirty hand here the Boss don't get his cut. You take a stone from the forest, you better give back to the forest. Like as the Boss is the forest, man. You take a whore up the river, you get a visa from the Boss. Ain't nobody get laid in the forest and the Boss don't get his dime. They say he keep it all up in a stash upriver. Green paper all round them walls. Green paper so thick like as you need a shovel, man. But nobody know. Ain't nobody see it and come back. Boss Macquarie, he say how it is, man. And you know what they say, you know-nothin' joke. Old Road stops grinning and gets serious. They say like Boss Macquarie ain't happy, now.

I shiver in the afternoon heat. I don't give a damn, I say to Old Road. I need to get to Marlow's. We had a deal. You not listening man, Old Road says. You don't wanna mess with the Boss. How much to go on to Marlow's, I say. Old Road looks up at the treeline, the shacks, the uncertain pastel-smudged sky. A thousand, he says. I rummage in my money-belt. Five-hundred, I

51

say. Get in that boat, Old Road says. Don't say I don't warn you, man. You crazy, man.

Old Road fires up the old outboard and casts off. What does Old Road know. Once I have the stone, once I've given Goldhaven the stone, once Goldhaven has paid out my share, I'll be able to buy Old Road and his silly pirogue many times over. Not that I'll want to. I don't know yet what I'll do with the money. Perhaps I'll get a new car. An SL convertible. I'll cruise up the driveway to one of those golf clubs, walk up to the table where the Indians are having one of their Sunday afternoon cabals, drawing dynastic diagrams on napkins and haggling over dowries, and hand over my letter of resignation. No, drop it on the table with a so long, boys. They'll gawp, speechless, then call security. But I'll be long gone, off down the coast to Deauville. Perhaps not. An SL is the kind of car the Indians would get their wives as an anniversary present. Perhaps I should get one for Kaat, instead. And send my letter by priority mail. I will picture them gawping as they read it. I have no idea if Kaat would want an SL. There are a lot of things I don't know about Kaat. I know the way her shoulderblades stand out when she lies face-down in bed, like the rear fins of a Cadillac El Dorado. At least that's what I imagine. I have never seen a Cadillac El Dorado. I like to pass my fingers over her smooth naked skin, the twin peaks, the broad plains in between, lightly rippled. Stop it you're tickling, she will say in her no-nonsense Flemish way. Perhaps she would not want an SL. Whatever. I would take Kaat to the poshest Flemish designers in the centre of town. The kind of places where the Indians might buy rags for their daughters. Kaat has the perfect figure. I don't know if Kaat is pretty, but she has the perfect figure. Her legs would look great, swaying in some diaphanously purple silky haze. Or whatever. Perhaps she'd walk up to the Indians' table with me, showing off the purple silky haze, as I deposit my letter of resignation with an indifferent wave. Or maybe not. It's not really about the money. Until Goldhaven walked up to me, I didn't really know what I'd come to Antwerp for. I thought it was about the money. And then he said those words. Pink, Goldhaven said. I don't know about you; but me, it does it for me every time. What, I asked, dumbfounded that Goldhaven was even talking to me, and he smiled, subtle and knowing. Had I ever wondered, he said, what it would be like. To get my hands on a big pink stone. To hold what no one had held before me. To feel what no one had felt before me. To caress what no one had caressed before me.

And then I knew. To feel the cool flinty surface. The Indians have never let me near their stones, have never let me near their safes. I used to dream of running my hands through their inventory, unwrapping those little origami envelopes, putting faces, facets to those initials they make me add up. They would not. What do you know about stones, they'd ask again. Let's keep it that way, they'd repeat. As we chug along, the brim of my hat pulled far down over my face against the sun, I start composing my resignatory epistle. I am pleased to, it'll start. Oh how it'll please me. Forget about the SL. Perhaps I should rent a Maybach for the occasion, and pull up in full sight of the Indians' table.

4

So this is it. From the river, Marlow's looks like any of the settlements that dot the forest in these parts. Trees, trees, trees. The landing, a tiny striplet of silt, covered in bottles and rusting tins and organic trash. Clouds of buzzing flies, too, bigger than at Cayata. I go dizzy. My neck hurts. I have a temperature. Perhaps one of the beasties that bit me the other night had some bad thing in its tiny insect gut.

Marlow's is the end of the road. If I don't find Jocelynho here, I will not find Jocelynho. Old Road, I say, what comes after Marlow's? What's the next town up?

Ain't no town after Marlow's, Old Road says.

Old Road says he will stay a night or two – a hammock under a shaky porch, that is all there is

– and then begin the long trip back to Cayata. I have a night and a day to find Jocelynho.

I walk among the huts. There are no buyers here and no shops. There are natives in sling-shot hammocks, and pork-knockers fresh from the forest, green-fingered and malarial and just as ragged and penniless as when they set out. There is no brothel and no policeman in Marlow's, and the guns are not concealed. There is no dump, and no cemetery. The jungle is everywhere, slinking its long stalks far into every hovel; raining sticky organic slime down on every inch of sodden ground. Hairy brown ghosts sidle up from the shadows, unwrapping their greasy grey bundles, hoping to tempt me with their paltry green-coated trash. Seen Jocelynho, I ask? Viu o Jocelynho? They have not; and if they had, they would not tell me.

Night comes without warning and quickly. For ten dollars I manage to get a hammock under a porch of sorts. There are no nets in Marlow's, and for all I know the one I brought from Antwerp now adorns the den of a pink-eyed monster deep in the green tangle. I didn't use to dream, and now the choicest nightmares are crowding in on me. Large pink crystal octahedrons dangle forever out of reach, teasing me from heads of broccoli tall as the cathedral in Antwerp, or swishing past embedded in the bumped backs of black caymans rushing to feed on the many limbs the river bears on its way to the coast. But I'm after a Brazilian by the name of Jocelynho. I glimpse him from time to time in the distance, a tall figure in a black cape crossing the river in a long dugout, standing forward of the ferryman, his face turned away from me. Goldhaven you bastard, I mutter into the mist as Jocelynho disappears yet again in the green curtains by the riverside, you made it all up, it's a joke—

I wake to the sound of gunshot in the distance, and sit up with a start in my hammock. Marlow's goes on going about its business. Clouds of lazy insects lift from my arms and a night's rich feeding. A man stands in the middle of the muddy track looking at me, a cigarette in the corner of his mouth, black shoulder-length hair, immaculate white shirt open to the fleece on his chest. Had a good night, Goldhaven asks, and I fall out of my hammock.

We stare at each other for a minute or so; Goldhaven grinning down at me as I rub my sore elbow and curse.

What are you doing here, I ask.

And what are you doing here, Goldhaven asks back.

I went to Cayata, I say. Jocelynho wasn't there. They told me I might find him upriver.

I know, Goldhaven says.

So what's the plan now, I ask.

Goldhaven takes a long puff on his cigarette. The plan? From what I remember, you have a job to do. Find Jocelynho and take the stone. Get the stone out of the country. Take the stone to my office in Antwerp.

So what are you doing here, I ask again.

I have business here, Goldhaven says. Anything wrong with that?

So why don't you get that stone yourself?

I'm a busy man, Goldhaven says. Now, I think Jocelynho can't be far. Are you up to this? Should I find somebody else to do it?

No, no, I'll get on with it—

Oh, and one more thing, Goldhaven says. You never saw me here. Otherwise, our little deal falls through.

But—

And yes, Goldhaven says. I can see that your stay here has been prolonged a bit. You will have some additional expenses. With a smile, Goldhaven hands me an envelope. I open the envelope. By my reckoning it contains some five thousand dollars. When I look up, Goldhaven is gone.

There's not a soul to be seen in the main street. The miners must have gone off to their diggings. The pork-knockers must have slunk off to do what they do, going through the tailings, wading through the mud with their pans and sieves. I have no idea how to make contact with Jocelynho. The heat is coming up. I take out my copy of *Babbon's St Andrew's and the Maritime Territories*. As travel guides go, Babbon is a waste of space.

Small in stature, fierce-eyed, taciturn, their skin the hue of a burnt pasty, the natives propel our pirogues with short wooden paddle-sticks, all the while humming a low chant evocative of friars singing in the Gregorian mode.

Etc. I might as well have taken the Antwerp telephone directory, and that has pictures in it, at least. If it wasn't for Old Road, Babbon would be rotting to sediment at the bottom of the Malakuzi. Just out of Cayata, I took Babbon's book from my holdall, flexed my arm, ready to throw Babbon out into the middle of the stream. But before I could chuck, the boat rocked violently, and Old Road was on top of me from behind, wrestling my arm down, tearing Babbon from my hand, cursing like a madman. You crazy, man, he shouted, quite beside himself with rage, you throw book in the river, you bring bad luck. What the fuck, Old Road, I said. You never do that no more, Old Road said fiercely and returned to his perch at the back of the pirogue.

What's all this about, Old Road, I tried again,

but Old Road only gave a hostile grunt. Babbon's book, with its red cloth cover and rubbed gilt embossing, could be mistaken for a bible. Maybe that's the only book Old Road knows. Can Old Road read? I have no idea. I don't like books. There were not a great many books in the house I grew up in. A few fake-leather-backed Reader's Digests, rarely opened, on the mantelpiece. Next to that, *British Birds. Birdwatcher's Britain. Fun with Feathers: Quick Spotting for Beginners. Bodine's Inventory of Winter Migrants & Occasional Visitors.* Etc. My dad's logbook, his most cherished possession. Nothing to entice me away from my Atari. Babbon's book has not made me change my mind. But I have not tried to ditch Babbon again.

I don't feel good about Goldhaven's sudden appearance, and his equally sudden disappearance, or his money. I hang around in Marlow's for another day, buying shots of moonshine from the pork-knockers at a shack on the edge of the forest. Have they seen Jocelynho? No, they haven't seen Jocelynho. Do they know where I can find him? No, they say, shrugging their shoulders. Maybe Jocelynho has gone into the forest, one of the pork-knockers says. Maybe Jocelynho has turned into a green-face. What? I say. Green-face, the pork-knocker says. You spend too much time out in the forest, you turn into the forest, is what people say. Your face grow green, man. Your fingers go knobbly. Like roots. They say. Your skin go like wood. You sit on them trees there, looking. You get wood-juice flowing out of your mouth. They say.

So have you ever seen a green-face, I ask? The pork-knockers look away. You see a green-face, ain't good to talk about it, they say.

In the evening, as I settle in to my ten-dollar hammock for another night, a ragged little boy comes up to me. Você the one que quer o Jocelynho, he says, in a broken mishmash of English and Portuguese. Yes, I say. Tomorrow, he says, you come with me, and holds out his hand. I give him five dollars. So where is he, Jocelynho, I ask. Onde está? Amanhã, he says. Tomorrow.

I pick up Babbon's book.

The natives, having disappeared knowingly in the forest shortly after our arrival, returned but a short while later bearing a cornucopia of fruit, some known to us, some, I suspected, never yet tasted by a European palate – amongst these, a variety of purple-skinned banana, sweet and firm-fleshed; and small globes shaped not unlike gas-lights, their skin a deep vermilion, and closest in taste, perhaps, to our own quince-fruit; and lastly a most curious type of berry, certainly unknown to any but the savage races

who haunt these forests; and whose exact shape
and constituents your correspondent can barely
contain his impatience to communicate to the
Royal Botanical Society, in conference, for they
resemble nothing so much as a human skull,
being covered throughout, but for a small plate
at their upper-most elevation, by a white
membranous skin, with two depressions just
below the stem like eye-sockets.

And so it goes on. I drop Babbon and fall asleep.

When I wake up, after another sweaty night, netless, at the mercy of the buzzing legions, it is mid-morning. I should be taking a Malarone but can't find the packet I bought back in Hopeton. The old bites on my arm have swollen into purple-ringed volcanoes; the new bites are just starting to erupt. I see the boy from the evening before, crouching in the shadows on the other side of the muddy track. Hoy there, I shout, and the boy winces, puts a finger to his lips, gestures mysteriously, points in the direction of the river. I get out of my hammock, and when I turn back to the boy, he has disappeared. I walk down to the river. There is no sign of the boy. A pirogue of sorts is chugging up the river towards me. It is piloted by a man in a dark green T-shirt and mirror shades with a neatly cropped white beard.

He looks about him a few times, then draws up by the landing, and beckons to me to get in the pirogue. Jocelynho, I ask. The man in the green T-shirt says nothing, and casts off. The river is steaming, blowing layer after layer of dirt-white cloud up into the canopy. Upriver, a dense curtain of steam hangs across the water. Aonde, I ask the man in the green T-shirt. Para là, the man grunts, pointing vaguely into the white. Some twenty minutes later, the pirogue turns suddenly into the low-hanging branches by the riverside, sending scores of purple birds shrieking and flying off. The man in the green T-shirt points into the green maze. What, I say, where? All I can make out in the penumbra is a tangle of roots and leaves and hanging shapes. The man in the green T-shirt points again. Vai com o cão, he says. I get out, step into the mud by the water's edge. Something wet and rough rubs up against my ankle. I look down and see a mottled ball of fur snorting in the mud; a frizzled stub of a tail; occasional flashes of jagged, crooked white teeth. The furball gambols up into the green thickets, yapping from time to time, bouncing on the spot to make sure I am following. I can barely make out the trees in the twilight of the forest floor, but the furball seems to know where he is going. After a while, the furball stops, and jumps yapping up at my trousers. I feel a tap on my shoulder. Someone is standing behind me, but I cannot see his face. He seems to be wearing a hooded gown of sorts, or a sack. Jocelynho, I ask. The figure gives off a deep grunt that I take to mean assent, and thrusts something soft and warm into my arms. It feels like fur, an animal skin; a dead animal perhaps. The figure lifts its arm, pointing at something in the depths of the forest. I strain my eyes to see in the penumbra, and see nothing. When I turn around again, the hooded figure is gone. The furball barks, a wet, sick, gargling bark, and bounces off in the direction I came from. Jocelynho, I call out, Jocelynho, but there is no answer. The furball barks again. Something brushes against my cheek; I feel a sudden peak of pain next to my mouth, slap my face hard, feel the warm squirt of fresh blood. I thrash hastily through the bush after the furball, through the swaying knots of organic matter, the webs, the cocoons, the nests, the traps, the whole green mess eating and sucking and draining and splaying and tearing and rotting and growing, and watching, and waiting, biding its time.

The pirogue is still there when I reach the muddy riverbank. The man in the green T-shirt sits impassively, staring into the white haze. I jump in the pirogue, and we cast off. I sit clutching Jocelynho's bundle in one hand and my bloodied cheek in the other. The quiet inside the white haze is broken only by the hoarse cackle of the engine. I look at the bundle. It is not an animal; and it is not dead; nor is it alive. It is the skin of an animal, old, used, ragged, and tied into a bundle with a piece of string. I see patches of forest frizzle into view, briefly, then fade back into the milky soup. The heat is biting deep into my eyes. Streams of sweat roll off my forehead, washing into the red on my cheek. At times I think I see black-caped figures sitting in the trees that shimmer in and out of view. Vulture-like, they are perched in the topmost branches, their heads covered, jaggedy rags hanging from their arms. My fever has come back. There is an ache in my back, in my muscles, in my eyeballs. We emerge from the cloud, and Marlow's comes into view. There is no one on the sandy landing; the path running through the centre of the village looks deserted but for some feral fowl, half-chicken, half-harpy, pecking at the thin sand between the huts. The pirogue pulls up by the landing just long enough for me to jump out. In the shade behind one of the huts, I unravel Jocelynho's bundle. The Indians do their best to keep me away from the front office, but I have seen a few stones. And none bigger than the one that tumbles from Jocelynho's rags now, eluding my shaking hands, falling with a big splosh into one of the puddles at my feet. I pick it up, wipe it with the rag. It is dirty, dull, the shape of a ball of aluminium foil carelessly scrunched up. A hundred carats at least, I guess; perhaps a hundred and fifty. I am no judge of colour, but I fancy I can see, under the dirt-brown surface, a shimmer of violet. I hastily wrap the stone back up in Jocelynho's rag and stash it away among the tangled branches of a cayabanda tree. There are voices on the other side of the shack, Portuguese. I step out into the sun and the sand. I have the stone. I am alive. I feel the heat. I feel the blood racing. I feel the prickle in the purple eruptions on my arms. I need a ride.

5

I wish I could call Kaat. Do I wish I could call Kaat? When Kaat calls me, it's usually for one of two reasons. She needs me to come to some dreary function with her folks. Or she wants to make love. When I call Kaat, it's usually for one reason. Sometimes Kaat will say sure, come over. Sometimes she will say, I'm busy, in her no-nonsense Flemish way, and that will be that. I wonder. I do want to call Kaat right now, but my phone hasn't had a signal since I left Hopeton, the gauge on the display suddenly going down to nil as the plane climbed up over the sugar-cane plantations, following the river upstream, and the forest came into view. And even if the phone worked, Kaat would most likely be at work. Kaat does the accounts in a posh tennis and fitness club somewhere on the road up to

Antwerp. I have never been. You can't come, she said, when I asked, once, if I could pick her up after work. The employees are not allowed to have visitors. They wouldn't even let you pass the barrier at the entrance to the park around the club. And that was that. From what Kaat has told me, the employees are not allowed to use the facilities, either. The closest they get is standing on some hidden gallery, behind a two-way mirror, looking down at the cool blue expanse of the pool on one side, and the pedalling and churning and swivelling metal of the gym on the other side. It's a pretty upmarket place, from what Kaat has told me. Range Rovers and Jaguars in the garage. The kind of place Goldhaven might frequent. In fact it might well be a place Goldhaven frequents. There's a club member, Kaat told me once, that all the female staff members are wild about. Tall, long dark hair, gorgeous abs. Impossible to tell his age. Something of an air of mystery about him, not your average middle-aged worn-out businessman sweating to hang on to his youth. Always has a 'hey' and a smile and a wink for the girls at reception when he comes in. And a scar, it seems, on his cheek, pink and crescent-shaped, leading to the wildest conjectures among the staff. It didn't click at the time, when Kaat told me in her usual Flemish deadpan way, but now it's all come back.

Or perhaps Kaat is hanging out with her friends. She does not have many friends. The ones I have met are like Kaat. Simple and to the point. But they do not have Kaat's legs. And they talk too much. They went to school with Kaat, mostly, out there among the gnomes and petunias. And ever since, they have dreamed of becoming the Flemish Barbie type, the type that will get picked up, one day, by Goldhaven. Perhaps. Once in a while they go off on shopping sorties together, late Saturday mornings spent gazing at the window displays in the fashion district in Antwerp, dreaming and giggling; they will have their nails done in a department store on the Meir, end up going into the C&A, buy a cheap bikini here, a blouse there; and then they will have an overpriced Kriek in a café on the market square, still giggling. If they get really bored, they might talk about me, what little there is to be said. I can picture their conversation. They think I am dull and a loser. I have no future. I drift along. I do not show my feelings. Perhaps I have no feelings. How can Kaat put up with me. And Kaat would sit there, smiling, and most likely she would not bother to respond. But the bottom line is, her friends would not be wrong. Back then, they would not have been wrong. How things have changed. I have the stone now.

And I am stuck. The landing is empty. Old Road has disappeared in the forest. There is nothing for it now but to wait. In the twilight, I wave a fistful of dollars about, sit down to eat chicken and beans and drink a beaker of rum. The mosquitoes hover about me at a distance, waiting for their meal. I am starting to blend in now, my trousers torn, my shirt muddied, my face scratched and full of dark stubble, my arms peeling, moving from angry scarlet on to native bark colour; but the mosquitoes can smell the freshness of me; the confusion; the fear. During the night, they will feast on it.

There is no TV in Marlow's, there are no entertainments, no newspapers, and no one to talk to. There is nothing but the jungle, and Babbon's book. I open it at random.

The natives were roused by a howling noise not far off in the forest and on rising had been smitten to abject fear on account of a shape they fancied they spied flitting from branch to branch above our encampment. To such superstitious non-sense, I knew there was but one riposte, picking up my Winchester and letting off a fair volley at random into the darkness above our heads.

Darkness falls like a leaden curtain; and soon even the flicker of torches and oil lamps around the hovels fades out. I fancy I see the occasional glimmer of red or pink or orange eyes in the darkness. There are grunting noises behind the huts, where the jungle starts; then a fierce growl, then a high-pitched shriek; then nothing. I hear, faintly, a lone gunshot ringing out in the distance. Silence.

Someone steps up to my hammock from out of the shadows. The boy who has been bringing my food and my drink for a few dollars a time. Don't stay here, he whispers. What, I say. The Boss, he whispers, and puts his finger to his lips. The Boss don't know, but when the Boss know, the Boss be real angry. The Boss don't like strangers round here. What do you mean, I say. Who's the Boss. But the boy is gone.

I try to stay awake, thinking of the Boss and the miners and their knives and their guns. I doze off; hear the humming of the mosquitoes about my head; will myself awake; succumb again. The night is made of sweat and ache, and dreams wild as riot. I am crawling through the white haze of the river, and the grey silt of the riverbed. I am beached below the landing, a great white whale scarred by incisions made by giant dragonflies with iron claws, with purple juice oozing from my blowhole. A man is walking on water down the river, a giant of a man, tall as trees, a giant with glistening black locks hanging down about his strong shoulders, and a white shirt open to the black curls on his chest, veiled in the river's drifting fog. The giant is smiling, his sharp teeth big as boulders of ivory. The giant stoops to plunge his hands into the river, and I see his long fingers dig deep into the sand, the sediment of dead leaves and trees and pirogues and bones and stones. Ha, the giant roars, and it makes the trees shiver and the waters gargle. The giant stands up, and raises his left hand high above the trees and the haze. In the palm of his hand, the giant holds a rock, pink, translucent, cut into a thousand facets. I flap my fins feebly, try to move my stranded hulk off the sand and clutch at the stone, but I sink deeper and deeper into the mud. I am an ammonite; a fossil; a relic; drawn down into the depths of the Earth, becoming one with the layers of lava and rock, a speck of carbon sandwiched between the silicates. I can hear the humming at the centre of the Earth, the Earth-fairy's song.

The fairy's voice is gentle and clear. It is English and educated. She is standing by my hammock and comes slowly into focus. Hope I didn't wake you up, she says. No, I say. That's quite alright. They said there was another English person in the village, she says. I thought I should say hello.

She is pretty, but not magazine-pretty. Straight, short brown hair, a stub nose, nice eyes, early thirties. Sand-yellow trousers and a white blouse. Trekking-shop smart. She looks perfectly out of place. Blow-dried, and clean, and fresh, untouched by the mozzies and the forest and the darkness. I wish I could touch her. You're not a miner, are you, she says. Don't know a thing about mining, I say. Such a shame what they're doing to the forest, with their digging and their mercury and all that. Don't you think?

I suppose, I say. Coffee?

I climb out of my hammock, feel ashamed of my sweaty clothes and my bitten skin and my sunburned face and rough beard. I arrange my chair and table, pick up an old wooden crate from the muddy track. I wave a couple of dollar bills. Café, dois cafés, faz favor, I cry to no one in particular. Have a seat, I say. A cup of thick, bitter coffee appears, then another, and my dollar bills are gone.

You seem to know your way around this place, she says, and smiles. Been here long? A couple of days, I say. I think. It's easy to lose track of time out here. What are you doing out here, I ask. Conservation project, she says. Who eats whom. What happens if you take one of the predators out of the chain. That sort of thing. Sounds grim, I say. Not really, she says, with a smile. I slurp my coffee, and hope she won't ask me what I'm doing in Marlow's. What about you, she says. Oh, I say, and remember what Goldhaven had told me when I last saw him, properly, back in Antwerp. Be discreet. No fuss. Say you're a tourist. I'm a tourist, I say. A tourist, she says. There are no tourists out here. Across the border, maybe, she says. Brazil, or Guyana, or Colombia. But not here. How absolutely remarkable. Where are you headed. Nowhere, I say. I'm following in the footsteps of Joshua Babbon. Joshua who, she says. I get out my copy of *Babbon's St Andrew's and the Maritime Territories*. You must be joking, she says. I might write a book about it, I lie. *In the footsteps of Joshua Babbon: a pilgrimage.* If I get back. And why wouldn't you, she says. He didn't, I say. Well now, she says, and smiles a funny smile. It's been nice talking to you. What's your name, she asks. I think of what Goldhaven told me back then. Never give your real name. Make something up. Tom or Joe or Jim or whatever. Uh, Charlie, I lie. And whyever not. Charlie's as good a name as any. Well, Charlie, she says. I'm so pleased to have met you. I'm Hazel. I guess I'll see you around? It's likely, in these parts, I say.

6

Hazel's gone. Blow-dried and clean. I think of
Kaat, and feel a kick of excitement, and something, maybe, like guilt. I prefer numbers to people,
normally. I suppose that's how I got to know Kaat.
I spotted Kaat's legs, crossed, smooth in flesh-
coloured tights, across the room at a course on
extra-territorial tax accounting. Kaat sat there,
never once opened her mouth, and I just thought,
wow. We ended up sitting across the table from
each other at lunch, and barely talked. I could not
take my eyes off her. I have no idea what she was
thinking. We did not talk much then, and we do
not talk much, now. It was not long before I got
to peel the skin-coloured tights off Kaat's legs, and
more, and I was not disappointed. What Kaat sees

in me, I have no idea. Perhaps she likes the fact that I have nothing to say. I am not interested in talking to Kaat, most of the time. And I spare her my talk, mostly. We rarely go out together. A movie, perhaps.

We sat in the sand dunes at De Haan, once, and looked at the North Sea, flat and still and grey as a sheet of metal in a scrapyard. Sandpipers waddled about like toddlers by the tideline. There was a beauty in that, I suppose, and no need for words. But we meet in Kaat's flat, usually, or mine. Things are straightforward, there, while the Belgian rain beats against the windowpanes. The valley between Kaat's shoulderblades. The gentle slope of Kaat's hip as she lies on her side and looks past me at the wall. I don't know what she is thinking, and I feel no need to ask her.

There's still no sign of Old Road. Things seem to be happening out in the forest. I hear shrieks. I see smoke curling up from behind the trees downriver. But it does not concern me. There is nothing to be done. A very large black and brown leech has attached itself to my thigh. I manage to flick the leech off my thigh, but the wound is oozing. I have no painkiller, no disinfectant. Goodness knows what the leech has injected into my leg. I have nowhere to run, and nothing to do. I wish Hazel would come back. I have only Babbon for company, here.

I sought to draw from the remainder of the night a little repose and solace; and after completing the preceding day's notations, by the light of an oil-lamp, with a short comple-ment on the latest nocturnal disturbance, cradling the Winchester in my arms, rested my head upon a bunch of leaves from the tree they falsely call, here on the seaboard, a martyr's palm, on account of the curious disposition of its branches.

And so on, and so on. I am sick of the tropics. Scabs come and scabs go. I have a giant blister on my ankle, the size of half a tennis ball, a neat globe, opaquely translucent, filled with liquid and with blood. Slime-covered lizards fall out of my clothes in the morning. I have strange headaches, on and off. I have finished composing my resignatory epistle to the Indians. It begins with, I am pleased to be able to inform you, and ends with a gracious, I am pleased to forgo any compensatory etc, which I intend as a polite way of saying stuff you, I don't need your money any more. I wonder, for a moment, what would happen if I did not hand the stone to Goldhaven, on returning to Antwerp. I could try to flog it myself. I could call in to the Indians as a mystery man from outside. You want a hundred and whatsit carats, pink. Meet me at the next performance in the sea lions' enclosure at the zoo. The Indians will be mighty annoyed, and mighty intrigued. They don't deal in this kind of rough trade. They do everything a hundred percent legit, all stones certified, reputable suppliers. They do corporate social responsibility and fund-raisers. They sign up to mining transparency, they even, almost, publish what they pay. They sit on the boards of all kinds of institutes. They have their polishing plants back home inspected for child labour. But can they resist a hundred and whatsit carats, pink, nice shape, no inclusions?

I'm there at 1730 hrs precisely. The amphitheatre above the pool is almost empty. A whistle and the sea lions fall into line. There's a pretty zookeeper in a tight polo shirt and shorts, thirtyish, her brown hair tied in a ponytail. The sea lions nuzzle up against her thighs. They jump and frolic and wiggle and make the bell go off and get herrings. A man sits down next to me. They've sent a brother-in-law. Not even a cousin. But that's their business. Probably want to stay at a few removes. He's not a director, for all I know, has his own little set-up, acts as a sub-agent from time to time. So, he says, the corners of his mouth twitching with distaste. I take out my bulging envelope, show him the contents. OK, he says, and fingers the stone, takes out a loupe, looks deep into the insides, figures out its mineral intricacies. OK, he says. How much. Ten, I say. He untenses and smiles. OK, he says, relieved. He takes a bundle of dollar bills from inside his jacket. I count. Ten thousand. The clowns. No, I say, you've misunderstood. Ten million. He tenses up again, twitches. He takes out his phone, makes a call. Hindi, Gujarati, Urdu, what do I know. Seven, he says. I think for a moment. OK, I say. Tomorrow, he says. OK, I say, I call you. And the next day, I'm there again, the pretty zookeeper about to start her show, the sea lions rubbing their snouts against her thighs. They've sent someone else now. A cousin. They wouldn't trust the brother-in-law with the seven million. The stone, he says, and I hand him the envelope, and he hands me a suitcase full of money. And without a word he is gone. I smile at the pretty zookeeper, and I think she smiles back, and the bell goes, and the sea lion gets a herring. I walk out of the zoo, and meet Kaat. What do you want, she had said when she picked up the phone. Nothing, I said. I want to buy you a present. Kaat was so surprised she just put the phone down. And then I see her on the platform at Central Station, and she looks at me with a look I've never seen before, quizzical, almost tender.

I think not. The Indians would turn me in, more likely. I just need to get out of here and get on that plane and find Goldhaven and get my share. Old Road has returned from the forest, but he lies dozing in the sun and is not about to cast off. Every couple of hours I go down to the river to harass him.

Nobody harasses Old Road. Fuck you, he says. You wanna get the hell outta here, you wait your turn. Nobody tell Old Road no shit, man. You don't know shit, man. This no time to move, man. You better listen to the people who know. You better listen to the people who know like to put an ear to the trees. And you wanna know what the trees say, is like as I tell you down in that Nickery. The Boss not happy, man. When the Boss not happy, you stay well put man. What do you mean, I say. Shut up, Old Road says. You not listenin'. Boss Macquarie not happy. Things not straight in the forest. Things been taken. Some no-good beetlebrain takin' stuff, not givin' Boss Macquarie his dollar. Worse, man. Beetlebrain never tell Boss Macquarie about the Nickery job. They just go in with their rudeboys and shoot things up. And worse, like. Word is they dress up in them rags and do that make-up shit to look like it's the Boss his men who done the job. There be some crazy jellywits out there, man. They say the Boss been in a fury up in his cabin, someplace out there. Old Road beckons at Marlow's and beyond. There be some ugly shit going down for this. Old Road looks worried. He points the other way, downriver. The column of smoke rising above the trees. Never been this bad, man. Word is Boss Macquarie's blown his whistle. What does that mean, I ask. Old Road frowns. Still not listening, know-nothin'. The Boss blow his whistle, his legion peel out from the shadows. Fall from the trees. Like angels, man, or somethin'. And then they roll on, man. You ever seen a column of warrior ants on the roll, you know. I don't, I say. You don't know shit, Old Road says. You besta stayed down your wormhole in the city, man. Boss Macquarie, he pissed. And with that, Old Road reclines on his narrow patch of sand and puts a discoloured old page from the *Atlantic Standard & Telegraph*, the only daily paper in St Andrew's, over his face to screen out the sun, and to tell me our interview is over.

A chopper on a roof, people piling in. Saigon Falls, it says.

I wonder where Hazel is gone. I would have noticed her, if she was still around. Where would she hide, in Marlow's? A Brazilian miner could, or a pork-knocker. But not a pale-skinned thirty-something with a stub nose in a freshly pressed white blouse. And I would know if she had left. There is only one way out of Marlow's, and it involves the river, and nothing goes down to the river without my seeing it. I wonder if she is on to me. I wonder what she made of me. I imagine she saw right through the

Babbon lark. *In the footsteps of Joshua Babbon?* Not very likely. Perhaps I should have posed as a birdwatcher instead. Not exactly original. Movies and dime novels are littered with them. But I would do a credible twitcher. I'm after the only remaining population of Lafayette's lesser spotted cockareens. The Northern Amazonian sub-species, with the pink patch on its belly. Round, a double pyramid. At least a hundred and fifty carats. Whatever. All that hanging around in hides, with nothing but bird books to read, when all I wanted was to be left alone with my Atari. Half a dozen other twitchers crammed into the little wooden hut; the smell of wet wool and mint cake. What are we after today, Dad? A solitary spangled green jay. A what? Blown over by an Atlantic gale. About four thousand miles off course. Here you go, page 245. Rare winter visitor to the British Isles. It looks like a thrush, from a distance. Through the telescope, it looks like a jay. So what. Yelps of excitement in the hide. All I feel is cold, and a little sorry for the poor bugger. Expects to touch down in Barbados, sub-tropical fruit trees, nuts galore, eager spangled green jay females. And here he is in a sodden bog. I feel for him. That's me. Way off course. I would not mind seeing Hazel again.

But there's nothing for it but to wait. A man comes up to my hut, a mud-stained scarecrow in rags, Worzel Gummidge with green skin and dull black eyes. He stands there eyeing me from the muddy track, leans against the shaky wooden post of the porch. The miners make a wide circle round him. The man stands there, waiting, smoking something long and brown and floppy, a kind of cheroot, its bitter smoke wafting over to me. He stands there watching me. He does not blink and he does not move. I remember what Old Road said about Boss Macquarie's men back in Little Nickery. The scarecrow fits the bill.

I wave my dollar bills, and nothing appears; no coffee and no beans. Around my porch a sanitary cordon has formed. The miners have retreated to their huts, their diggings, their forest outposts. They have dived for cover, ready to hit the ground.

I lie in the darkness, not moving, under Worzel's watch. The night is hot and heavy. Instead of the usual rise of hungry snorts and panicked screeches, the jungle stays silent. All the braying and moaning and snapping has been put on pause. There are no stars and no moon. All is black but for a ring of red embers at the end of the scarecrow's cheroot. I am tired, all of a sudden, my eyelids sagging, the darkness seeping into my temples, my arms going numb. I fight it, will myself to stay awake. But there is no fighting the darkness. It wraps you up and pulls you in. But I have a travelling companion now, stub-nosed in a freshly pressed white blouse. What?

Don't hit me Kaat, it's only a dream. I'm getting a few on my radar now, mixed in with the nightmares, though I'm not really given a choice. Kaat drifts off again, north by northeast, tactfully steps off the seaboard, though I can tell this will cost me when I'm back home. And anyway, there's nothing in the contract about stopovers and lay-bys. The contract's silent on this kind of stuff, deadlines and modalities. There is no contract. But there was something, after all, in the way she looked at me, not quite flirtatious, but knowing. Come on, 'Charlie', she's saying now, putting a stress on the inverted commas; but I don't really mind, she's a bit of a tease. St Barts, she says, or Barbados? Perhaps she's the kitesurfing type, pale-skinned and lithe. I don't surf, but I'm a fast learner. I could settle for this, I say. Another caipirinha? Yes please. But first, I've got a bit of business to take care of, back in Antwerp. Of course, she says, in the footsteps of Gibbon and all that. Babbon, I'd say. It's become our little joke by now. I wonder how long a million would last you, here at the Baie des Anges Resort & Spa. Or whatever he'll give me for the stone, back in Antwerp. Unless I end up going for flippers and seven big ones instead. Not that I know myself. There's only one way of finding out. Keep my spot by the pool won't you, I say to Hazel, and then I get up.

7

Except I can't get up because someone's stuck the cold snout of a .38 in my ribcage. It's Worzel. He stands there eyeing me, waiting. He's finished his cheroot. It's very quiet now. The river has stilled its gurgling. The trees are not swaying, the macaws have stayed their gibbering. You take something from the Boss, the scarecrow says at long last. His voice is hollow and brittle, like a patter of mice scurrying over broken glass. No one takes from the Boss, the scarecrow says. Up, he says. What the, I start, and get a painful poke from the .38. Whither, Worzel. Worzel won't say. I am frogmarched up the dust and detritus of Marlow High. There's no one out. The miners are observing the curfew, stuck in their hovels, waiting for Worzel's shadow to pass. Whither. Into the tangle and skein. Into ingestion, digestion, sediment. We walk. There is no path. Worzel does not need a path. I have no time to think what manner of sucking, biting, drilling bodies are attaching to my legs as we go deeper and deeper into the green. Worzel stops. There is a man sitting in the branches of the nearest tree, just visible, where the canopy starts. He has a machete in one hand, a bottle in the other. He does not move. There is a wall among the foliage, rough wooden planks and a door barely visible beneath the vegetable weave. Worzel knocks. In, a voice says. Worzel pushes me through the door. A thick brown penumbra and a zoo-like pang pervade the hut. Somewhere in the depths of the hut, something snorts. Something that's not human. There's a scratching of paws on the wooden floor, like a dog shovelling air on its shit. But this scratching is big and fierce.

You like it up here, a voice comes out of the darkness. A shape, big, horizontal, with a shimmer of something lighter at one end. White hair, blonde hair. My eyes settle in to the darkness. A man in a hammock. He's not looking at me. He's not talking to me.

They all like it here, the man says. His accent is local, lilting, singing, Caribbean. His voice is the deepest I've ever heard, a low growling thunder at the bottom of a barrel. His face shimmers pale white in the darkness.

But I like it even better. Nobody knows how to like it as good as the Boss, the man says. What you got for me, huh? What you got on that Nickery job?

Nothing, I'm about to say, but the man in the hammock is not talking to me. You don't talk now, he says, but you talk later. They all talk later.

He been watching down Marlow for days now, Boss, Worzel says.

Yeah watchin' and all, the figure in the hammock says. Ain't nobody but the Boss does watchin' round here. You know what they say round here, he says.

I say nothing, and get a shove in the back. The figure in the hammock is talking to me after all. Nothing, I say, I don't know.

Don't know nothing, the figure in the hammock says, and chuckles darkly. They say there been a big stone in that job. Size a man's fist. What you know about that, don't-know-nothing?

The man in the hammock spits. Something hits the floor. In the penumbra further down in the hut, I can see something stirring, scratching the rough planks that make up the floor. A gleam of white teeth, a glint of cat's eyes. If it is a cat, it is big. Very big.

They say them goons go in dress up like my men, the man in the hammock says. What you know about that, don't-know-nothing?

I don't know anything, I say.

Don't-know-shit, the figure in the hammock says. You don't talk now, you talk later, the figure in the hammock says.

Worzel gives me a rough tug from behind. My audience is over. For now. Worzel takes me back out of the shack, further into the cleated green, reaches into a dense growth of lianas. There is a rough gate, and crude latticework woven from greenery. Worzel pushes me inside, looks at me, expressionless, and pulls the gate shut. I'm on my own. A bird cackles, somewhere close by. My ankle feels sticky and itchy. My temples are exploding. I pass out. I never used to dream. I have the choicest nightmares, now, and they are quite something. I see green shapes flitting in the trees. I see mummified explorers, their crinkled faces ash-grey, drifting in ghostly pirogues down the river, their bodies drained by giant leeches, rolls of parchment sticking to their skulls. Babbon babbles in the darkness. The harpies howl. And here's the Boss's hut again. A roughly cut door. A feline pang inside. Rough shelves, hewn from branches, bending under the weight of all that green paper. Legal Tender Notes issued under Abe Lincoln. War Reserve Issues. Silver Certificates. 1934 series. More recent bills, too, tonnes of mouldering paper. A flick and a hiss, and flames rise from the shelved greenbacks, the tangled lianas that crowd down from the ceiling. Boss Macquarie rises with a curse. There is a fierce scratching of claws at the back of the hut. There is smoke all about, wet chlorophyllic smoke enveloping the forest in confusion and panic. Sentinels drop from the trees, the Boss lets out a furious roar, and junglelife scampers panicked down to the river.

8

When I awake, I hear rustles and swipes, see wings beat past above. A snout appears in between the bars of the gate, an ugly black thing covered in bristles, tiny teeth just visible at the tip, then disappears. The heat is getting worse. My shirt is drenched. I realize something is wrong when the animals beat up a panic. A flight of bright-coloured macaws. A stampede of something big, and heavy, brushing against the side of my cage from the outside, snorting. Screams and grunts and coughs from behind the green curtain. And smoke curling in through the webbed lianas, the sprouting thorns. A strange crackle of wet leaves, like bacon tossed into the pan. I take a few steps back, charge at the latticed gate, which does not budge, only bulges slightly, elastic. I fall on to all fours, try to keep my nose to the ground. A long green snake rubs past my cheek, makes for a crack in the tight latticework. Should I scream? Not much point in screaming. I think of Kaat. I think of the stone. The stone will stay where it is, forever, behind the shacks on the outskirts of Marlow's. It will be covered by layer upon layer of potato peel and empty cans of feijão and sedimenting trash. Kaat will fall in with some dull sod from her home town in an Audi TT. She won't cry for me. Perhaps a hundred years from now, when the river has reclaimed its banks and the shacks of Marlow's are washed away and down and out into the Caribbean, some prospector will hit upon the alluvials in these parts, and chance upon the stone, Goldhaven's stone, my stone. Perhaps. More likely, it's all for the birds.

And then the cage door swings open. No one to be seen. The hut, in flames. Some deep primeval voice inside, cursing. Smoke everywhere. Things falling out of trees. The tip of a blackish tail, zigzagged, disappearing in the greenery. Whatever it is that's going on between the Boss and the other lot, it's pretty serious. I run, to where the sun filters through the smoke and the shades, to the river. All Marlow's afoot now, milling in the sandy high street, flies all abuzz, dogs barking, cats jumping from roofs on to the heads of startled miners, everyone looking, half-expectant, half in terror, up to the bristling forest. I dive out of sight behind a shack, make my way along in the shadows. My bundle's still there, untouched. I feel inside for the stone. I stuff the bundle under my shirt, dash out to get my holdall from the shack where I hung out, and jog down to the landing.

Old Road sits there by his pirogue, untouched by the agitation. A small queue has formed on the sand. There are three seats in the dugout, and there are four potential passengers on the beach. The three others are diggers, each scared by the commotion in Marlow's, each clutching a small rucksack, each with a waist swollen under their dirty shirts, like mine, by a stash they are trying to get back to the buying offices downriver. Old Road has been emboldened by the competition, and has put up his prices. 200 US for the two-day trip to Cayata. I brandish my greenbacks. I am desperate to get out of Marlow's.

The diggers are furious with Old Road, and with me, for spoiling prices. Tempers and voices are rising. One of the diggers has grabbed Old Road by his collar and is pointing at me. I can only make out half of the quickfire stream of creole that passes between them, but I understand it involves a proposal to arrange alternative means of transportation to Cayata for me, by means of dunking me head-first in the tea-coloured current, and against payment to the boatman of an incentive of 201 US, to be split equally between the three diggers.

I up my offer to Old Road to 800 US, for a solo ride, and with that the deal is clinched, and Old Road lifts up a grey canvas cloth stashed at the back of his pirogue and produces a revolver of sorts; a museum piece, but the sight of which is enough to get the three miners to beat a provisional retreat. You not gettin' away wi' this, you be sure of that man, one of them curses at me. We be back, you know. And with that, they march back up the beach into Marlow's. Old Road stashes my 800 away in his shirt-pocket, carelessly. I see another bulge there, another, bigger, roll of notes. Someone got to him before I did, and paid him for a ride they did not take. Old Road, I say, somebody pay you to wait there? You talk too much, Old Road says.

Just then, Hazel appears on the landing, pristine and prim like a doll just out of its box. So, she says, you're still going in the footsteps of that Baboon of yours? Babbon, I say. Yes, sort of. Hazel looks at the bulge under my shirt, where I have hastily stuffed the bundle with the stone. What's that, she asks, are you sick. No, I say, I'm fine, and curse under my breath. Hazel turns to Old Road and flashes a schoolgirl smile. So where are you guys going, she asks the boatman sweetly. Cayata, Old Road grunts, no places left.

I hear the sound of an engine, in the distance, approaching. A plane, perhaps. But there is no landing strip in Marlow's. The nearest strip is at Cayata, and from there it is a long trek up the river. No, not a plane. A helicopter. I see it briefly behind the trees, circling, looking for a place to land. There are no helicopters in St Andrew's. One or two old Army Hueys stranded at Willaerts Field, going in and out of use every couple of years, in and out of spare parts.

The chopper hovering over Marlow's now is not a Huey. It circles over the huts, once, twice; then comes into full view again, hovering some twenty metres above the river. It's a Squirrel, perhaps, in civilian colours; and with a Brazilian registration. The pilot must be an ace, or an ass; the machine is coming down over the small strip of sand and silt at the landing, now, probably the only open spot just wide enough to take the chopper's blades. It's churning the waters of the river up into a storm; the trees by the river are swaying heavily; and the puddles in the main street are sloshing their dark-brown contents up against the walls of Marlow's huts. Old Road hangs on to his porkpie hat and stares. The chopper stays down, its skates barely touching the sand. Bye, Hazel says, and runs up to the chopper, crouched; throws her backpack in through the open door, jumps in. The chopper lifts up, dips its nose, and goes off north, downriver. Shit, I say. They'll be in Cayata in ten minutes. And we're going to take, what, Old Road? Shut up, Old Road says, and lifts the canvas cloth at the back of the pirogue. You talk too much, you swim.

94

9

She has her own chopper. She didn't offer me a ride. She could have offered me a ride. She didn't. I'll never see St Barts. I'll never learn to kitesurf, and I'll never get a caipirinha at the Baie des Anges Resort & Spa. What a woman though. She has her own chopper. But the fact is, she didn't offer me a ride. Old Road and I float down the river in silence for a day, maybe two. The heat is getting to me. Shapes blur, merge; hours and days flow into one another. My arms are swelling up again. I have a headache that will not lay off, a gloved fist pounding my right temple from the inside.

Why is it taking so long to get to Cayata, I ask Old Road.

Old Road laughs. You think them river always

flow one way, man, you got it wrong. This river real special. Ain't no stupid physics in charge of *this* river, man.

So, who is in charge of this river then, I ask.

Man, you never listen, Old Road says.

Oh, I say. The Boss, right.

And I got news for you, Old Road says. He left the forest, man.

Good, I say. Just as well.

Old Road curses. You don't get nothing.

What, I say, what about Boss Macquarie. I'm glad he's gone. The further the better.

Oh man, Old Road mutters. Every time you open your mouth, is like a sloth farting. Listen up. Boss Macquarie, he left the forest. Boss Macquarie never leaves the forest. Never. When the Boss leaves the forest, bad news. Boss Macquarie just left the forest one time, long ago. They say.

What, I say. Why.

What they say is, they give the Boss a big pile of paper to do a job.

A job, I say. Where. What kind of job.

A job, Old Road says. Up North, they say. Over the border, over the sea. Hewston, or Nouston, or something. Cowboy country. What do I know.

Why on earth would Boss Macquarie go all the way to Houston to do a job, I say.

Enough talking, Old Road says. You wanna know

stuff that don't concern you, you go do your own investigating and shit. Go talk to the trees. Mingle, and stuff. Old Road chuckles, and pulls his porkpie hat down over his eyes.

I try to picture Boss Macquarie on a plane to Houston. What do I know about Houston. Ground Control and Major Tom. I've been to New York, once, and that's it. I didn't like it, particularly. I was on my own. I had not met Kaat, yet. I didn't like the flight over, boxed in, rude hostesses, plastic meals. Boss Macquarie doesn't like it. He's looking down, for the first time, too, crossing half an ocean, all cute little turquoise lagoons and atolls. Max Macquarie really doesn't give a shit, just wants to get it over with. He's longing for the trees and the animal groans and the humid bosom of the forest. Here he is, landing in Houston. I imagine someone has bought him the ticket, with a slip of paper bearing a name and an address. And a thick brown envelope. How much does Boss Macquarie get for a job like this? How many noughts? It's a straightforward job for the Boss. The kind he's performed a dozen times, no doubt, in the shadows behind a shack, at the end of a winding forest track, in a tuft of macaranda bushes, in the slippery silt of the landing in the river's bend, under the canopy of a giant parrot-claw tree; with a machete, an old carbine, a roughly knotted length of sisal, or his bare callused hands, hard as steel. I shudder.

Here's Boss Macquarie rolling through downtown Houston in his cab from the airport. What's Houston like? Oilfields and cactuses? No, dull slivers of glass. The Boss doesn't much like what he sees. He spits, with precision, at the rearview mirror. Shit, man, the cabdriver says, and pulls over. You do that again, I call the cops. Drive, Boss Macquarie says. There is something in his voice that makes the cabdriver step on the gas. Thirty-eight forty, the cabdriver says when he's reached the address on Macquarie's piece of paper. Boss Macquarie counts out the dollar bills, single dollars all. A wad he's pulled out off a shelf in his hut, mouldy and smelly, guarded by the cat. Keep the change, Boss Macquarie says. What the shit, the cabdriver says. What's this now. Thirty-nine one-dollar bills. But not just any old kind. I know what they are. 1934 silver certificates, obsolete as a dodo. How do I know? Kaat's father has a collection. A humidity-controlled mahogany cabinet, in his bungalow, guarded by a detail of gnomes. And every time I come to visit, I have to marvel at the historic shillings and guilders. The cabdriver doesn't see the point, though. Hey motherfucker, that's play money, he shouts, but there is no sign of Boss Macquarie now. An empty street, fences, driveways, long sloping lawns, New World-Tudor facades. Dammit, the cabdriver says.

Boss Macquarie has entered the house, found his mark, done the job. It's a ghastly thought. It's what Boss Macquarie does. He's out by the back garden. An identical residential street, sloping lawns, fences, driveways. Boss Macquarie flags down another passing cab. Where would Boss Macquarie go, in a place like this, with a job like the one he's just done? Continental Starlight Suites, Boss Macquarie reads off the piece of paper the man from up North gave him. People can't help being struck by Boss Macquarie's accent. There's something jarring and incongruous. And something imposing and majestic. It happened to me in the cabin. It shuts you up. The cabdriver just won't shut up, though. Yo where you from man, he breaks out with a smile, never heard no white man talk like that. Drive, Boss Macquarie snaps, and the cabdriver hits the gas. A scream rings out over the neighbourhood of sloping lawns and neat driveways. You hear that, man, the cabdriver says. Drive, Boss Macquarie says.

The Continental Starlight. Fifty floors. Boss Macquarie's room is almost at the top. A corner room with wraparound views. Highways encircling the hotel on all sides, snaking off into the distance to tangle with yet more highways, downtown erupting on the horizon, its grey canopy piercing the smog. Max Macquarie takes one look, misses the green stalks, the chomping and tearing, the hungry feeding grounds of the Malakuzi. What would Boss Macquarie do next? He's thirsty, of course. Boss Macquarie needs a drink. I can't see him heading out into the concrete tangle again. So he goes down to the lobby. No difficulty picturing this. They're all the same. Subdued lighting and big C-prints of sunflower petals. Velvety loungers, and Boss Macquarie in one of them. What can I get you sir, the waitress says – no, she sings, with a Texan lilt. I can hear it, alongside the chugging of the outboard, and the gentle splashing of the tea-brown water. I don't know what a Texan lilt sounds like. It's something about being out here. It's getting hot again. Whisky, Boss Macquarie says. Would you like that on the rocks sir, or neat, the waitress sings. Is she pretty? I think I can make her out, straight out of some Confederate vampire soap. Visions and stuff. Not bad. But Boss Macquarie is not impressed. Whisky, he grunts, and the waitress jumps back, startled. Ye-yes sir, and off she goes. Shame.

Let's see if I can get a reading on the nature of Boss Macquarie's job. If Old Road won't tell, I'll have to do my own investigating. Talk to the trees. They're impenetrable here. A thick green wall, straight up to the canopy. But I can see it now. A giant screen covering the wall, split between half a dozen channels, comedy, news and sport flickering interchangeably. The Astros getting whacked in one quadrant; next to it, a local news reporter mouthing silently into a microphone. I remember the headlines from that one time in New York. A funny kind of grammar. Tycoon Slain in Mystery Rogerstown Killing; HPD Say No Clues. Boss Macquarie gets his whisky. How can he hope to stay discreet, though? Try as he might, he can't fail to attract attention. It's something about him, a presence. I felt it in the twilight, up in the hut, hard and radiant. There's a racket at a nearby table; a rabble of pale-faced square-mugged collegeboys in sneakers and sweat-shirts, a few drinks down and dopplering up. Hey hillbilly, they holler at Boss Macquarie, waiting for Mama to pick you up, show you the big city lights. Stupid, insane laughter. Kaat and I would have walked out there and then. We can't stand that kind of nonsense. It's what I like about Kaat. But what would Boss Macquarie do? Boss Macquarie would turn his head, slowly. A lion vexed by a fly. You don't wanna mess with the Boss, Boss Macquarie would say. The collegeboys will laugh. Jeez man, one of them might say, a smug overgrown teenager with an Astros cap, what a freak. White trash, another collegeboy will join in, laughing. Fuckin' albino Rastafarian, another will add.

I don't want to picture what happens next. I open my eyes.

What you say, Old Road says.

Nothing, I say. I didn't say anything.

You did, something about a picture, Old Road says. You losing it, man. You not made for this place, man.

Whatever. I close my eyes again. Back to the lobby of the Continental Starlight Suites. I've missed a frame or two. Good. A white-haired man of indeterminate middle age sitting impassively sipping his neat whisky. Two collegeboys, sweatshirts and baseball caps, on the floor, groaning, their faces streaming with dark scarlet goo. One of the lower quadrants of the TV wall in a pile of tangled electrodes and shards. Boss Macquarie will finish his whisky, pay and go back up to his room. Forty-seven channels flickering past. Boss Macquarie will sit there, bored. Boss Macquarie will never return to Houston. He has not enjoyed his outing. It's like Old Road said. Boss Macquarie will vow never to leave St Andrew's again. Here's one last glimpse of him now, one last time, on the flight back South. Looking down at the blue maze of the marinas around Miami, the turquoise shimmer around the Keys, spitting on the floor. Boss Macquarie is a creature of the forest. Boss Macquarie is at one with his biotope. You cannot take the creature out of the biotope without fucking up big time. Boss Macquarie never leaves the forest. If he's left the forest, it's not good news. More likely than not, it has something to do with the stone. And that is really not good news.

Yeah, I say, out loud, and Old Road sits up. You're right. It's not good news.

What you talking about, Old Road says.

Boss Macquarie leaving the forest, I say. It's not good news.

Man, you're slow, Old Road says.

I sit dozing, let my arm dangle in the tepid water, awake when Old Road shouts *cayman*; and doze off again. We get to Cayata in the afternoon. I say goodbye to Old Road. You still don't know shit man, he grunts, and is gone. It rains, on and off, but the sky seems loaded with gloom. At Cayata's general store, I ask to borrow the owner's satellite phone, the only one in town, and put a call through to the air charter company at Willaerts Field. Tomorrow, maybe. Maybe? If the rains stop. Otherwise the plane won't be able to land. OK. How much? Three thousand. OK, I say. I hope Goldhaven will give me a decent cut when he sells the stone.

Night falls quickly. I put up in one of the cubicles of the brothel, again, try to nurse my swollen, sun-scorched arms. I think I hear a chopper in the distance, once. I dream of Kaat, crawling in to my cubicle through the dirty curtain-rags. She turns into Hazel when I reach out to touch her, then morphs into a black reptile with a jagged tail. I dream of Goldhaven, stalking me with a black cape, swinging from tree to tree, the body of a harpy, the head of a man. I am a sloth, so weary, so slow, moving from branch to branch, an inch an hour, hearing the flap-flap of Goldhaven's black cape coming closer behind me, almost feeling his razor-sharp talons striking my back.

I wake up in mid-morning. The sky is as gloomy as before. Occasional raindrops fall, fat as grapes, but the big bladder in the sky is holding back for later. There is a faint murmur behind the trees, rapidly coming closer. My Islander comes into view, three thousand dollars worth, a small down payment for riches beyond belief.

The Islander banks, does its usual sweep above Cayata, comes in low over the trees. The landing gear comes out, late, just in time. It touches down heavily in the soft mud of the rain-soaked piste, dirty water splashing up under its wheels, skids to a halt, finally, at the very end of the piste. The pilot is not happy.

Gonna have a tough time getting back in the air, he says. And the weather's no good. Gotta hurry, or the rains'll catch up with us.

I climb aboard, clutching my holdall, with my precious bundle inside. A small crowd of diggers and hangers-on has gathered by the side of the plane, waving dollar bills, begging to be taken aboard. No, the pilot says, we'll be too heavy if I take more than one. There's water dripping out through the seams of the ceiling lining. More, now, a right little water-fall. I count out three thousand US and hand them to the pilot. He takes the thick wad of notes without a word, puts it in his shirt pocket. There's another bulge in there already, even thicker.

Now you better pray, the pilot says.

The engines start up again. The Islander crawls back to the start of the runway, trawling through the mud. The pilot looks worried. With a deep howl, the engines rev up, and we're off. The plane wobbles from side to side, dips through the soggy depressions in the piste. Now, the pilot says, and the plane slowly lifts its nose, bounces back down on the mud, lifts up again, and with a loud roar clears the tips of the trees, just.

Your prayer done good, the pilot says.

The plane circles over Cayata, once more. I look down on the shacks, the bend in the river, the snaking tracks leading off to the workings, the occasional clearings in the forest with their pits and chutes and sluices. And then we're off over the unbroken forest again, crate after crate after crate of dark green flowerettes stretching to infinity. You better hang on, the pilot says. A wall of black cloud towers straight ahead of us, solid, streaked with grey lines. You better do your prayer again, the pilot says, and I can see the sweat running down his forehead.

Shouldn't you turn around, I ask.

No better behind us, the pilot says.

I look around, and see a bundle of dark-grey puffs massing at our rear. When we hit the rainstorm, it knocks the little plane off balance, and we almost hit the swaying canopy below. There are sheets of water coming down now, pounding the plane; the trickle from the seam in the ceiling liner has turned into a steady gush; there is water splashing about my feet. We're in the thick of it now. All we can make out ahead is twilight and rain; and looking down, even the trees are blurred into a vague green mash.

We're not gonna make it to Hopeton, the pilot says. Got to take her down somewhere.

For five, ten, twenty minutes we jolt around in the storm, then the pilot shouts, hang on tight now, and takes the Islander on a steep dive towards the treetops.

I've seen a strip round here somewhere, once. Keep a lookout, he shouts.

We fly just above the trees, looking for a break in the dense canopy.

Over there, the pilot says, pointing to what looks like a clearing, just visible through the curtains of water around us. He takes the plane off on a sharp turn. Flying over the clearing, we can make out a short landing strip, a few huts, some machinery.

The Islander circles above the clearing, once, twice.

Hope these people are friendly, the pilot says. But we got no choice.

The landing strip looks short, and badly maintained. Little lakes and streamlets have formed across its reddish surface. Tufts of shrub have sprung up in places. The plane is hit by a gust of wind as it comes down, and slithers sideways through the mud. One of the wheels is knocked away, the left wingtip scrapes through the mud. Bits of wing splinter away, the left-hand engine hits the ground, projecting propeller fragments up against the fuselage. Spinning around like a wobbly top, the Islander smashes into the trees. One of the wings breaks off; branches come boxing in through the windows; and still the Islander keeps spinning, furrowing into the soggy soil until the fuselage hits something big and hard and everything goes green and fuzzy.

Two

Facts about Goldhaven

The river glistens in the moonlight, wending its way through forests and soggy meadows, past the ghosts of bare-bosomed maidens shivering in crumbling towers, weary dragons perched high up on their crags, cobwebs blowing in the frosty night. It rolls slowly down to the sea, carrying sediment and broken wardrobes, worn-out tyres, and now and then, a corpse. It's swallowed its share of bodies over the years. If the beemer went over the edge, it would nose-dive into the black water and burrow into the soft sand, its backend sticking out like some monstrous gastropod. If only Goldhaven could open the door and jump out as the car went down, he might have a chance. Goodness knows how deep the Rhine is. A couple of metres, or as deep as an Olympic diving pool. What does Goldhaven know about the Rhine? Fuck-all. Goldhaven tries his door once more, to no avail. He tries to shift over to the passenger side of the beemer, but it only makes the see-sawing worse. A train glides past in the distance, silently, blurry little yellow rectangles flowing by behind bushes and trees. In the mirror, Goldhaven can see Zog Shikzahl going about his business, merciless and slow, not quite human. Goldhaven tries to figure out where he went wrong. Getting on that plane to Moscow was a bad move. Goldhaven might have known there's something wrong with chiselling stones out of the frozen ground where polar bears and wolverines roam. Goldhaven should have stuck with what he knows best, places where the soil is red and juicy and bountiful, places where you drop a banana skin and before you know it there's a banana tree shooting out of the ground. Luscious places full of life and light. The beemer see-saws again. Goldhaven looks down into the dull black mirror of the Rhine. There are currents down there, patterns, shapes. Stuff that congeals. Faces. Rocks and trees and rivers. Fish and seaweed, slivered into rolls. What's this now, a Nile perch? This is the Rhine, right? More commonly called *capitaine*, notable for its enormous gob and firm white flesh. Goldhaven, this is your life, they're all saying, flitting past before you go down. What the fuck, Goldhaven says, and the beemer's nose twitches, downwards—

1. Once upon a time, Goldhaven's favourite colour was white

Here's Goldhaven, wearing a crisp white shirt, khaki shorts and a pith helmet, stomping about in the mud near Likuana. He likes to call this his garden. All about him stretch the fields, the watering holes, little craters filled with pallid white water and toiling bodies. The stench is enough to make a hippo puke, but Goldhaven is happy. No one's been here before. Goldhaven has found what the boys back home call a Lolita. A seam that no one has mined. The locals used their witch doctors to help them find the deposits, sheer hit and miss. Going through the tailings alone would be enough to let a man retire to his own island at thirty. Goldhaven is delighted with his Lolita. And the locals are delighted with Goldhaven.

Goldhaven pays twice what the syndicates offer. Il y en a pour encore 15 ans, au moins, Goldhaven's man is saying, an amiable local fixer called Jean-Baptiste. The dumb saps from the villages have wasted decades pottering about with their ridiculous beach buckets and spades and home-made sieves. Goldhaven has put up the money for a couple of Caterpillar D2s to come in and start shifting the top of the pipe. The yield is promising, and in the meantime Goldhaven has negotiated buying rights on all the stuff coming in from the pits. As for the boys with the AKs and the bloodshot eyes – at least they keep the riff-raff away. They take a cheeky cut, the AK boys, and what with their gunplay and their coarse manners – pop-pop-pop – they make even Goldhaven nervous at times. But the stuff comes out of the ground, shiny white and dull ochre, and is carried up to Goldhaven's makeshift HQ, a container in a clearing halfway up the hill, with a good view of the river and the workings, and a few old mine-warning signs – skull and crossbones on a loud red and yellow background – planted on sticks in the ground around the container to keep any unwanted visitors away. There's the chug-chug of the generator in the background powering the air con and the grading lamp, and a skinny guy wearing nothing but flip-flops, boxer shorts and an AK stands on guard by the door, and now and then Goldhaven hears an argument outside, when one of the riff-raff comes too close, and then there might be a few dull thuds, or a couple of sharp pops, like balloons drifting into a flame, and that is that.

Goldhaven is happy. He's got it all sorted, down to getting his goods out of the country. Without the right paperwork, the shiny little mounds on Goldhaven's table would be worthless. An amateur might try to get the stuff out by post. Mixed in with parcels of yam or beans, bundles of stripy rags, chains of polished bone, or baked into the innards of little clay animals. But Goldhaven is no amateur. Goldhaven has settled on the old slavers' route that leads due north, through the bush, up to the border with Costa Vermelha and beyond, to the Indian Ocean, and on to the capital, São Bento. It's passable in a 4x4, and it has never knowingly been blocked by anyone who could not be bought off with a tip in the lower three-figures. Once over the border, the slavers' route runs on an old deserted causeway past the swamps that make up most of Costa Vermelha before reaching the capital. São Bento lies scattered across half a dozen islets in a mosquito-infested estuary. Anyone in their right mind is well-advised to stay clear of Costa Vermelha. And most people do. There is no resident diplomatic corps in São Bento. Even the Portuguese cover Costa Vermelha from distant Maputo. There are no foreign journalists in Costa Vermelha. There are no journalists. Costa Vermelha is perfect for Goldhaven.

For his first visit to Costa Vermelha, Goldhaven comes in by plane. Nothing too flash, just a little twin-engined Cessna. Goldhaven has no appointments and no credentials, but this does not put him off. He rents a limo, the only one in town beside the president's. He finds a couple of motorcycle outriders for a small fee. In their day jobs, they work for the president. But the president has nowhere to go. There is all of ten miles of paved roads in Costa Vermelha. So in goes Goldhaven, kicking up a bit of a racket, with flashing lights, dogs scattering into the sun-blasted warren of shacks, zigzagging among the potholes. He has the limo sweep right into the courtyard of the presidential palace; has himself announced as the CEO of a major mining corporation listed in Jo'burg, Toronto and London. The president is woken from his siesta by the agitation down in the courtyard, and instinctively reaches for his gun, and the briefcase in which he keeps his diplomatic passport and a couple of undated plane tickets to Paris and Rio. Agitation, in Costa Vermelha, can mean only one thing. It can mean only that someone who thinks he's the next president is storming up the steps to the palace with a couple of dozen mercenaries in tow. But what's this now. An investor. In-what, the president screams at his butler, perplexed. What do you mean, an investor. No investor has taken the slightest interest in Costa

Vermelha since the president took office. No investor had taken the slightest interest in Costa Vermelha since independence. Costa Vermelha has never produced anything more valuable than sweet potatoes and shellfish. Goldhaven comes straight to the point. Is His Excellency aware that Costa Vermelha is endowed with huge mineral reserves. No, His Excellency is not aware. As far as he knows his country harbours nothing more glamorous than a very large swamp, a few subsistence farmers and a handful of shrimp fishermen. But Goldhaven has the goods to prove that Costa Vermelha could be the next big thing. Goldhaven extracts a little leather pouch from his case. The harvest from an exploratory dig undertaken by an unnamed acquaintance, and which Goldhaven wishes humbly to present to His Excellency as the rightful trustee of his country's mineral riches. And then Goldhaven produces a little projector from his case, and a laptop, and without asking permission beams a map up on the only white patch on the wall of the president's audience hall, right next to the president's portrait in lurid oils and dark blue gala uniform with a Spanish sabre. A map, and diagrams showing the prospective wealth of Costa Vermelha's sub-soil: blue patches, red patches, and plenty of shiny pictograms. Dig here, and you'll laugh all the way to your penthouse on Avenue Foch. His Excellency doesn't have one, yet. A crumbling bungalow in the second tier of houses, with only a sliver of sea-view, in Antibes, and even that is being squatted more or less non-stop by a dissolute gang of nephews and their hangers-on. But a penthouse on Avenue Foch? Goldhaven doesn't put it in quite those terms, but His Excellency is enchanted. His Excellency is a little troubled by the question of how one can mine in a swamp or an estuary, but Goldhaven has brought a picture that puts the president's mind at rest. A photograph of a dredging barge, the size of five elephants, a floating shed complete with suction pipes and washer plant. I can have this over in Costa Vermelha next week, Goldhaven says, and ready to start work. And I will name it in your honour, your Excellency. His Excellency is delighted.

Goldhaven, too, is delighted. And then he gets down to work. He arranges for the dredging barge, a hollow shell long pilfered of all inner parts, and barely in floating order, to be shipped from Durban to São Bento. He has it moored in the marshes of the estuary, among the little islets they call the Ilhas de Santa Isabel. The shrimp fishermen have never seen anything like it. Goldhaven has the barge painted over; and then he has it named the *Presidente Ribeira*, and it looks more than respectable in its new livery, ready to steam up any river and clear things out. Goldhaven has a couple of derelict shacks by the

São Bento airstrip fitted out as comptoirs, complete with grading lamps and scales, and an official authorization signed by the president. And then Goldhaven has the president print his own export permits. The arms of the Republic – a shrimp salient, etc – are embossed on the receipt stub, and the president's benign smile, wrinkles carefully airbrushed out, runs across the full width of the permit. Justiça e Direito, the Republic's motto says just below the president's chin.

Let's get this baby rolling, Goldhaven says, and a deafening bashing and clanging grinds into motion somewhere in the bowels of the barge. Goodness knows what they've installed in there. Goldhaven doesn't want to know, but it sounds good. A bargain for the couple of hundred he's doled out to one of Jean-Baptiste's cousins. Like a home-made industrial drum machine, little pointy hammers coming down on a rusty old pipe section, metal sheets coursing with the rhythm. You can hear the racket halfway across the Bight, the off-duty shift-workers way out on their rigs a couple of countries further along the coast roused from their siestas; expatriate wives on the golf course in Mombasa distracted into swinging their balls way off course into the lapping waters of the bay. At the far end of the barge, something has been lowered into the grey muck of the swamp. A giant vacuum cleaner tube, folds of flex nosing down like a greedy sandworm. Goldhaven has hired two of the AK guys from Likuana as hands on the barge, busying themselves by that monstrous hoover, groaning and shouting and waving handsignals to each other over the din, kitted out in smart white overalls and hard hats. Goldhaven has even thought of a logo. Eldorado Continental Inc., it says in stitched blue letters on the overalls, with a stylized outline, that big generous bulge in the shape of an elephant's ear, the only continent worth looking at.

And off it goes, the drumming of the infernal machine in the guts of the barge churning up to an ear-busting climax. There's an AV production team busily filming away on the nearest spit of dry land, and a cavalcade of 4x4s doubled up all the way back to the capital. Goldhaven has had a makeshift jetty put down across to the barge, rough planks and poles thick with dollops of red carpet. Goldhaven himself is looking neat in a natty beige blazer, white open-necked shirt. He could be the star of a deodorant commercial, spotless and cool in the heat. The president has come in a dark three-piece suit, his aide-de-camp two steps behind him with a dark briefcase, looking sombre and worried. Things have been a little edgy. But now the president has a smile on his face. A little light relief from the swamp. The guys in the white overalls emerge from a door in the fat bulging flank of the dredge, carrying a metal box. It's Goldhaven's very own theatrical touch, even if the guys in the overalls are overegging the amateur dramatics, groaning and panting as they lug the box over the jetty, depositing it with a flourish at the president's feet. Senhor Presidente, Goldhaven says, opening the lid, the AV team leaning in all excited with their camera and mike. Bem, the president says, muito bem, and the attendance breaks out into spontaneous applause.

The goods Goldhaven has chosen to inaugurate his pipeline and barge are still caked in Likuana mud. But what does the president know. What does anybody know, or care. The cameras are rolling, and everybody is smiling. The shrimp fishermen in their shanty towns, huddled around a lone TV set wired up to some overhead web. The presidential guardsmen in their barracks, lounging on the back of their technicals. The company is not smiling, its intel corps monitoring the scene from some underground bunker somewhere in the suburbs of Nairobi, but who's to care. The president is thrilled. Uma verdadeira maravilha, Senhor Goldhaven. Off it goes, the first parcel of genuine Costa Vermelha production, with a beautiful export permit signed by the president in person. Where to, the president could not care less. Eldorado Continental Trading, or something of the sort.

2. Goldhaven likes fish, preferably raw

A fuzzy image down in the black Teutonic soup. Black hair, flowing, and a white stain of moonlight. It's Goldhaven again. It could only be Goldhaven. No one else would choose to eat a tuna roll with cream cheese and frizzled cucumber for lunch out here at a hundred and ten in the shade. Not a couple of inches from the equator. Not in Costa Vermelha. And anyway there's not much shade to speak of, here. But Goldhaven is basking in the sun, stuffing his face with nigiri and big fat rolls and cornets. Not for Goldhaven the deep chill of the air con and the hum of a generator in the background. It has only just opened, the sushi place, São Bento's first. Goldhaven turns it into his HQ when he comes to town, and his boys order hamburgers and down big pint-sized bottles of Vermeka lager, and everyone has a good time. Goldhaven is basking in it, the glow, the heat, the ascending curves, the dizzying growth rates. No one has ever seen anything like it. No one has ever done anything like it. Goldhaven is the man. The man with the pith helmet, his white shirt open to the third button from the top, not a spot of sweat in his armpits, a sliver of raw African snook poised on his chopsticks. A skyscraper is rising from the swamp, faster than it takes the sun to revolve around this fetid equator, casting a shadow over the shantytowns and the fishermen's huts. It's going up on some dodgy Chinese credit line; no one knows who is planning to take over the thirty floors of office space; and no one cares. It will bear the president's name. The ballroom will be named after Goldhaven. A hell of a boom is ripping through Costa Vermelha. And the sushi's good. Water-borne, vector-borne, airborne, sushi-borne: anybody in their right mind would stay away from this stuff and stick to the scrawny local chickens, well-roasted, or simmered into a stew for five hours. But Goldhaven is untouchable. Cops and bugs never could get to him. Nor can the company. It has its spies hiding in the undergrowth; telephoto lenses twitching from behind the shutters there on the second floor, right next to an ancient flaking mural of the president, the shrimp salient, etc. Goldhaven doesn't care. Goldhaven is the man. And Vermelha Bonds are it. They've just gone on sale on the Jo'burg exchange, and sold out in a day. No one really knows what they're backed with. No one has actually been to São Bento. And no one cares.

Goldhaven has cleared his platter of sushi. Time for another. Goldhaven is eating faster than they can pull the *perca-do-nilo* out of the swamp here. But Goldhaven is no fool. He knows it won't last. Regulatory entities have mushroomed all along the pipeline. Spoilsports and busybodies, obsessed with cleanliness. Most of them have never even set foot in Africa. But it's too late to turn the tide. There's a whole industry of them out there. And now Goldhaven can hear the hum of a small twin-engined plane out in the Gulf. Goldhaven puts his chopsticks down. There are no planes out here, except on Tuesdays and Fridays, when the twice-weekly flight to Jo'burg comes in, the crew ready with big canisters of repellent at the door to fend off the clouds of hungry mosquitoes. The president has a plane, too, a Gulfstream. And Goldhaven has his little Cessna. The Costa Vermelha airforce has an old Pilatus, grounded since 1977. That's it. Goldhaven has done his homework. So what's this now. Goldhaven catches a glimpse of it between the roofs of São Bento, flying low. A Beechcraft. It's gone again, but Goldhaven can hear it, like a lawnmower going round and round in circles. This is the end. One brief glimpse of the Beechcraft, and Goldhaven knows. An inspection mission, sent by the spoilsports and the busybodies. Serious bespectacled types with gemology degrees, coppers, statisticians. The plane just keeps circling, flying so low that any moment they'll be taking the roofs off the fishermen's stilted shacks. Goldhaven can picture them, peering out of the goggle windows, swearing in the heat. Something with the air pressure system. They've forgotten to bring their air-sickness bags and the stench in the cabin is getting bad. Where on earth, they're asking the Director of Mineral Resources, who is strapped in a back seat with them, where on earth are those diggings? Pointing at GPS coordinates on some print-out, waving copies of Costa Vermelha export permits in his face. Yes but yes but, the director is stammering, looking very pale now, there is an explanation, you see it's, uh, it's subterranean limnic digging we do here, honest, pointing down at the Ilhas de Santa Isabel and the *Presidente Ribeira*. Ah well, Goldhaven thinks. Goldhaven keeps a low profile. More sushi for dinner. Goldhaven has no illusions. Soon, the local stock of Nile perch will get a chance to recover.

The next morning, there's a sharp metallic noise over in the swamp. Ping-ping-ping. Goldhaven knows exactly what it is. Goldhaven has perfect pitch. *L'oreille absolue*. The sound of a small hammer, probably made of a silver alloy, a geologist's hammer, no more than an inch in diameter, coming down on the tinpot hull of the dredgeboat *Presidente Ribeira*. Uh-huh, the spoilsports and busybodies will go, just as we thought. A curious compound this, 90 per cent rust, 10 per cent yacht paint, a very hardy variety. But you can't fool us. A gentle tap, and it comes apart like dust. Uh-huh, Goldhaven thinks, as a girl in a white lycra dress pours him a coffee and starts massaging his shoulders, running her slender fingers down into the frizz on his chest, this is it. Almost. He can see them back in Antwerp, in London, in New York, in Dubai and Tel Aviv, riffling through parcels of his finest São Bento production, jotting sizes and qualities furiously on their charts, scratching their heads to work out origins.

Goldhaven knows, and gets on with it. Back to Likuana, back to his garden. For a while, the stones keep coming in. Goldhaven empties the little packages on the table in the container that serves as his office and digs, and does his sums. The likely proceeds, the number of permits he'll need up in São Bento, the likely side payments. The stones come in, and Goldhaven stashes them away in the old safe at the back of the container. And then one afternoon, a real African beauty of an afternoon, pale blue with a hint of orange round the edges, something happens. Goldhaven has just come from swiping his fingers through a week's run-of-mine. Only another suitcase or two, Goldhaven says to Jean-Baptiste, and you'll be rid of me. Jean-Baptiste laughs, and then out of the pale blue of the afternoon sky, there comes the dirty chug-chug of rotor blades. They close in fast, till they're right above Goldhaven, chugga-chugga, making the rusty old container creak and shudder. An Mi-8, white-painted, with two large black letters written on its fat belly. It pauses over Goldhaven's garden, hovers there, immobile, for a minute or two; flies off slowly in a wide wobbly circle, tracing the line of the artisanal diggings all along the river's winding oblong; and comes back, till its big clumsy wheels almost touch the roof of Goldhaven's container. And then it lands right in Goldhaven's garden, coming down heavy in Mi-8 fashion, almost horizontal, its fat wheels skimming across the soil, skidding to a halt above the pipe. So here we go again, Goldhaven says to Jean-Baptiste, and walks over to his safe. It would not be the first time that the local peacekeeping detail comes barging in on Goldhaven's operation. They like their souvenirs, the local battalion, wide-eyed country boys more used to manning the glacier-line in Kashmir.

So Goldhaven flogs them some of his surplus. Bagfuls of dirt-khaki boart for the men; and for the occasional officer, a nice little two-pointer so full of inclusions that back in Antwerp he couldn't sell it to a drunk donkey with a gun to its head. It provides a neat outlet for the production Goldhaven has a tough time offloading elsewhere, and it seems to keep the guys with the blue helmets off his back. But when the door of the Mi-8 swings open and the ugly old bumblebee, with its porthole windows and its crudely bolted clamshell doors and its TV-tower cockpit, disgorges its passengers, Goldhaven can tell something's not quite right. Apart from the Ukrainian engineer, the disparate characters stomping along the diggings are in civvies. A tall old guy in glasses and a baseball cap. An earnest-looking young woman with a rucksack. A young guy with a beard and a case full of test tubes and strange chemicals. And a black guy in a flowery shirt who is definitely not from these parts. South African, Goldhaven guesses. Tanzanian. This lot are certainly not part of the local Bat. They don't have the military look about them. Kitted out with nets they could be a bunch of amateur lepidopterists out to catch a long-tailed heliconius. But then the old guy walks up to Goldhaven. Goldhaven, he says, without a word of introduction, and sticks a grubby piece of paper signed by some committee chairman in New York in Goldhaven's face. And then they're all over Goldhaven's garden, measuring and sampling and taking pictures and talking to the local hands. A couple of hours later, they've choppered back out. The dumb mugs digging the soil and churning the sieves in Goldhaven's garden are thrilled to be famous for five minutes: Ouais, on sera à la télé demain! But Goldhaven knows. That night he packs his stuff, empties the contents of his safe into the false bottom of his Louis Vuitton case, and after a last night of tropical fun in the little town they call Likuana, Goldhaven turns his back on the diggings by the river.

Stoical, Teutonic, the dark waters of the Rhine flow past, majestic and dull. But what's this now, freaking along in a tiny vortex, dancing a breathless tarantella down to the sea? The spinning coil of a body plunging from great heights, breaking the surface in a thousand little squirts? No. It's just the jut and slice of superyachts churning the waters of the Gulf. In Costa Vermelha, the boom goes on. The airport road has had a makeover. Four lanes, and the president's nephews are boy-racing up and down in souped-up roadsters, slow goats and donkeys scattering in a panic. The president proceeding at a more stately pace in his limo, recently updated, an S-class stretch, reclining in the cool leathers, casting a paternal eye over his possessions, the shacks and the shrimperies, the buying offices that have sprung up along the palm-fringed approach to the airport. The motorcade drawing up outside the VIP lounge. The president stepping out onto the red carpet, lackeys bowing. At a table in the far corner, the props have been laid out for the president's favourite trick. Scales, a grading lamp, a transparent envelope with a gluestrip at one end, a blank permit, a presidential seal. A lackey with a bottle of champagne, which will be invoiced to Goldhaven's company. But where is Goldhaven? Goldhaven is never late. He should be here by now, immaculate in a dark suit with a white open-necked shirt, waiting with a knowing smile and a little suitcase, his security detail lounging in the background, two guys in crisp olive-green fatigues and shades, AKs slung over their backs. Apart from the Presidential Guard, no one is allowed to take guns into the VIP lounge. They always make an exception for Goldhaven. But where is Goldhaven? Onde está o Sr. Goldhaven, the president screams at the Minister for Presidential Affairs, who accompanies the president to these signing ceremonies. Where the fuck is Goldhaven, the Minister for Presidential Affairs screams at the Secretary General of the Presidency. The secretary general has no idea. Goldhaven moves in mysterious ways. He's taken over a suite of rooms in the centre of town, above the sushi place, where he comes and goes at leisure. No one has bothered to keep tabs on him. The secretary general breaks out in a sweat, starts barking orders down his cellphone at the Colonel of the Presidential Guard. Engines rev at the barracks behind the Palace, and a dozen pickups swarm out across the territory of the Republic, zodiacs rushing out to the fishermen's stilted villages and searching the rickety huts. O que, the shrimpers ask, confused, and the guardsmen don't really know what they're looking for, a giant shrimp perhaps, a Goldhaven, grande, preto e branco, but they haven't seen anything of the sort, though even here, out on the stilts above the fetid waters of the bay, Goldhaven's money has been trickling down in impenetrable ways; flatscreens swaying on the fickle walls, liquors never seen before in these parts progressively blurring the shrimpers' steady hands. But where is Goldhaven? Goldhaven's gone. The secretary general screams archaic curses down the phone at the Colonel of the Presidential Guard, no longer in Portuguese, falling into some rich ancient idiom now, calling monsters and snakes down upon the colonel's head if Goldhaven does not report to His Excellency within the next thirty minutes. A truckful draws up outside the sushi place, storms in, smashes up the sushi counter for starters, rushes Goldhaven's place. It's clinically clean, no personal effects left, all the closets and drawers scrubbed. But where's Goldhaven? Onde está o Goldhaven? Don't know sir, don't know nothing sir, the Chinese sushi chef stammers. Não ha, the truckful calls in to the Colonel of the Presidential Guard, who stares pensively at his Glock for a moment before taking a bottle of mangrove moonshine from his desk. One more place to look. But the colonel need not bother. His windows start shuddering just then, and an ear-splitting racket goes up all over town, a clanging and banging and bashing and rolling, unmistakeably the dredging barge *Presidente Ribeira*. The phone rings, the secretary general, screaming at the colonel, Can you hear it, Yes, do you fucking think I'm deaf, Mind your language, but neither cares really, now, with nothing but that infernal racket in the background. It has to be Goldhaven. Only Goldhaven knows how to get the dredging barge to work. No one else would dare to touch it, go anywhere near the *Presidente*. Perhaps Goldhaven's got his appointments mixed up. So unlike him. Perhaps Goldhaven is about to haul a singularly massive harvest from the swamp. So big there'll be a cut for everyone, and the higher up the feeding chain, the bigger the cut. Colonels, secretaries general, etc. So what are you waiting for, idiota. And off they go, goats and donkeys bolting out of the way, as the Presidential Guard in full force converges on the *Presidente Ribeira*. In they go, in circular formation, pickups bumping over the salines, a couple of Tatra trucks rumbling right up to the shaky planks of the walkway where Goldhaven first received the president. The colonel surveys his troops, a crescent moon of firing points around the steep white walls of the barge. Come out now, the colonel bellows through an old megaphone. But nothing stirs, just a red-cheeked tern rising from a railing on the roof of the barge with a high-pitched cry, kee-kee-kee, just audible against the clanging of the machine. OK, the secretary general says, sheltering behind the colonel, vamos lá, idiota. Just you wait, the colonel thinks, I'm the one who gets the last laugh. Not very likely; but right then, he orders an advance, blowing his whistle, and then the Presidential Guard goes over the top, through all of two feet of fetid water, with startled flamingoes lifting off and crossing the border into less bellicose jurisdictions. A volley of AK butts comes down on the venerable old vessel, and then the *Presidente Ribeira* crumbles, all of it, big chunks raining down into the muddy slush, big pieces of hull, fiercely oxydized metal that has served dredging ore in the Congo, up and down the Volta, among the crocodiles of the Niger river. Till there is nothing left but the naked frame, and there in its bowels, Goldhaven's machine. A rotating drum, something sloshing about inside it, random rocks most likely, hammers on the outside banging against some rusty tubes, the Presidential Guardsmen squirming as they hold their ears in agony. So, er, what exactly is the purpose and finality of this revolving piece of mining kit here, the secretary general wants to ask, though not in those terms. There is no one to ask. The thing is driven by a crude two-stroke engine, a stripped-down old outboard by the look of it, and it's been triggered by a timer. There has to be some kind of a chute somewhere; some kind of suction apparatus; some kind of a bucketline, or whatever. The secretary general doesn't know a thing about mining, but this much he knows. The Presidential Guard rummages and kicks and butts, yet there's nothing to be found. Yes, there is. Sitting on a rusty ledge overlooking the machine. It's Ken, in a tuxedo, his standard kit, but he's without his usual bow-tie, his flamboyant white shirt opened down to the third button, and Barbie is kneeling in front of him, in a nice pink frock with rhinestone sew-ins, her hands lifted in adulation, or surprise, or whatever, and she's looking at the biggest rock she's ever seen, the size of her head, at least, a sparkling acrylic pebble, princess-cut. And there's a tiny banner pinned to Ken's tuxedo, written in the most dainty little handwriting, *Obrigado, folks!*

They shoot it up, there and then, the Presidential

Guard, once they're back on dry land, emptying their clips and then some to cut it into pieces, but it's a resilient old bugger, the dredging barge *Presidente Ribeira*. And it won't just sink, not in these few feet of stinking water, so they have to send in the corps of engineers and organize a proper fireworks. And make up some story about Goldhaven having booby-trapped the thing. There is no way the president can be told about that little Ken & Barbie tableau. The president is in a foul mood anyway. Where is Goldhaven? Goldhaven's gone.

3. Goldhaven was a company man, once

What manner of fish are these, anyway. They're not *capitaine*, that's for sure, though they could be, ugly big-mouthed bastards the shape of aardvarks. Where have all the Nile perch gone. Goldhaven's gone in deep, this time, crawling through the sediment, the upended staff cars and panzer-wagen, Napoleonic carriages, crusader shields rusting back to ore, whatever it is history's thrown at these parts. Goldhaven's sitting in the swaying beemer, and he's working his way through the sinister black sediment at the bottom of the Rhine. Goldhaven's gone in deep. It's all coming back. Goldhaven as a company man, looking down. He's got a crystal tumbler in his hand. Twenty-two floors below, Nairobi does its stuff, gridlock and crying hawkers and rhinos stamping in their reserve, but up here in the Council's conference room, the screaming midday sun is muffled by the Venetian blinds, and everything is swathed in calm. The patriarchs gaze down on Goldhaven from their heavy gilt frames. Sir Henry Holroyd-Broughton, Bart, lion-slayer and Lord of the Valley. Sir Philip Holroyd-Broughton, Bart, who could have persuaded a rhino to buy a horn and owned the largest collection of Mantegnas outside the Uffizi. Sirs Aubrey, Giles and Roderick, steel-gazed and fast-chinned all, moustaches fit for scrubbing down a regiment.

The patriarchs are not easily pleased, stern old buggers, stiff upper lip and all that, but they like what they see. Goldhaven's about to get a medal, or whatever it is they do around here. At this rate, Goldhaven will be invited to take a seat on the Council, some time soon. In more than fifteen years of buying, he's earned the company a fair packet, working its most difficult stations, running its operation up North, chartering planes in Dar es Salaam, old Antonovs with Belarusian and Bulgarian crews, riding shotgun on the rickety old birds as they go in to the makeshift airstrips around Huét-Makinga, subjecting the goods to a first quick check on a makeshift table at the airfield, while the Antonovs churn the sickly sticky tropical air with their crude propellers. No one remembers Goldhaven's company days now, least of all the company. Which is funny, because for fifteen years, Goldhaven had the freedom of the twenty-second floor, fraternizing at will with the Council, up in the dim light of the sanctuary, with ice cubes clinking and the occasional soft sound of fragile pages being turned in ancient leather ledgers; and for fifteen years, Goldhaven had the run of the estate up in the highlands. It's a privilege the company granted only its very best agents. They'd be picked up by a small plane in Nairobi and ferried upcountry, to a clearing in the tea plantations that stretch across the foothills, and there'd be a ranger waiting with a Land Rover, and then the Land Rover would wind its way up through the thick forest, lightly skirted by butterflies the size of paintings, watched by shaggy inkpot monkeys with tails like quills, into the cool and shady heart of the range.

There'd be a handful of pith helmets up on the special rack by the cloakroom already, and a game of croquet going on at the bottom of the garden. Khaki flannels and billowing white blouses; a Holroyd niece, maybe, over for a taste of Africa, the tame and the rough; and a stone to take home perhaps, as a souvenir, cut but unset. Drinks on the flagstone terrace. Goldhaven leaning against the cast-iron pillars of the conservatory. Colonial Arts and Crafts, half-timbered Gothic, leaded windows overlooking the dense spread of the central highlands, rolling down to the plains on all four sides. On a clear day you can see the jagged peaks of Mount Kenya, hundreds of miles away. Limestone lintels that must have cost their weight in gold to lug up this hill. Lackeys in white uniforms patrolling the grounds with silver salvers. Goldhaven knows how to play the game, among the agents and their trivial weekend talk. He's English enough to pass for a pukka sahib; and he's French enough never to lose that slightly detached air of amusement playing on his lips. He'll join in their pastimes, obscure card games with names like Pilgrim or Fool that haven't been played outside the highlands since the 1920s. Whispers in the library. Opalescent sunsets, the howls of Ethiopian wolves echoing from across the range. The company of agents at table, black tie and garnet cufflinks. Cigars have been cut and lit, big fat torpedoes out of a rosewood box with gold bands. The cicadas are out, stuck against the flyscreens like fat little vessels on a nautical map. Talking shop is taboo; but hunting tales are not. Grouse partridge quail. Goldhaven sits in silence, drawing on his torpedo. What's a bag of some flapping moorland fowl against wrestling an eight-foot reptile straight out of the natural history books. Goldhaven's stories precede him. African cedar-wood logs crackle in the rustic fireplace. It gets cold at night, here on the heights of the range. The Holroyd niece is swooning.

But that was then. Purged and deleted. It ends one Friday afternoon in Nairobi. Goldhaven has touched down on a commercial flight from down south, and walks across to the light aircraft lined up at the far end of the airfield, Pipers and Beechcrafts ready for their short weekend hops to parks and lodges and treks. There's a Cherokee in the company's colours waiting, as it always is, but when Goldhaven wants to hand the pilot his weekend bag, all he gets is a cold stare. You're not on our passenger list, the pilot says, and of course he doesn't have a passenger list. Surely a misunderstanding, Goldhaven says, but there's another agent who's just come in off a plane from Kampala, and he's had his bag stowed away and the pilot has put the hatches down and the propeller's starting up. Goldhaven hops on a taxi downtown, to the Holroyd tower, and it's the same, a cold Can We Help You Sir from one of the two prim women in black woollen suits who've been sitting behind the big mahogany reception desk for as long as Goldhaven can remember. Goldhaven's been going in and out of the Holroyd tower for years. He's never had to so much as show a badge. And here's a security detail emerging from behind the two prim woollen women, and they mean business, and before he can say Holroyd-Broughton, Goldhaven's sitting on the hard, thick-bladed lawn outside the Holroyd tower with his bag upside down, and the doors are closed and the security detail are watching him with their arms crossed from inside.

Goldhaven goes back to his hotel. He has a drink, makes a couple of phone calls. The next morning, he's on a plane to Kinshasa. Ça va, chef, his driver greets him as he comes out of the crumbling airport building. Ça va, Goldhaven says, mieux que jamais. Goldhaven goes back to the field, doing what he has always done best. And for a while the company seems happy to indulge him. Down in Tchikapa, up in Equateur, over in Kisangani, back in Mbuji-Mayi, round the sticky velvet lounges of Kinshasa. Goldhaven keeps buying up what he can. Flawless white. Mud brown. Tiny specklets, sugar-crystal sized, and fist-sized lumps. The couriers keep coming to Goldhaven's hotel room, South Africans mostly, balding bulldogs with little to lose. And Goldhaven finds that his account is kept buoyant, as it has been these past few years, cash deposits only, no transfers, no trace. Perhaps Goldhaven's just been moved from one account to another. If that's what it takes to keep the old boys in Nairobi in the comfort zone, and the corporate risk managers happy. What does Goldhaven care? Goldhaven's methods are as effective as ever. The stones keep going out, and the money keeps rolling in, more than ever before. This is as good as it gets.

Cut loose by the company, Goldhaven carries on doing what he does best. Pay the best dollar, the best nouveau zaïre, for the best stones, and never mind the rest. In Kisangani, in Mbuji-Mayi, in Tchikapa, moving from town to town. Relying on his reputation, and his steady network of friendly comptoirs. Wherever folks are willing to accept the simple and honest currency of good, solid cash, Goldhaven is The Man. The Prince of Prices. Goldhaven keeps his white Land Rover, and his safari helmet, and his colonial poise.

But one day, something happens. Goldhaven is dozing in his hammock, in a shack on the outskirts of Tchikapa, or Kisangani, or Mbuji-Mayi, taking it easy after a taxing few days in the bush. As ever, the courier said nothing the day before, acknowledging Goldhaven's haul, a banged-up little aluminium case, with a nod from the open door of the Caravan and a worried look round the scrubby fringes of the airstrip. The courier had fear oozing out of his pores, the fear of other takers suddenly bursting onto the scene from behind the bushes, taking out the propeller of the Caravan first, then making straight for the suitcase, the courier's handgun no match for their combined automatics. Goldhaven smiled at his twitchiness. No one in their right mind would take from Goldhaven. What happened afterwards, once the Caravan was up in the air, or trying desperately to pick up speed over the pebbles and the soggy red soil, was not Goldhaven's problem. Either way, the money will be deposited in Goldhaven's account, anonymously, and that's all that matters.

Goldhaven lies in his hammock, and thinks about the glass and steel tower, the estate in the highlands. Goldhaven has never been one for regrets; and he has none now. But he does wish he had tried his luck with the Holroyd niece, that time after dinner. Goldhaven lies in his hammock, and listens to the tropical noises around his hut, the indeterminate animals, the squabbles and the laughter of the locals, the pots of his cook banging in the kitchen, and suddenly there's another noise, a right storm, coming closer, just above the corrugated iron of Goldhaven's roof, his whole shack shaking and vibrating now, the pots in his kitchen tremoring into symphony. Uh-huh, Goldhaven thinks, his perfect pitch kicking in, a medium-sized Antonov, an AN-26 most likely, not every day we have those coming in to Tchikapa, or Kisangani, or Mbuji-Mayi, or whatever. Out of curiosity, Goldhaven wanders over to the airfield. The Antonov has a Kenyan registration, and Goldhaven's come just in time to see the cargo ramp going down, and a man in colonial outfit, khaki jacket, shorts, safari helmet, walking down the ramp. A dead ringer for Goldhaven, though Goldhaven's never seen him before. Well hello there, Goldhaven says, I thought I was the agent for this station. The man looks at Goldhaven briefly, and then a white Land Rover noses out of the Antonov, rolls down the ramp, and the man with the safari helmet gets in next to the driver, and off they go. And that's the last Goldhaven sees of the man. Until one day, it's about 112 in the shade and everyone is pinching their eyes against the biting heat, Goldhaven goes to a little dig some twenty miles out of Tchikapa, or Mbuji-Mayi, or Kisangani, from where one of his stringers has called in a nice stone. But as his Land Rover approaches the churned wasteland of the pits, it has to swerve out of the way to avoid smashing into another Land Rover, the mirror image of Goldhaven's, coming in the opposite direction on the narrow track. Merde, the driver curses, qu'est-ce qu'il fout ici? What indeed, Goldhaven thinks, but looking back he can just make out, in the passenger seat of that other Land Rover, the mushroom shape of a pith helmet. Walking up to the rendezvous point he's agreed with his stringer, Goldhaven knows what is coming. Désolé chef, Goldhaven's man says. Ils sont venus avant. Comment, Goldhaven says, qui et comment, though he knows the answer. Ben je sais pas, Goldhaven's man says.

And so it goes on, wherever Goldhaven goes, anywhere worthwhile, the other guy shows up, in

144

the same safari helmet, and the same white Land Rover, and the same colonial poise. And the other guy starts doing Goldhaven's usual rounds, the usual trading centres, and the backwaters and shitholes, too. Goldhaven begins noticing uneasy flinches as he talks to some of his contacts. There are fewer stones on the table when Goldhaven comes by on one of his tours. And for those that are there, the sellers are asking ever higher prices. Goldhaven has always made a point of treating his sellers well. You've got to schmooze them, he'd say, at least at the beginning of a relationship, get them well hooked. So Goldhaven will readily pay well over the odds. Goldhaven knows his price lists well. He knows what is reasonable and what is not; and he knows what is plain barmy. And ever since the other guy has started to show up, prices on Goldhaven's patch have gone plain barmy. Alors, qu'y a-t-il, Goldhaven will ask one of his sellers, over a beer, in the seller's office, with the humming of the air con and the chugging of the generator in the background; and the seller will as likely as not turn his face away and turn his hands up, Que voulez-vous, cher ami, il y a moins d'offre ces jours-ci; c'est plus dur pour les creuseurs, vous savez, ils doivent aller toujours plus loin. And Goldhaven knows that the seller is lying, and the seller knows that Goldhaven knows; and that is that. And then one by one, the comptoirs that Goldhaven

145

has been working with inform him that they are putting other arrangements in place. And Goldhaven can guess what those arrangements are, and what they involve. Just face it, Goldhaven's friends in Antwerp and in London will advise, cut your losses and get out; there's plenty of trade for you here; you can't win. And Goldhaven knows that some of them are concerned, though they would never admit as much, at their association with a renegade such as himself, and at what they think the company might think, or do. So everyone is telling Goldhaven to call it a day, quit, kick the habit, stop fighting against the odds. But Goldhaven does not give up. Not then, not so easily. Goldhaven gets in his Land Rover, drives into town, parks in the dusty square outside the prefecture, goes into the flaking colonial-era building of the Regional Directorate of Mines, and walks into the office of the regional director. Ça, c'est des pratiques franchement in-acceptables, he says, dropping his pith helmet on the regional director's desk. Have a seat, cher ami, the regional director says, what are we talking about, exactly. This invasion, Goldhaven says, Est-ce qu'on peut pas faire quelque chose. Oui, on peut faire quelque chose, the regional director says, mais ce sera pas facile. Bon, Goldhaven says, c'est déjà ça. Et ce sera pas donné, the regional director says. How much, Goldhaven asks. Eh ben, the regional director says, leaning back in the swivelling chair in his bare, bullet-marked office, fiddling with his enamelled cufflinks, pulling the sleeve of his immaculate sky-blue shirt down over the gold watch on his wrist. Il faudrait renforcer le dispositif régional antifraude – cela implique la création de plusieurs postes additionnels – il faudra demander l'autorisation au ministère – cela implique un effort administratif considérable – How much, Goldhaven asks again. The regional director picks up a lone sheet of paper and pencil on his desk, and starts doing his sums. Cent mille, he says after a while. Soixante-quinze mille, Goldhaven replies without hesitation. C'est bien, the regional director says.

And Goldhaven shakes hands with the regional director, and goes back to his hammock, and waits. And in the meantime the sorcerer opens his box, and runs his fingers over the assorted bottles and jars, the powders and ointments and drops. The bark of the chuga-chuga tree, ground to dust. The petals of the equatorial bellflower, worked into a purple paste. The scales of the greater crested palm-lizard, smashed to tiny flakes. The juice of the hema-gora nut, distilled to tenfold potency. The sorcerer murmurs his spell, and takes a pinch of this and a hint of that, and in a garish thimble mixes it all, and says another spell, and off it goes, on the back of a motorbike, in a satchel, through the chugging traffic and the red dust, the rich red dust, every choking handful replete with cobalt, copper, manganese, cassiterite and stardust. And the next time the man in the colonial outfit passes through on his round, in his white Land Rover, with a radio welded to the boot, and a suitcase full of nouveaux zaïres, and a smaller case full, perhaps, of greenbacks, the regional director gives a banquet. And the man in the colonial outfit is a little surprised, but he duly takes his seat as the guest of honour, and gives a speech. Promising riches and harmony, like Goldhaven always used to. In the kitchen, meanwhile, the cooks go about their business, coating and frying their plantains and their oiseaux sans tête, well done, well cooked, roasted, cremated, the way the white man likes it round here. And someone, in the kitchen, uncorks the sorcerer's concoction; and drinks are served, and the man in the colonial outfit remembers his drill, drink what your hosts drink, no less but certainly no more, but does not, when he is served, keep an eye on the movements of the waiter's hand, and so the man in the colonial outfit raises his glass again, insouciant, and drinks—

Goldhaven knows nothing of this, and would not care to know. For a while, thereafter, the sources unfreeze, the springs unsilt around Goldhaven's round. Goldhaven is once more the Prince of Prices, the Man with the Mostest. Tiens, tiens, he will say

148

to his sellers, who are again piling the goods high under their lamps when Goldhaven steps through the door. On dirait que ça pousse de nouveau chez les amis dans la brousse, and, Qui paie mieux que moi, hein?

And then, a month or two after the banquet, Goldhaven is lounging in his hammock again, dozing after a good round in the bush, picking up the goods just like in the old days, ouais c'est vous le chef, il y a personne qui paie comme vous, listening to the ambient noise, the children playing and the women chattering, and there's a humming noise that gets louder and louder till it comes down roaring right over Goldhaven's hut, and everything goes into a shudder, and Goldhaven, perfect pitch and all, knows exactly what it is, it's a fully-loaded AN-26, coming in to land at the airstrip, and Goldhaven gets out of his hammock, walks over to the airfield, gets there just in time to see the loading ramp come down. Really, Goldhaven thinks, except this time, it's not one but three Land Rovers that rumble down the ramp, and three identical-looking agents in colonial suits who walk down the ramp, and close on their heels come three very tall African men, definitely not from these parts, wearing large floppy hats, with large Browning pistols barely concealed in the pockets of their baggy shorts and an emblem like a Masai spear embroidered on their sleeves. Well now,

Goldhaven says, and they walk past him, and they ignore him, and one of them says something to the other two like, Right chaps, meet at the rendezvous point at 1500, and Goldhaven knows there's an unlimited supply, where they come from. After that, every time Goldhaven goes out to the villages, to the diggings, they've got there before him; they have suitcases full of cash; and after a while Goldhaven is no longer welcome in the villages and at the comptoirs, and in any case the transfers to his account have stopped, and the couriers no longer show up, and Goldhaven is reduced to scooping up the trash the men from Nairobi have left behind. And then Goldhaven decides to throw in the towel, and move on.

4. Goldhaven is not a thug

So is this what it's like, when you're out of the game, sleeping with the fishes. There's a slickness to it, a fluidity in the darkness, a bit like moving through a bar with the lights dimmed, past all the other suckers, zooming in, heading for your soft white beacon. But there is no beacon here, when you're sleeping with the fishes. Goldhaven sits in the beemer, perched on the edge, a total write-off, and at the same time he's moving through the pondlife down below, silent and grandiose. Goldhaven is free to make new friends. And he does. Goldhaven first meets Colonel Lakamba at a national day reception in the gardens of the embassy in Paris. Lakamba is standing at the centre of a big throng of admirers, hangers-on, parasites, officials of the Ministère de la Coopération, technical advisers to the Présidence de la République, Lebanese mobile-phone entrepreneurs, decorative interns. For some reason, the conversation turns to mining. Your exports are systematically under-valued, Goldhaven says, you're missing out on 50 per cent of your revenue. The officials frown, and wonder how the man in the Versace satin jacket and open-necked white shirt showing off the black frizz on his chest has managed to gatecrash the party. Goldhaven has scrounged the invitation off a contact in the Embassy in Brussels. It cost him an extended lunch at Les Bols d'Argent, but it's turning out to be a worthwhile investment. Monsieur, you seem mighty confident, the Colonel says. What do you know about our production? Goldhaven knows everything. Yields, size distributions, average prices per carat going back to independence and before. And he's able there and then, champagne flute in hand, decorative interns gawking on, fountains bubbling prettily, attendant bureaucrats mentally composing worried telegrams, to roll out a demonstration to the effect that the coffers of the state have lost out to the tune of three hundred million dollars since Lakamba's people seized power some five years ago. Three hundred million, Goldhaven says, that's thirty hospitals, a hundred schools, the highway to the northern border resurfaced twenty times over, more than the annual

budgets of the Ministries of Education, Social
Services and Public Works put together. Lakamba
is a little turned off by the statistics, but the three
hundred million have him interested. Let's talk, he
says, the next time you're in Port-Doré. Here's my
card, Goldhaven says, but the Colonel has already
turned his back to the conversation, and Goldhaven
only just manages to slip his card in the hand of
one of his assistants, a giant called Fidèle whose left
cheek is scarred by a bracket-shaped beetle bite. C'est
qui ça, someone would ask; Ah, c'est notre homme
ça, Lakamba would say, il va vous arranger tout ça.
On vous appelle, Fidèle says now to Goldhaven, and
that is that.

Goldhaven gets his call three weeks later. When he
gets off the plane in Port-Doré, a motorcade of half
a dozen shiny 4x4s take Goldhaven straight to the
Minister's office at the Ministry of Mines – where
Lakamba spends half an hour a day, perhaps, when
he is in the country, to sign ministerial orders, receive
gullible delegations from H Street, and the like – and
thence for dinner to Lakamba's house. Lakamba could
have been president, but he knows better. Everyone
wants to be president. Lakamba chose to be Minister
of Mines. He resides in a neat 1970s carbuncle next
to the US ambassador's residence, overlooking the
Atlantic Ocean, its own little stretch of beach cordoned
off round the clock by an unsmiling detachment of

the Republican Guard, a gallery overlooking an inner courtyard and a pool where drinks are served, pink champagne on tap as has always been the Port-Doré tradition. A l'amitié, Lakamba says. After dinner, Fidèle slips a little piece of paper with a number written on it in Goldhaven's hand. Il manque trois millions pour les autorisations à l'exportation, he says. Goldhaven knows he will have to call in a few favours back home. He knows better than to argue.

The next morning, Goldhaven heads out to the field. He sits next to Fidèle on the plane. Fidèle is in jovial mood and intent on entertaining Goldhaven with tales from the bush. C'est là qu'on a attendu l'Aube de la Nation, he says, pointing down at an indeterminate point in the endless green spread below, fighting the emperor's men. How many years, Goldhaven asks. Five, Fidèle said, maybe six. What did you eat, Goldhaven says. Ça, pas de problème, Fidèle says. Il y avait de tout. The Colonel looks after his people. C'est un bon chef. Un grand chef. Il y avait de tout. La bouffe. Les femmes. Tout.

Uh-huh, Goldhaven says. The plane lands in a swirl of red dust, on a piste that has seen better days; scraps of colonial tarmac still visible under the post-colonial sediment; the rotten shell of an airport building still bearing, in sculpted gesso, Marianne in profile, a Third-Republic beauty stained orange and black by decades of tropical precipita-

154

tion. A column of pickups stands waiting in the red dust, a technical in front and a technical bringing up the rear, manned by men in T-shirts and baseball caps and holding AKs.

On a mis à notre disposition un détachement de la Garde Républicaine, Fidèle explains. Le ministre attache beaucoup d'importance à votre visite.

The road to the mine is a washed-out gully of red dust, with occasional tufts of tarmac remaining; the pickups negotiate them one by one, twisting and turning with the lay of the road, at snail's pace. Il y a beaucoup de choses à faire ici, comme vous voyez, Fidèle says. The convoy comes to a halt. There is a rusting gate; crumbling concrete washed dirt-white; a guard-house; more men with AKs; large black letters over the gate, reading, with gaps where the letters have fallen, *Min d Sa n -T o me*. Goldhaven has been here before, a long time ago; and he might have been working for the company at the time; but the mine is even more decrepit now than before. Of the five known pipes, only two are being worked; and even those are merely being scratched on the surface. From what Goldhaven can see, much of the good ore is being thrown on a slag-heap. The equipment is old, cobbled together from cast-offs from the copper mines in the far North. Du boulot, oui, Fidèle says; and, Voilà, avec vos investissements, on va mettre tout ça à jour.

On its way to the sorting plant, the convoy climbs a small hillock, turns a corner to the part of the mine known as the East Quadrant. Goldhaven tells the driver to stop. Et ça, c'est quoi? Spread out before them is a lunar landscape of red soil, pockmarked by a multitude of craters, some of them actively worked, some disused and filled with dirty water; and swarming all over them are gangs of ragged locals, themselves covered in red soil, bearing sieves and shovels and spades. Fidèle looks embarrassed at this; barks something at the men with the AKs. A volley of pop-pop-pop is fired in the air; and like startled rabbits the mud-splattered miners scurry for cover, disappear among the knots of bush dotting the mine. Il faudra faire quelque chose, Goldhaven says, sternly. Oui, il faudra faire quelque chose, Fidèle agrees. On pourrait détacher un escadron de la Garde Républicaine, Fidèle says. OK, Goldhaven says. It will imply certain overheads, Fidèle says. OK, Goldhaven says. D'habitude, ils tirent pas dans l'air, les gars, Fidèle says, and Goldhaven would rather not know; but the next time he comes to visit, there are no muddied locals in the enclosure.

5. Goldhaven does not like the company

There's nothing down here, really, nothing of interest, no staff cars and no panzerwagen, nothing but slimy black shapeless things neither plant nor beast nor fish. Goldhaven scoops up handful after handful of black silt, looking for the goods. But it's a wash-out, really, the Rhine. Just like the Saint-Thomé mine. From Antwerp to Tel Aviv, from Dubai to New York, everyone knows the Saint-Thomé mine is a wash-out. A source of industrial trash, a relic, depleted long before the revolution, run down by the excesses of the emperor, who'd chopper in to Saint-Thomé once in a while in a Chinook with a revolving bed, to take home a couple of suitcases, candy to throw in the deep end at one of his pool parties, and watch

157

the attendant generals, ministers, ambassadors strip off their dinner jackets and dive in a greedy frenzy after the dull round pebbles. Everyone knows, except the company. The company knows better. When the emperor's Chinook thundered in, the company had a team hiding in an old bunker by the airstrip, training their field glasses on the emperor's convoy as it slowly made its way into town. The company had a team on the ground inside the mine perimeter, their faces black with boot polish, pith helmets covered in camouflage nets, khakis adorned with twigs and palm leaves, hiding in the undergrowth by one of the unworked pipes, jotting down movements and coordinates, sinking probes into the rust-red soil. The company had a man in the throng with the emperor in the superintendent's office, looking important and official, and getting a reading on the goods laid out for the emperor, computing average sizes and grades, sending a quick field report back to Nairobi before the emperor's Chinook had even left the airstrip. The company waited, biding its time, waiting for the emperor to exit.

No one gets to rush the company. The Saint-Thomé mine? The company's agents would shrug their shoulders and sip their champagne, and watch the boat race sweep past, or the derby at Chantilly, and not let anything on. The Saint-Thomé mine? It might get a mention, in passing, late at night in the library, when all the guests have retired to their rooms and only Council members and the odd Holroyd-Broughton are left. Ah yes. The Saint-Thomé business. I see. Good.

The company takes its time, and keeps people guessing, and then it gets the goods. The company sends a delegation to Port-Doré. The president plays hard to get, at first, and the Minister of Mines is unavailable. The company ups its offer. The company extends an invitation to the president, the minister and an unspecified number of hangers-on. A plane is dispatched to Port-Doré. A working visit to Nairobi, followed by a retreat in the highlands. Perhaps it's the cool air of the range; or perhaps it's croquet on the lawn; or perhaps it's the pheasant shoot the company puts on in the valley below the estate. Or perhaps it's the package put to the president over a particularly fine glass of XO. Roads docks airstrips. Some budget support, for good measure. The men with the pith helmets play a very long game.

Bastards, Goldhaven thinks, now he sees the whole sequence in stereo, perched up here in Zog Shikzahl's vicious Bavarian cradle, and sorting through the Rhenish muck. Goldhaven is not happy. No sooner has he set foot on the tarmac in Port-Doré than things go to pieces. There's a reception committee waiting at the bottom of the stairs, but it's not the kind Goldhaven was expecting. They have not come with the usual convoy, Land Cruiser, tinted glass, motorcycle escort, chilled bottle of pink champagne waiting on the back seat with the Colonel's compliments. They've come in an unmarked pickup, hired thugs, paid-by-the-hour accessories to the Ministry of Mines police. Goldhaven is manhandled roughly into the cabin of the pickup and rushed off into town. Pour qui vous vous prenez, où on va, Goldhaven asks the goon who has jumped in next to him, mirror shades and garish purple shirt over his bodybuilder's torso. Tu la fermes, the goon says, and that is that.

The pickup swerves into the Ministry of Mines compound. They should have deposited Goldhaven at the front entrance, where he should have been met by the head of protocol. Instead, Goldhaven is taken to a staff entrance at the back. Allez, en bas, the goons say, leading Goldhaven to a grim-looking meeting room on the ground floor. Qu'est-ce qui se passe, Goldhaven asks. I'm supposed to have a meeting with the minister at three. Vous allez voir, the goons say, and leave Goldhaven alone with a couple of very large, translucent geckos chasing each other over the ceiling and the stained walls. Goldhaven tries to call Lakamba's office on his mobile, but there's no signal. An hour passes. One gecko eats the other gecko. And then Fidèle appears. Eh, ça va, mon ami, Goldhaven says, and offers his hand, but Fidèle looks troubled.

Ecoutez, il y a un problème, he says. Our contract has been cancelled. Cancelled, Goldhaven says, comment ça, cancelled. Force majeure, Fidèle says. The minister's will. Nothing I can do about it. You're lucky the minister is not asking for back royalty payments. So, Goldhaven says, c'est quoi cette connerie, I help you build up production from the pitiful state it was in, I invest a lot of my own good money, and my friends' money, to be told the contract is cancelled?

Fidèle is apologetic. Ça arrive, cher ami. The minister has his reasons. A new investor, Goldhaven asks. Somebody topped my deal? How much? Je n'en sais rien, Fidèle says. Goldhaven can tell he knows. I want to see the minister, Goldhaven says. If there is a reason, the minister might as well explain it to me. Fidèle doesn't like this. Ecoutez, I'm trying to be helpful, my friend. But no one insults the minister, OK. And not just anyone gets to meet the minister.

Not just anyone, Goldhaven says, so now I'm just anyone, huh? Let's get this over with quickly and without too much pain, Fidèle says. You owe the ministry a month's production. We suggest you regularize this quickly. I owe what, Goldhaven says. True, he has a month's production, part of his regular deal with the ministry, waiting and ready to go out at the airport. But the stones are already spoken for further down the pipeline. We know you have a shipment at the airport, ready to go out, Fidèle says.

The minister has asked me to recover it. That's my shipment, Goldhaven says, as you know perfectly well. Even if you are cancelling my contract, that shipment is mine.

Bon, allons voir, Fidèle says, and unfolds a dubious-looking, handwritten docket one of his sidekicks has passed him. Selon les termes de l'ordonnance ministérielle no. 37/46 du 3 mai, sont retrocédés à l'Etat, en accord avec le code minier section 376.4, les usufruits de toute production minière ou hydro-carbonique dont le titre a été transféré à une tierce personne, etc. Usufruit my arse, Goldhaven says, in English, but Fidèle has already motioned to his side-kicks, and Goldhaven is bundled out of the ministry and back into the pickup. With Fidèle following in another car, Goldhaven is rushed back to the airport, taken to the customs lock-up where the shipment from the centre of town has just arrived, made to initial an even more dubious document signing over ownership of the shipment to the state, as represented by the Ministry of Mines, and presented, after a cursory Adieu, mon ami, with another piece of paper by one of the goons. What, Goldhaven says, a depor-tation order? You've got to be kidding. Goldhaven gets on the plane, looks out of the window, the swaying palm trees, the pockmarked concrete, the mangy strays foraging by the terminal building, and puts two fingers up to Port-Doré.

6. Goldhaven knows how to handle a gun

There's a busy throng of traffic now, ghosts rushing into stories, knights to perdition, tragic maidens to sainthood, all of them swaying to the same Wagnerian jig. Goldhaven weaves in and out of the bustle, sits watching from his perch, watching and waiting, with open arms, his scales readied, a bottle of pink Ruinart on ice. It's over. Likuana, Port-Doré. Over. Stuff has been appearing in the papers; racy exposés, gory full-page ads. Goldhaven's position in Antwerp is getting pretty tenuous. Goldhaven couldn't care less. Goldhaven doesn't read the papers, when he can help it. Goldhaven will always be the Prince of Prices. The Man with the Mostest. Where others ask questions, Goldhaven opens the door to his safe. He's been lying low for a while, doing a little legal trade here, a little grey business there, but nothing that would warrant cracking open the Ruinart. He's been loitering around the bourse, speeding down the motorway to Knokke, lounging in the expensive deckchairs of the promenade, ogling the young mummies on the private beaches of the Zout, striking up a conversation here, a risqué chat-up there, having tepid adventures with housewives up from Rhode-St-Genèse in their black 4x4s. Goldhaven is bored, but he's got to keep his head down for a while, wait for the dust to settle.

And then a man walks into his office. A dusty African with a beard, harsh and full, and a glower in his eye, sharp and suspicious. So, the man says. So, Goldhaven says, and opens the drawer in his desk where he keeps an old Army-issue FN Five-seven. What can I do for you. The man takes an envelope from his pocket, an old brown padded envelope, and empties its contents on Goldhaven's desk. Uh-huh, Goldhaven says, and puts the Five-seven back in the drawer.

Goldhaven hates the place the moment he gets off the plane in Karraïne the next evening. The people are sullen. The air is sullen. The few wisps of scorched brown grass by the side of the airport terminal are sullen. Karraïne is like its name, a rasping abrasive spike of a place. There is no wink-

164

wink, how can we help you Monsieur, in Karraïne. And you are as likely to find alluvial mining in these parts as in Trafalgar Square. But Goldhaven is intrigued. The stones the dusty man with the beard dropped on Goldhaven's desk looked as clean a batch of run-of-mine as he has ever seen. Goldhaven is back in the game.

Goldhaven spends the night in a Chinese-owned concrete hulk of a hotel, and he's almost the only guest. There is a nightclub down a bunker at the back of the hotel, where the clients are frisked on entry, sullen men in freshly-pressed olive-green fatigues depositing their sidearms at the cloakroom, and the party goes on while Karraïne gets taken, is liberated, gets taken again, and liberated again in the space of a long, whisky-drenched weekend. A few bored French engineers sit at the bar, their legs dangling awkwardly from the shiny stools, staring into the black velvet gloom. On the dancefloor, polished to a deathly black pallor, a girl with straightened black hair in a white mini-skirt and lowcut white T-shirt sways in a trance to an old Madonna song.

Goldhaven sits at the bar and orders a glass of pastis. Salut, he says. Salut, the engineers say, raising their glasses. Drôle de ville, hein, Goldhaven says. Ah, ça! Drôle de pays, the engineers say. Je suis un humanitaire, Goldhaven says, putting on a phoney English accent. Je travaille avec les Nations Unies.

Ah, that's good, they say. Where are you heading? Out North, Goldhaven says, to where the refugees are. Ah, the engineers say, you're lucky, you've got your own airline. Our plane's got engine trouble, we're stuck here in Karraïne. Good luck, Goldhaven says. The chat has been worth his while. He swings over to the girl on the dancefloor. L'amour a frappé, he says with a wink.

There are baronies here on the riverbed, muddy fief-doms, rotten boroughs marked out in bones and piss. Goldhaven has seen them all as he peregrinates through his life, jumping from decade to decade in the batting of a bare eyelid, the swishing of a tailfin. Margraves and Counts, Imperial Knights and Prince-Bishops. There are Kingdoms, too, in the sands. Bobou Amer, the seat of the Warris Kingdom, sits in a depression on the edge of the most desolate mountain range in Africa. Like the last twitches of a heart going into full arrest, the dry peaks of the Warris Mountains jut up into the dusty plains around Bobou, home to vultures and sand-textured reptiles that have yet to find their place in any zoological textbook. Bobou Amer is as ancient as the Kingdom. Like the Warris Mountains, the adobe roofs of Bobou look from afar as if they have been etched out of the desert with acid, or gnawed at by termites. The only concrete structure in Bobou is the airstrip. It owes its neat state of repair to the small French army post that has been sitting ever since independence behind a discreet earthen dam at the far end of the runway. Once in a while, the French will sortie from their fortress in a convoy of a couple of jeeps and an armoured recce vehicle or two, and rumble around the streets of Bobou Amer and surrounding villages, showing the flag, getting out once or twice to chat and sip a lemonade with the village elders. No one much minds the French around here. For now, the only certainties in the Dur Warris are the French, and the Kingdom, and war. The detritus of war lines the landscape around Bobou like fag-ends in an alleyway. Burnt-out technicals in ditches punctuate the bumpy track into town. War washes over the Dur Warris year in, year out, like the rains, like a plague of locusts.

Goldhaven travels to Bobou in style, aboard a shiny white UN Beechcraft flying the rotation between Karraïne and the refugee camps lost among the badlands of the Dur Warris. Goldhaven was disturbed at first to find that the generous bundle of notes he pushed across the table in the UN compound in Karraïne did not get him on the passenger list. It took a few phone calls to friends of friends in Kinshasa and a ride round the backstreets of the Boulevard Frantz-Fanon to get Goldhaven his ticket, in the shape of a beautifully-produced, and suitably expensive, diplomatic laissez-passer issued in the name of one Björn Blomenvasa, official of D-2 grade in the employ of the International Development Support Agency. Goldhaven conceived Björn Blomenvasa without much reflection; and chose IDSA at random from a long list of acronyms and agencies helpfully proffered by the artisan recommended to him by his Kinshasa contacts. Professeur Bonnefoi Malunko, maître-documentaliste, read the plaque by his door on the first floor of a tumbling building with a seedy bar on the ground floor, and Goldhaven is well pleased with his new identity. The shiny red document decrees that Blomenvasa should be granted all facilities for speedy travel, not to mention immunity from legal process. Goldhaven has never seen anything like it.

The King of the Warris, too, knows a thing or two about immunity. He sits in a palace made of mud on a red rocky crag on the outskirts of Bobou where the wind sings among the broken stones. His Majesty is the descendant of one of the oldest line of kings between Cairo and Cape Town. For twelve centuries his forebears have kept the peace in these parts, with their cavalry, their sabres and their torches. For twelve centuries, the Kingdom's horseborne reapers have staked their claim on everything that moves across its lands, on lead and wood and wool and slaves. There is no pink champagne to be had in the royal palace. A single naked lightbulb illuminates the audience hall. Goldhaven has not come to marvel at the Kingdom's illustrious history. But the palace is Goldhaven's first port of call in Bobou. Goldhaven has done his homework. And he has a scribbled recommendation from the dusty man who came to his office in Antwerp. Goldhaven, too, is a King. The King of Comebacks. The Lord of Last Laughs. He has come with a suitcase full of emerald scrip, and no intention of departing empty-handed.

Goldhaven gets straight down to business with the King. J'ai bien aimé ce que j'ai vu, à Anvers. Il me faut plus de ça. Je paierai bien. Je paie mieux que quiconque. The King is non-committal. C'est bien. On est content. You will wait a bit, we'll let you know. You stay in Bobou, we come to you. But Goldhaven is not content. Not a bit. He has not come all the way out here to gaze at the camels and the moon rising over the tumbling medieval ramparts of Bobou Amer. Your Majesty, there is a misunderstanding, he says. Your man told me you had more of these. Lots more. Beaucoup beaucoup pierres, he says. That's what I do. Beaucoup de pierres. De bonnes pierres. Et je paie plus que les autres. Now it is the King's turn not to be amused. Vous voulez faire des affaires avec moi, you follow what I say. The King's adviser, crouched on the floor by his side, chips in. Vous savez à qui vous avez affaire, he says. His Majesty is sovereign over 70,000 people, he is the chief of the Warris, the Daïn, the Kring, and lord over the cities of Bobou Amer, Tuf Bahda, and forty villages. Nothing moves without his Majesty's accord. Rien. You do not like the way we do things in Dur Warris, you go back to Europe.

Goldhaven is down, but not out. He decides to stay the night in one of the UN guesthouses in Bobou, brandishing his red laissez-passer to silence any questions why he has not come with the requisite security authorizations signed by New York. In the evening, with the red satin covers of his laissez-passer emerging conspicuously from his back trouser pocket, Goldhaven mingles with the expats on the patio of the guesthouse. Goldhaven is in luck. There are no IDSA staff in Bobou, nor are there any sanitation experts, and barely anyone has so much as heard of IDSA. Goldhaven regales the crowd with stories of trekking through the Kasaïs in the service of the MDGs, repairing a well here, installing a hand-pump there. By the end of the evening, thanks to a dozen pint-sized bottles of airlifted Skol, he is chums with some people from the refugee agency, whose local knowledge of Dur Warris is second only to that of the King's men. And such a damn poor patch of the planet, too, he says. They've got nothing at all, nothing but baked earth.

Not true, one of the UN guys says. They do. They don't talk about it, but they do. Oh yeah, Goldhaven says, yawning. Yeah, the UN guy says, one of the refugees showed me once. Really big stones, too. But they don't want anyone to know. Seems they're really afraid of the King, the army. So, uhm, Goldhaven says, lifting the bottle of Skol to his mouth, where do these stones come from then?

Nobody knows. Probably on the other side. But nobody knows for certain. Gosh, Goldhaven says. By the way, I need a lift up North, got to get around some of the villages to check out the scope for new projects; I've got some good Swedish money lined up. Any chance you guys going out there soon? Sure thing, the guy from the refugee agency says. We're heading out to the camps again tomorrow, better take advantage while the ceasefire lasts. They say the war might start up again any day. It's a deal, Goldhaven says, and clinks his bottle of Skol. Let's hope we manage to get something under way before the war starts up again. Yeah, say that again, the guy from the refugee agency says. What he doesn't know is that wars tend to happen with disproportionate frequency in places visited by Goldhaven. But so do outbreaks of Ebola, and endemic malaria, and structural illiteracy. Goldhaven has never knowingly started a war.

7. Goldhaven has a scar

Down here it's mud, mud, mud everywhere. Everything turns to slurry and slime and sludge, shading from chocolate brown to charcoal black, enveloping everything. There's nothing that hasn't been captured and sandwiched here. Whole villages, civilizations, unclassified bugs, ship-sized Saurians, unlucky wizards still humming with static. Every stratum of history, every forgotten species, every freak disaster. There's nothing but mud now, and layer after layer of crap. Goldhaven strolls past in a leisurely aquatic glide, inspecting all the specimens, the conquests, exploits, casual mistakes. And mud is everywhere. The ruts in the lousy track have turned into a deep brown churn of muck. The rains have started. The way out to the camps is tedious. The

4x4 slips and swims along at snail's pace. After four hours, the first white tarpaulins come into view, water bladders, hastily constructed food warehouses. OK guys, this'll do, Goldhaven says, and with a wave he's off, into the warren of tents and huts. Goldhaven knows his way round places like this. He has an instinct, acquired in years of doing business in the field, for sniffing out the elders, the bigwigs. More important, he has an instinct for sniffing out the guys who really make the running, the guys with the guns. More important still, he has an instinct for sniffing out the guys who bankroll the guys with the guns.

The guys with the guns have blended in neatly, in this camp, careful not to attract too much attention. But Goldhaven is on to them in no time at all, and introduces himself as a friend of the cause. And then he gets down to business. Stones? Yes, it turns out they know all about the stones, and are readily charmed into talking. The pits run along a wadi just across the border. They have been worked for generations; and for generations, the locals have sold their bounty to a white man who comes in a flying machine from afar. White man, Goldhaven asks, what white man? White man in round hat, with tall man carrying big gun. Aha, Goldhaven thinks. Things are coming into focus. And the white man, does he say where he goes with the stones? He says he uses the stones for big magic. He pays good money. How good, Goldhaven asks. Not good at all, it turns out. I offer you five times as much, Goldhaven says. The guys with the guns, who are not readily given to incredulity, look at each other. Wait here, one of them says, and disappears in the warren of tents. He returns with an old man in a white gown who looks Goldhaven up and down. Why should we trust you, he says. We get good money for our stones. I will pay you much better money, Goldhaven says. The white man with the tall man from afar will not be pleased, the old man says. I am not afraid of the white man, Goldhaven says. The white man will work his magic on us, the old man says. I am not afraid of the white man's magic, Goldhaven says. In my country, I am a king, a sultan, a sheikh. He takes out his red laissez-passer. I am big with UN, he says. White man makes trouble, I call in UN. Big noisy flying machine with guns and thunder. The old man looks dubious. How much, he asks. Ten good stones, Goldhaven says, and opens his suitcase, this much.

The next morning, after a night spent in one of the huts under the protection of the guys with the guns, Goldhaven, wearing a boubou and chèche, heads off across the border in a caravan of a dozen camels. The guys with the guns don't seem too bothered about patrols. It's ceasefire time, and the perfect moment for trade and trafficking. The French, who

174

are alone in keeping an eye on the border with their planes and their patrols, are not interested in a few refugees on camels.

Just the other side of the border, there is a village. A boma of thatched huts; some of them bare and bearing traces of smoke from one of the many eruptions of bad blood that have swept over the region; a few skinny goats and sheep; camels tethered in the shade. Under the canopy of a baobab, Goldhaven meets the elders of the Kaja-Dahu, tall, unsmiling men in white boubous with grey beards. The elders, too, are swayed by the sight of Goldhaven's suitcase. But there is a problem. The King of the Warris has already been promised a cut. Not just a cut. Another 50 per cent on top of what Goldhaven is offering. Not good, Goldhaven says, and gets up. Wait, the elders say. They huddle together for a while, talking agitatedly, then go up to Goldhaven. The King will not be happy, they say. We can deal with that, but we need to improve our defences. Defences, Goldhaven asks, what defences? The King will not be happy, they say again. And they name their price, a third on top of the figure Goldhaven has named. Goldhaven does his figures. A complex pipeline; tricky logistics; and the King will not be amused. In these parts it is not a good idea to get on the wrong side of the King. It might prove difficult to get the stuff out through Bobou Amer. There will be multiple authorities to pay off. Goldhaven has no idea how he will bring the stuff to market. No provenance, no paperwork, no nothing.

Goldhaven can hear the hum of a small plane in the distance. Friend or foe, Goldhaven asks. White man in big hat and tall man with big gun, the elders say. OK, Goldhaven says, you have a deal. And – do not mention me to white man with big hat. Goldhaven withdraws to a shady corner between the huts. The plane, a single-engined Cessna with a Kenyan call sign, comes swooping in over the boma, almost touching the top of the baobab, then lands somewhere in the bush. The guys with the guns move off on their camels, to return ten minutes later with the passengers – a deeply tanned white man in khaki trousers and shirt and a comical pith helmet, and a very tall African man in a beige uniform with an oversized gun holster on his belt. Goldhaven can overhear most of the conversation. The white man greets the elders profusely, in English. The elders reply curtly. The white man hopes that fate has been good to the people of the boma since his last coming. The elders reply that this is a matter between fate and themselves. The white man opens the large leather satchel he is carrying. The elders remain impassive. The white man stops, asks if the wadi has been generous with its gifts since his last coming. The elders reply that the wadi no longer bears gifts for the white man in the flying machine. The white man loses his temper, starts shouting at the elders. The guys with the guns draw closer. The tall man in the beige uniform draws a Hi-Power from his holster. The guys with the guns start pointing their AKs. All right, all right, the white man says. I am sure you have your reasons. We can talk. The elders gesture dismissively. You are not welcome any more, they say. The white man closes his satchel. I will be back, he says. The elders look on in silence. The guys with the guns wave their AKs, and the white man in the pith helmet and his guard walk hastily out of the boma. Ten minutes later, and the Cessna is in the air again, circling the village before flying off at low altitude. Good riddance, Goldhaven says, to no one in particular.

There is a feast at the boma, that evening, but the elders are not smiling. The meat has the consistency of an old tractor tyre. There is not much fun to be had in these parts. At least the stones are good. Big, nice colour. No wonder the white men with the flying machines have kept their little arrangement a secret from the world for half a century.

For a month, two, three, Goldhaven comes and goes between the boma and the Dur Warris, crossing the border at will, waved on by the guys with the guns; flashing his red laissez-passer to stay at the guesthouse in Bobou and drink Skol with the aid workers; hitching rides on the UN shuttle to Karraïne; and making sure to stay well below the King's radar. But one day, crossing the border in an old Landcruiser he has bought in Bobou, Goldhaven is stopped by a flying patrol from the French army garrison. The red laissez-passer works its magic; but the lieutenant is not happy. Vous savez pas que c'est la guerre, hein, Blomenvasa? On vous conseille de rentrer directement à Bobou.

Never mind about me, Goldhaven says, I know my way around here, I have a project to visit the other side of the border, a well, I've finally managed to get it to flow, they need me there. Vous avez pas entendu, the lieutenant says again, taking Goldhaven by the shoulder, we strongly advise you to go back to Bobou. There's been shooting here these past few days. The King's men have started raiding villages on the other side. Ca pète de tous les côtés, d'accord? With that, Goldhaven is sent off on his way back to Bobou Amer. Back at the camp, he looks for the guys with the guns, only to be told they are out at work.

War, in the Dur Warris, is a haphazard affair, and involves occasional futile chases in technicals across the arid plains; the arbitrary encirclement of villages and rustling of cattle; the momentary seizure of sub-prefectures; and declaration of all-out victory; but its victories and defeats are never decisive or definitive. So Goldhaven, who is used to operating in such shifting terrain, takes care to avoid the usual tracks when crossing the border, and manages, more or less, to pick up his regular parcel from the boma. For the elders, it is business as usual. They do not blame Goldhaven for the King's hostile attentions; and they seem grateful for the additional flow of greenbacks into their war coffers.

But the sediment is merciless down here. Everything is catalogued, everything goes in the inventory, every little scrap of calamity is sealed and numbered. The good times and the bad. There's no place to look away, and cringing won't do. They're expressionless, the slithery scaled buggers down here, and they can't close their eyes on your shame. Goldhaven does not feel shame, stuck up here in his cage, but he can see the shame clouding the smooth flow of the Rhine now, little white specks and flakes on the dull black surface. It hits Goldhaven on his way to the shower block. He's just stepped out from the guesthouse with a yawn, another hot and tedious day breaking over the badlands. There's a bright light, up so close it makes Goldhaven's eyes ache. A white woman in her twenties, short brown hair, khaki shorts, white T-shirt, not bad-looking. She's got a camera, and she's thrusting it in Goldhaven's face. Mr Goldhaven, can you tell me what you are doing in Bobou Amer. Her accent is English, educated, supercilious, know-all. What, Goldhaven says, in a Swedish accent, or possibly Danish, or Norwegian. I'm Björn Blomenvasa. I'm a senior official of the International Development Support Agency.

Oh come on Goldhaven, she says, I know exactly who you are. Don't deny it. Whawhawha, Goldhaven says. I'm providing sanitation infrastructures for the people of the Dur Warris region. Wells bore-holes latrines. Goldhaven takes out his red laissez-passer. Björn Blomenvasa, he says, official of the D-2 category.

So you deny ever having had a commercial relationship with the Kaja-Dahu people? Rubbish, Goldhaven says. The only relations I have had with people of any description are of a sanitary nature. Now if you would allow me to go and have my shower, Goldhaven says, stepping forward. But the woman does not budge, keeps sticking the camera in Goldhaven's face. Goldhaven pushes the woman aside and walks on. The night has been hot. He needs a shower. But then there are whistles, half a dozen UN security staff come jogging up, nightsticks are drawn, a right fracas. Goldhaven has a big gash right down his cheek, bleeding profusely.

Goldhaven knows this round of the game is up. Before there can be an internal inquiry, a DSS team dispatched from New York, credentials investigated, IDSA HQ contacted and found not to exist, Goldhaven has gathered up his kit, stashed the last parcel from the boma away at the bottom of his suitcase, and hitched a ride on the shuttle back to Karraïne. Ça va pas, ask the French engineers whiling away another evening in the bowels of the nightclub behind the hotel. Vous avez eu un accident? Oui, c'est ça, Goldhaven says, I bumped into a fucking wild hog up in the North. Crazy country. Crazy country, the engineers concur, drôle de pays. Goldhaven waves a bundle of CFA francs at the girl swaying by herself on the dancefloor. Ce soir, l'amour va frapper, OK?

8. Goldhaven is not a sissy

Mixed in with the other crap in the sediment there's a raft of nightmares. Goldhaven hasn't chosen these, and they're not something he usually loses sleep over. They're paperwork, mostly, extracts from files, interview records, panel reports, more unpleasant full-page ads, signed by dozens of minor celebrities. And a nasty letter from the bourse that lands in his letter box one morning, the cowardly postman evaporating into the Antwerp drizzle before Goldhaven gets a chance to throw it back in his face with a return to sender. A disciplinary hearing. A threat of exclusion. Fuck them, Goldhaven says. Who needs a bourse when you've got guts and flair. Goldhaven gets another letter. A summons from the federal organized crime squad. Fuck, Goldhaven says.

He puts on a tie and calls his lawyer. Goldhaven goes to Brussels. Goldhaven hates Brussels: there are no rivers in Brussels. The meeting room is cold, impersonal but for the shields and flags of various police squads, exercises, cross-border programmes lining the walls. Crossed swords, the scales of Lady Justice, framed in olive branches. Variations on this, in all manner of national colours. Cops don't have a lot of imagination. A tape recorder has been set up on the table. Sit down, the chief inspector says. Goldhaven can sense the Feds' excitement. They've been waiting for this. They've been waiting for a big fish like Goldhaven. The industry has turned squeaky-clean and sterile. Like any other industry. Big corporations, transparency, beneficiation. Every little crumb certified and traceable. But to have an old-style buccaneer like Goldhaven in one's clutches, for once. They've been preparing for this day, building up their file, constructing their case. Honing their technique, sharpening their claws, practising their Dirty Harry frowns. For years they've been whiling their time away with small-time tax fiddles, the occasional polisher with sticky fingers. And now the big fish has swum into their net. The big bad croc. The big black cayman himself.

You are not being charged at this stage, the chief inspector says. This is an exploratory conversation. If my client is not being charged, Goldhaven's lawyer says, there is no point in continuing. I suggest we terminate this meeting and reconvene when you have made up your mind what you want from my client. Wait, Goldhaven says. I'm happy to talk. I have nothing to hide. I want to know what I'm being accused of. Goldhaven's lawyer looks unhappy, tries to whisper in Goldhaven's ear. But Goldhaven wants to face this like a man. Goldhaven is not going to be a sissy hiding behind technicalities. Good, the chief inspector says. Let's begin shall we. You recognize the location where these photographs were taken, presumably. The chief inspector places pictures of Goldhaven in Likuana on the table. Well, I suppose I do, Goldhaven says. And what if I do? This is Likuana, is it not, the chief inspector says. What were you doing in Likuana, Mr Goldhaven. I was tending my garden, Goldhaven says. I beg your pardon, the chief inspector says. I was tending my garden. Cultivating my patch. I'm a great fan of African horticulture. Have you ever tried creating a landscaped garden in Africa? It's great fun. People are ever so interested, and ever so helpful. The crowds that come along to help you. The plants that people want you to plant. The whole village had ideas about perennials. And some kid who absolutely wanted me to plant some succulents. Everybody wanted to work on the water feature.

Then what are these, the chief inspector says, and

puts a sheaf of photocopies on the table. Receipts for the purchase of Caterpillars in Dar es Salaam. Gravel pumps and jigs in Jo'burg. A mining dredge – a dredge, of all things – in Durban. Ah yes, Goldhaven says. To create a proper landscaped garden, you need to sort your pebbles into the right sizes. And you certainly need some decent earth-moving equipment. Ponds, borders, hills, gazebos. Right? You are aware that Likuana is in an area that was not under government control at the time of your presence there, the chief inspector asks. If you tried to reduce Africa to the bits that happen to be under government control, Goldhaven says, you might as well stay at home, Chief Inspector.

Goldhaven's lawyer intervenes. Chief Inspector, I draw your attention to the fact that it has at no point been illegal under Belgian law or the decrees implementing UNSC sanctions to be present in or indeed conduct economic activities in the area around Likuana. Your insinuations are most improper. The chief inspector starts rummaging in his file. We have witnesses who can attest to your having directed the mining operations in Likuana. Goldhaven shrugs his shoulders. Roll them on, he says. Once more, Goldhaven's lawyer intervenes. Whatever you might be referring to concerns at most infringements of local mining regulations. I don't see how this is relevant to our conversation. The chief inspector continues. You are aware, presumably, that you were identified by the sanctions committee when it made a site visit to your operation in Likuana, Mr Goldhaven. Pages 23 to 34 of the report. Quite a detailed description, you might say. I take it you have read the report, Mr Goldhaven?

Goldhaven's lawyer begins to shift uneasily on his chair. All of this is highly irregular, Chief Inspector, he says. A committee report has no value as evidence in a court of law. You know that perfectly well. You bring this report into court as evidence, and I will demolish every line of it. I am sure the judge will not be too impressed by hearsay produced by a bunch of amateurs who spent all of, what, two hours on the ground?

It's OK, Goldhaven says. I want to answer the question. As it happens, Chief Inspector, I only read fiction. As a matter of principle. Comes in handy when you're wrestling a croc. I am not joking, Mr Goldhaven, the chief inspector says. How do you explain the fact that after your return from Likuana, your trades at the bourse suddenly increased by 400 per cent over your previous averages? The chief inspector produces a thick ream of print-outs detailing Goldhaven's transactions. I can trace everything I sold, Goldhaven says. I can produce a permit for every import. And I can assure you we will be looking at those permits very carefully in the coming weeks, the chief inspector says. Now, let's move on. The principal reason for our conversation today. What were you doing in Karraïne?

Kara-what, Goldhaven says. How do you spell that? We have the invoice from your stay at the hotel in Karraïne, the chief inspector says, producing another piece of paper. We even have the invoice from the nightclub. Shall I remind you? Ah yes, Goldhaven says. My holiday in Karraïne. Yes, I do remember now. Well, may I tell you a secret? Goldhaven leans over the table, conspiratorially. Chief Inspector, how shall I put this. I like African women, he whispers. Are you going to arrest me, Chief Inspector?

I'm only interested in some of your dirty little secrets, the chief inspector says with a frown. From Karraïne you moved on to Bobou Amer. What were you doing in Bobou Amer?

Now that, Goldhaven says, is where you've got your sources in a twist. I've never heard of this Boubou place of yours. The chief inspector places another document on the table. The passenger list from the UN flight that Goldhaven took from Karraïne to Bobou Amer. You were travelling under the assumed name of Björn Blomenvasa, the chief inspector says. Bjooorn Blooomenvasa, Goldhaven says, drawing out the Os. What a silly name. I would have thought of something more plausible.

I remind you Mr Goldhaven, that you were caught on camera by a journalist in Bobou Amer. In fact you were caught on camera in the middle of a rather graphic assault. A spectacular case of mistaken identity, Goldhaven says. And I really must object, Goldhaven's lawyer says. If Mr Goldhaven is accused of assault in Karraïne, I am sure we can wait for an extradition request to come in through the normal channels. Except that, if my memory serves me right, Karraïne does not have an extradition treaty with the kingdom. And I believe common assault is not covered by the kingdom's statute on extraterritoriality. The chief inspector is unimpressed. Counterfeiting of UN travel documents is an offence in the kingdom under the terms of the treaty on privileges and immunities, he says. Punishable by up to five years' imprisonment. You have no proof that my client ever travelled under the name of Björn Blomenvasa, the lawyer says. And even if he did, you cannot prove the charge of counterfeiting. Oh, but we've only barely begun, the chief inspector says. And anyway, this is all by the by. Mr Goldhaven, have you ever been to the land of the Kaja-Dahu?

The what, Goldhaven says. Do you make these names up yourself? You might not read the newspapers, the chief inspector says, but presumably you have heard of the conflict in the Dur Warris. A little local unpleasantness, Goldhaven says. There's plenty of that, in Africa and elsewhere. I don't see what it has to do with me.

Goldhaven's lawyer looks increasingly uncomfortable. I object to my client being questioned about current affairs, he says. He is a businessman, not a journalist. And his personal views on African politics have no bearing whatsoever on the matter you are discussing with him. It's OK, Goldhaven says. Even if I don't read the newspapers, I take more than a passing interest in African politics. So you deny ever setting foot in the land of the Kaja-Dahu, the chief inspector asks. You deny having had meetings with their elders, negotiating the purchase for cash of a significant proportion of their production? Now why would I buy anything from the Catcha-Doo, or whatever they're called, Goldhaven says. What could they have that I might be interested in? Cotton boubous? Millet? I'm not in the millet business. Far too unpredictable. I wouldn't have the nerves for all that price instability. The chief inspector looks at his colleagues. Do you have any questions for Mr Goldhaven at this stage, gentlemen? They shake their heads. Well then, thank you for your time, Mr Goldhaven. A most profitable conversation. You can count on us to be in touch. You will be informed through the usual channels if there is a formal indictment. And I suggest you consult your lawyer on the chances of that happening. Personally, I am rather optimistic.

9. Goldhaven always gets the goods

OK you win, Goldhaven says, yells, screams, at the top of his voice, I'll give you whatever you want I'll get the goods tell your people I'll get it now stop I'll get whatever they want give me a month—

The car stops see-sawing. Zog Shikzahl's face appears by the passenger window. You get the good. Much good. Next time you go in water. One month. Yeah yeah, whatever, Goldhaven says, now let me out of here. But Zog Shikzahl is gone, disappeared into the night, cuneiform, preceded by a gust of bad vibes. The faces in the water, too, are gone, just another bad memory. There's nothing but the bridge and the carcass of the beemer, pathetically perched. The surface of the river is dulled back to its oily black flow. Goldhaven tries the doors one last time, finds that they are wedged solid, sits still for an hour, maybe, shivering, then wends his way onto the back seats. He picks up the fire extinguisher, smashes the rear window, brushes the myriad little twinkling crystals out of the way, cuts his hand, squeezes out, awkwardly, the car see-sawing all the while, slides over the boot, down onto the tarmac. One hundred K or so of Bavarian Motorsport sits cantilevered on the edge of the bridge, the centre of gravity just behind the front wheels. Fuck. How do you explain that to the cops? Goldhaven could report the beemer stolen. But Goldhaven is anything but inconspicuous. His exit from that bar in Dusseldorf with Zog Shikzahl was nothing if not theatrical. And even if the clientele of the bar like to stay in the shade, the cops always find someone who will talk. The last thing Goldhaven needs now is yet another constabulary on his tails. He kicks the beemer's rear bumper, pushes hard against its back end, finds that it moves more easily than expected, grating but smooth over various spilled lubricants from the underside of the car. A few centimetres, halfway between the front and rear axles, and the beemer just lets go, tips headlong over the edge, a silent plunge, a splosh, and is gone, sinking gently even now into layer upon layer of sand, gravel, mucky alluvium. Who would look for a beemer on the bed of the Rhine.

Generations of tourists off to ogle castles and dragons and fair maidens will glide over it and not know. Goldhaven casts one last look into the black waters and shrugs. One hundred grand. Ten carats. Life goes on. Goldhaven has an idea.

A big stone is all it takes. One very, very big stone. Cleave it; cleave half of it again; frazzle the edges, dull the surfaces – Goldhaven knows a freelance polisher in the back streets here who can do wonders, turn brown clonkers into fancy marvels. Just one very big stone; the Russians can get their share, an astral shower of two-carat splinters, spread to a trickle, enough to make the Russians bite; slow enough to make them patient, and intrigued, and wanting more. It's where Goldhaven wants them; and just then he will split, Zog Shikzahl or no Zog Shikzahl. And Goldhaven will get his big stone, his big double-digit pink stone.

So Goldhaven does what he does best. Sits waiting. Looks good. Keeps his ear to the ground, the long tables of the bourse, and the polished black marble bars of Goldhaven's habitual after-hour haunts. Picks up the vibes. Some melée for a prom-queen crown. Not interested. A mountain of carbos for a year's production of drill-heads. Forget it. A couple of blue stones for a fancy big-name atelier in Paris. Not today, folks. Who's this now, passing down the aisle ponderously in a double-breasted suit. The chairman of the bourse's disciplinary committee. Ouch. Goldhaven turns his face full-on into the soft north light of the windows, a posture almost as flattering as the profile. From behind, Goldhaven could be any bourse dandy now, jet-black, a very sleek raven. The double-breasted suit passes, and Goldhaven swivels back to profile.

And then, one day, the answer comes to Goldhaven, calling from a public payphone all mysterious, Meet me down at Nellie's, and Goldhaven knows there and then he's got it made. Nellie's is one of those places your average dealer, peroxide-clean these days with permits and warranties and ethical audits, wouldn't be seen dead in. But Goldhaven is not your average dealer. The man sitting there at the back, under the football widescreen and clearly paranoid about microphones, is an amateur, Goldhaven can tell, from the way he fidgets and ticks. He's just a go-between, at a few removes from the people in on the job. Where, Goldhaven asks. Where on earth is that, Goldhaven asks. Stones, what stones, Goldhaven asks. What colour, Goldhaven asks. How big, Goldhaven asks. Goldhaven can tell it's the real thing. The guy is too nervous for a scam. And anyone who's anyone knows better than to pull a scam on Goldhaven. The man sitting here fidgeting doesn't really know shit, but he does know it's a weird job. A big up-front investment. Not too many questions asked; and not too many answered. It's better that way, for all concerned. And the pay-off's big enough to make it worth anyone's while. The down payment, for Goldhaven, is no big deal. He has a few nest eggs stashed away, in Belgium and in more benign jurisdictions. There's one catch, though. Whoever puts up the big cash, and harvests the big returns, also has to take care of getting the goods to market. The syndicate behind the job won't touch that side of things; too hairy; too many ramifications. The syndicate, from what little Goldhaven can gather, is just a bunch of local heavies who will be all too happy to pass the buck further down the line when the splatter hits the fan. That's fine by Goldhaven, too. Goldhaven has never shied away from the music, unlike the salon adventurers who crowd the bourse. And as for getting the goods to market – Goldhaven remembers his conversation with Zog Shikzahl. Дурак. Durak. Dumbo idyot. Now there's a thought. A dumbo idyot is just what Goldhaven needs for this job. And Goldhaven knows just the man.

194

Three

Down the River

10

The bird has impenetrable eyes, cast-over eyes, swished from time to time by some kind of membrane, and a long spear-like beak. It sits perched over me, inspecting the wreckage. So, uh, this is a bench here, split down the middle, cheap synthetic rag-doll filling spilling out like candy floss. This is glass, in a spangly milky way leading nowhere. This is a nice metre-long piece of fuselage, it's got part of the call-sign on it, a 9 and a Q, no country I know. And this here is a gyroscope, see how it turns upon itself, the still centre, etc. The bird affects interest, bends its neck into a curling snake, spins the outer wheel, and again the membrane goes swish-swish. This is wheel-rubber, coming home at long last, running off into the trees. This is kerosene in a drip, see how it flickers to a dead black rust. But who cares, I've got my bundle. There's no way I'm showing Big Bird here my pink wonder. But Big Bird plays in a different league anyway. He's plucked me by the collar of my shirt – torn, blood-splattered, enough gore to last a chapter or two of Babbon's little red book – and flung me out into the red clay of the landing strip. Where am I, I want to say, but my lips won't move. Shut up, Big Bird says, seven foot three and shoulders like a watchtower. A talking bird, whatever next, I want to say, but my lips won't move. This way, it nods. Where, I want to say. Into the woods, it says, and there's a chorus coming from deep in the trees. This way, into chlorophyll and pulp.

There's a sign over the treeline where we're heading, Welcome to the Arboretum, it says, in caveman letters, two monkeys astride it juggling their pink rocks. Where are you taking me, I want to say. Shut up, the bird says. The Boss will talk to you when he's ready. Oh, rodent voices coo in the branches, chipmunks or the like, he's being taken to see the Boss, and then a murmur spreads through the forest, the Boss, taken off to see the Boss. Furry shapes dash across the path around me, poke my legs with sharpened bamboo staves, hissing taunts of GI, hey GI, we get you. Sorry chaps, I want to say, wrong continent, wrong century, but no, they insist, the Boss rules this part of the forest. And it's true, there are skeleton choppers hanging from the trees, the odd Starfighter, the occasional hail of flintstone arrows raining down on us from the wings. Propaganda adorns the mangrove, big red drapes over the branches, set with Svarovski glitter, recalling the basics. The Boss is the Boss. Don't mess with the Boss. Naturally. I'm not political, I want to insist, really it's a misunderstanding, but the banners keep coming. Pink is for pussies. Size matters, and colour, and cut. Hey, I want to say, what are you suggesting, but the bird doesn't care for this kind of idle chatter, and from behind the dripping leaves, heavy with monstrous cocoons and amorous groans, I can hear Kaat giggling. What, I want to shout, I should have thought better of you, but she's gone into fade.

Along the way they point out a gallery: dusty glass cases on either side of the path, man-size; cardboard labels in a dusky nineteenth-century scribble. Joshua Babbon wears his with pride, though his sack of bones is much collapsed, his natural history erratic. You never did trust me, he says, and here's your comeuppance. Next, a tall man in a dark suit, showy white collar, raven-black hair, no need for a label though he's got his back turned to me. You're not, he's saying to no one in particular, really getting anywhere are you, and then there's a beep where my name should have been, and then he flicks his cigar my way, and fifty grand in expenses. But but, I want to stammer, I'm not expendable, really, and the next case is empty, but I can guess who it's for. Charlie, the old-fashioned scribble on the label says, and Farlow, or Harlow, or some such. Oh no, I think. Oh yes, the assembled fauna cackles. Who are you, a voice pipes up, thin and volatile. I stammer, and to my surprise I can speak, but I've forgotten the name. I don't know, I say. Who are you. I see it now, the size of a small pigeon, plumage indeterminate but rather jolly. I'm the pink cockareen, it says. Hardly, I say, surprised at my daring, you're not pink at all. Lesser spotted, it says, pointing out a pink spot on its tummy, octahedron-shaped, nice colour. There's canned laughter coming out of the under-growth, more taunts. And then a stern voice barking at the far end of the alleyway. Order, order. Who's that, I want to say, but I'm too weary to move my lips. Doesn't matter, Big Bird says, I can read your mind anyway. Order, order, that harsh voice bellowing again from down the alleyway. He's coming into focus now, an old man sitting on a pyramid, flowing white hair, waving a sceptre of sorts, or a paddle. I'm sure I've seen him before, a pin-up in Babbon's book maybe. No, he says, a frontispiece, engraved. Nonsense, I hear a croak from back in Babbon's case, the man's a fraud. Silence, the white-haired man roars and all is still in the menagerie. But, I want to say, but Big Bird leans over and whispers,

You don't speak in his presence, unless spoken to. Oh, I say, somewhat disappointed, but the Boss has cut me off. He's wearing a straw hat now, a perfect cone in the Vietnamese fashion. Steady yourself for the big question, Big Bird whispers, and here it comes. *What*, the Boss thunders, to a roar of applause from the gallery, critters and cryptids, reptiles, rats and raptors, even the odd botanical specimen flapping approvingly, *What manner of creature are you, exactly?* Oh no, I want to say, always that question, but my lips won't move.

I thought so, the Boss says, running his fingers through a vast red tome, you don't feature in my system. Now get out of my Arboretum. An awed hush runs through the massed fauna and flora, then frantic whispering. Kaat looks sad but not surprised, squeezed in between the meerkats and the kangaroos, and even Hazel looks disappointed, from her ringside seat somewhere between hawthorn and hebe. And then Big Bird picks me up by my bloodied collar, and I'm paraded out past the massed critters, orders and families and genera galore, out to the back entrance, where great auks and dodos await their turn to exit. At least we made it into his system, they tell me as I brush past. Good point, I want to say, but the air's thin up here, as I dangle from Big Bird's beak, arms and legs kicking, and here we are now, it says Exit, above the treeline, and No Re-entry, and there's a stagedoor, and out we go, and Big Bird's flung me off into the pale grey distance, and my landing isn't a pretty sight, brains and blood seeping out of my head, jumping fish, wiggling caymans, green goo, gushing out, running to the sea. It's cold and grey outside the Arboretum, everything's caked in concrete, a flyover obscuring the sun. I know this place.

11

It's Sunday morning in Mechelen. I feel Kaat's arm next to me. My knee rubs against her thigh. I don't want to get up. Rain outside. I don't know if Kaat is pretty, but I like the feel of her, up against the rain and cold. I run my hand up from her knee, listen to her breathing. The rain hammering against the window panes. A nasty rain, a hard rain, pounding my temples. Why is the rain so painful this morning. It's grey outside, and yet there's a blinding light here. My eyes are still closed. I don't get it. I've had the most ridiculous dream. Talking birds. But it's not as if I chose my dreams. Something's banging against my temples. How are you feeling. A voice, and it's not Kaat's, and it's not the talking bird. I open my eyelids, the light is too strong. I don't recognize these sheets, this pillow.

I'm not in Mechelen, and my head hurts. Not a head-ache, something much worse, a pounding and grinding. Rough landing you had there, the voice says. Wasn't much left of the plane. I open my eyes a little. A room. The sound of rain, drumming on the roof, water dripping somewhere. Better get some rest now, the voice says, moving further away. I can't make out if it's a man or a woman. A door is opened and closed. Where am I, I ask, but there's no one there. I try to sit up, but the pounding in my head is too strong. Nausea wells up inside me like a rotten fruit. I fall back onto the pillow. The ceiling is corrugated iron, green-stained. The last thing I remember is the plane, skidding on that muddy landing-strip. Bushes and trees, and suddenly the plane spun around, and then there was a big jolt. I feel my head. There's a thick bandage, thicker still just over my right temple. Shit. Where's my holdall, where's my bundle. I try to sit up again, but the nausea is too strong. I drift off again. I never used to dream. The rain keeps drumming down on the corrugated iron roof. I want to throw up but can't. It's not in my stomach, it's in my head, a lopsided heaviness that's yanking my brains around. I look around. A room, just big enough for a camp bed, a folding table and a chair. A gas light on the wall. A puddle in one corner, with a steady drip down from the ceiling. The sheets are torn and stained. There is no net. Excuse me, I say, but there is no one there. I get up and walk slowly over to the door. The door is a sheet of plywood. There is no lock. The nausea gets to me. I stumble back to the camp bed and collapse. I want to scream, but there's no sound. The patter of rain on the corrugated iron roof is all there is. Rain is all there was, that time in Normandy with Kaat. Rain against the windows of the cheap hotel over-looking the harbour. To think that they towed those concrete jetties all the way across the Channel, I said, bombs and shells raining down all around them. Incredible, Kaat said from the bathroom, they've got bath salts in the shape of rubies here. The room comes into focus. What does Kaat know about rubies. The walls really are cardboard-thin. There's green creeping in through a gap between the planks on one side. We made love in the bathroom, Kaat going on about the ruby-shaped bath-salts, and then things came apart. Rubbish piled up on the table. Animal noises wafting in from outside. Grunts and shuffles on the other side of the cardboard-thin walls. Oh shit. I should be in Hopeton by now, strolling through customs. An in-and-out job. Piece of cake. Let me take that jacket of yours, sir. Oh no jacket, just a bloodstained shirt, never mind, with the fare you're paying sir we won't ask any questions. Would you like some champagne sir. But my bag, where's my bag. Sorry sir, the steward says, no pink cockareens on this flight. Sanitary regu-lations. What, I want to say, and I open my eyes.

Nothing, but my bag's right there, by my bed. And the bundle's inside. I feel the stone. Thank goodness. The nausea comes back in a sudden rush. I throw up. I should be reading that menu now. Feet up, one push of the button for the perfect lounging sensation. The Boeing's engines firing up. Or maybe it's a chopper. I think I can hear a chopper's blades in the background, whacka-whacka-whacka. And then I drift off again. I'll have the beef tenderloin. And the Rioja. More bread, yes please. The vinaigrette. I'm through with this. I mean it. Once I've taken out the stone and got my money, I'll retire from the industry. I won't have to work, for a while. Perhaps I'll travel. Not to these nauseous tropics. Canada sounds nice. And then I'll see. I feel the stone again, hard and very big. A stone like this must come to market every ten years, at most. I would not know. I have asked the Indians if they will let me come to an auction. They have always found an excuse. You're doing an excellent job, they will say, mustn't get you distracted. I will show them, when I crunch the gravel, when one of the lackeys brings round my Testarossa. I'll stick a twenty-euro note in the pocket of his shirt and wave goodbye. So long, I'll say, and I will have spoiled their afternoon, and garbled their astrology. Welcome to the future, I'll say to Kaat, who's wearing tight white shorts so indecently short her legs run right up into the sky. I'm so tired.

I'd better have a story, for when they come back. The voice, whoever put the bandage round my head. Whoever pulled me from the wreckage. Friend or foe. It matters, out here. I'm a birdwatcher, I'd lie. How delightful, they'd say. You must be the first. Why here, of all places? A bird I'm after, I'd say. You wouldn't have heard of it. Try me, they'd say. Lafayette's lesser spotted cockareen, I'd say. The Northern Amazonian sub-species, with the pink patch on its belly. They say the only remaining population nests in these parts. If I'm lucky, they'll buy it. If I'm not, they'll throw the Linnaean book at me. It's big and pretty heavy. There's no such thing as a cockareen, they'd say. Least of all a Lafayette's. English usage, I'd say, one last try. Might be different in the States. Mexican laughing-jack, maybe? Hardly, they'd say. And then I'd be screwed.

There's a low noise from behind the wall, snorting and sawing. I manage to get up, walk over to the door. It's still raining. Over by the far end of the landing strip, I can make out a tangle in the bushes where the plane skidded into the trees. I walk along the side of the shack. There's another door, another room like the one I woke up in, with a camp bed and a table. The pilot is lying on the camp bed, snoring, his wet shirt thrown over the back of a camping chair. There's a big pile of money on the table, one-hundred-dollar bills. The pounding in my head starts again.

12

I never used to dream. It takes imagination. I have none. But something got shaken up when the Islander hit the trees. So where are you taking me, Old Road? Shut up and sleep, Old Road says as he takes the pirogue downriver, down rapids and water-falls, past stockades and through barrages of poison-tip arrows, through the estuary of the Malakuzi. We hop over the sea-wall, dash out into the open sea. Where are you taking me, Old Road? Out into the turquoise tub. Let's dabble in islands. Take this one here, Old Road says. Encircled by flying fish, giant terns skimming the water, sea-turtles casting their wavering shadows against the pale blue reef. Jagged cliffs at one end and a long lip of white sand extending around the lagoon on the other. A wooden landing pier; a band of friendly local scare-crows who haul in the pirogue, the smell of grilled jacaré, fresh and chewy. There are coconuts raining down into the white sand, and papaya, and starfruit. Who's that now. Short brown hair, khaki shorts, running into the warm blue water with her snorkel by her side, circled by choppers like dragonflics. Come, Old Road says, and the pirogue darts out into the reef where the big fish cavort, where Boss Macquarie is At Home today, offering witch-lobster canapés and slices of sea-gherkin. What you been up to man, Old Road asks, and the Boss grunts, Been wrestling with the white-tips. Tut tut, Old Road says. Gave 'em a fighting chance, the Boss says. Queensberry rules and all.

I want to dally a while with Hazel under the coconut trees but Old Road is a mean taskmaster. No time, man. This is the express, man. You wanna be slow food, you better go back to Marlow's, man. We got work to do, man. Where to, Old Road, I stutter in a blur. Up the white sand, into the picture-book jungle with a vengeance. Oh no, not the forest, I implore Old Road. Pretty palms and rainbow-feathered lorikeets, pristine streams with jumping fish and giant frogs glistening in gold and blue, lime-green tree-snakes dangling from the branches of rubber trees, chequerboard monkeys, pitcher-plants big as cars, their giant cups filled with fraying tapirs and fading sloths. Why, Old Road, why. Shut up, man, Old Road says, and look, and study. I consult my guidebook. A large octavo, red linen embossed in gilt, torn at the spine. Babbon's Book of Practical Caymans, it says in whiplash lettering. Open it, Old Road commands, and lifts a ragged old cloth at the back of the pirogue. What's that, Old Road, I ask, incredulous. A twelve-inch dreadnought gun, my friend. Is that a crystal octahedron glistening among Old Road's incisors as he grins at me? Nobody mess with Old Road, Old Road says.

And here we are now. A deep ravine; and on the other side of the ravine, tall spikes of rock jutting up out of a sandy desert of crags and crevices, yellow bluffs of stone half-eroded like giant termites' hills. Wooden crane-like structures emerging from the rock here and there, swaying in the wind. There is no wind. Piles of sand and gravel lie scattered like giant anthills and worm casts. There is a constant sound of clanging, hammering, the occasional dull explosion; and then the earth will shudder lightly, and a plume of smoke and dust emerge from one of the holes. There are holes everywhere, little man-sized rabbit-holes, or bigger craters bulging into the innards of the earth, or messy molehills where the digging has taken place from the inside, and the entire structure has collapsed on itself, and drawn piles of loose gravel down, down into the hole.

These miners, whatever they might be, they're in a league of their own. There must be thousands of holes; and below ground, thousands of miners, hammering and drilling, away from the scorching midday sun. What are they mining, I ask Old Road. Shut up, Old Road says. When cayman ready for you, he come for you from deep down below. And Old Road falls into a cavernous cackle that makes the nearest pit collapse into itself, a dust mushroom rising cathedral-high into the azure sky. I see, I say. What does Babbon say? Babbon has nothing to say. He sits grinning on one of the anthills a little further down, waving his big red book of poppycock, white bones bleached by the sun of the Malakuzi, teeth ground down by the monotonous fare the natives have been feeding him, seeds you can cut glass with, kernels hard as drillheads. Savages all. What's that, Babbon? Babbon has taken out his Winchester. Her Majesty won't stand for this, he says. I'll now proceed to read the riot act. He waves his big bad boatman's stick, fires petty little shots of lead up in the air. There's an echo all across the minescape. The orcs down in their potholes have taken their pieces out, their slingshots, and now the holes are spewing forth carbuncles. Carbuncles? Opals, perhaps, black and shimmery as Goldhaven's hair. But these are no ordinary opal mines. These, Babbon says in his tinderbox voice, Victorian-posh and graveyard-thin, are the opal mines of Pulau-Sulakko; and though the savages here did their all to expose a most savage disposition, the opals revealed themselves to be of exquisite quality, delicate in flavour, soft but firm in the hand, like the cheek of the savage I named Samson, and not unlike the fruit I have encountered in my youth on the wild slopes of Bein Mahon; and which the local peasantry in those parts know most flatteringly by the name of Babbon-berry—

A salvo from Old Road's twelve-inch gun puts paid to the babble. I want to go home, I say. Back to Kaat. She's got the smoothest legs in Flanders. No use moping about it, Old Road says. I'll take you on a tour. What's your name anyway, Old Road says. Durak, I say. Dumbo idyot. Can you spell that for me, Old Road says. Sure, I say. Дурак, etched in giant opalescent letters into the cliff face here, Gould's shearwaters tumbling all about it as Goldhaven's beemer goes over the edge. Идиот, I add, for good measure. Oh yeah man, Old Road says. I thought so. But never mind. Come, Old Road says, mind your head now.

And down we go. Drills, shovels, poles and ropes scattered about, the occasional flash as a charge goes off in a siding, and then the tunnel goes black with the plume, and then the rummaging begins. Jacaré! a cry goes up, and everyone dives for cover, scampers for the smaller shafts, waits for the big snout to pass. And off they go again, driving their shafts left and right and diagonal and up and down. A silent gasp of surprise resonates from one of the tunnels ahead. Oh-oh, a breakthrough. A breakthrough? Seems a crew ahead of us have burrowed out through the cliff face on the far side of the island, and tumbled with their brittle shaft into the blue waters below, patrolled by reef-sharks and skimmed by hungry frigatebirds. Ain't nothing beyond Marlow's, man, Old Road cackles. And down we go, the pirogue drilling vertical now, deep into the core of the island. Even down here, there are crews at work, below the bottom of the sea, with water pissing in through the drill-holes and sloshing about our feet. Duck, Old Road says. Where, I say, but Old Road has thrown his tarpaulin over me, and it's an armadillo's skin, meshed and metallic, and the bullets dance off it, greasy and dark. Shit happens, a voice drones on in the background, a natural-history voice-over, all neutral and bored. And every once in a while, it goes on, a drilling crew will break through the wall of a tunnel, and find itself face to face with the competition. And so the miners of Pulau-Sulakko come well-equipped to the fray now that the season has started. They bring ropes and poles and drills and buckets and spades, and they bring machetes; and old pirate muskets, and pistols from wartime stashes. Mining on Pulau-Sulakko has become an underground game of Russian roulette, a troglodyte's chicken game. Can I come out now, I say. Only a fool be scared of a cayman in a boat, Old Road says, his eyes glowing like red LEDs in the dark. The voice in the background goes fuzzy, then hums back into focus. There are pacific solutions to some of the encounters, it says, but more often than not, they end in bloodshed, with one side retreating and the other taking over the vacated tunnels and shafts—

A pocket of cold air gusts past, accompanied by a posse of gnomes. They've got pick-axes, ropes slung round their waists, red capes over their white manes. Stop, the chief of the gnomes commands, and leans over to me with a conspiratorial whisper. You know what, Durak, we just like the candy down here. It's our dirty little secret. It's the sign of a true Africanist. And with a chuckle he's off, leading his little militia into battle, off to tap the walls for any sign of thinning or brittleness, and then they'll post themselves, sidearm at the ready, by the suspect tract, waiting for a possible breakthrough. Enough, I cry, choking on the yellow dust, gagging in the dank darkness here at the heart of the opal cliffs. But Old Road is sulking, has steered the pirogue off into a branchline of the river, where the cliffs are made of blood-streaked marble and wiry little mosquitoes wait humming in the cracks. OK, I say, and pull out a fat wad of silver certificate bills, faded to pastel-green, and with the side-burned image of Joshua Babbon throning on a pyramid. Old Road grunts assent and fires up the outboard. It's sticky outside. Old Road steers the pirogue to the edge of the cliff. A flotilla of little boats lies at anchor in the large bay below; each waiting for its cargo, a crewman squatting in the hold with a rifle, or a flare, scanning the bay for scavengers. The waters are agitated; cut by jutting fins. There are rich pickings to be had now, and whenever the sound of gunshot rings out, reverberating through the trumpet-like hollows of the tunnels and shafts, the reef-sharks jostle for position in the wash below the opal rocks. And still more hopeful miners land on the island, moor their boats in the bay, and make the ascent up the crumbling cliffs. Old Road has joined the bobbing fishing boats down in the bay, is on the look-out for his next fare. And I stand alone in the opalescent quicksands among the pits. But no, I'm not alone, for Babbon's back, waving his little red book, white hair flowing down to his ankles, barely sheathed in some worm-eaten animal skin, mad eyes burning in their bare-bone sockets. For the savages, he starts, on reaching this strange excretion of some more energetic prior age of our dear planet, fell prostrate instantly and intoned a most unusual rhythmic howl, the like of which, &c. I shoo Babbon away, but he won't lay off, my mentor and guide, with an oil-lamp and a ghastly smile about his bare-boned mandibles. Night falls over the green slopes and jagged bluffs of Pulau-Sulakko. The flying squirrels emerge from their holes. The tufted nightjar cries and flaps its wings. And as the lights come out over the little boats moored in the bay, a deep growl rises from the very bowels of the cliff. It rises in pitch, spreads out into a popping and banging and cracking. Smoke rises from the pits, pink and purple and orange. Sparks fly out of the shafts, spinning and whizzing wheels of fire. Panicked miners jump out of their tunnels, run for the cliff face, slide down the rope ladders, abseil down to the sea, gesticulating wildly to their boatmen. Old Road's limo has drawn up by my side now, smooth and dark and long. Get in, he grunts. Take me home, I say, so tired. No, he says, someone you got to see, and the pirogue goes headlong over the clifftop and down into the bay, where the boats are whizzing around among the rocks, picking their crews up out of the water; and the sharks are coming in, too, hoping to garner a little business from the commotion. A storm is massing on the horizon, a rough black slate streaked with pyrite flashes. No, I say to Old Road, this is not the way; let's go back, back down the river; back to Cayata; but Old Road wags his finger, cocks his twelve-inch gun, and the pirogue banks and cuts on through to the eye of the storm. A vessel is bobbing there, all tranquil in the gentle sway while all about us fly islands, scraps of red linen, green rags, Babbon's bones. It's a handsome big-game fisher rigged up with disco balls and black-leather divans. Kobold, Antwerp, it says on the stern. There is no one on deck, but in the wheelhouse, a man stands by the glass, his back turned to me, all in black, shoulder-long hair shiny with a crust of carbo melée. Come on up, he says, and takes a glass from the bar by his side. Let's drink to success, Goldhaven says, turning to me now, and hands me a cocktail, gold-streaked and spinning on a tiny vortex. Now then, Goldhaven says, the stone, and I reach for my bag. I feel, and I grope, and I poke, and suddenly the storm comes crashing in on me, and the sky comes crashing down. The stone is gone. Tut tut, Old Road goes, and I hear Goldhaven's voice fading fast, Durak, dumbo idiot—

13

The rain has stopped. The sky has turned the colour of cracked old tarmac. There's a shrinking line of pipe-grey on the horizon. The trees are merging into a single lump of black. There's a dim light among the trees, over on the far side of the landing strip, where the plane slammed into the bush. There is someone else. I slip on my shoes and tiptoe to the door. The night, outside, is hot and vibrant with the scent of some animal. Something big and smooth that lurks panting in the shadows behind the shack. Whatever. I scamper across the wet mud towards the trees. The light disappears. A screech, like a door or a window. But in the darkness I can see nothing. The air is perfectly still now, there's nothing moving. I reach the trees on the far side.

There goes the light again. It's a hut, or a shed, just behind the treeline. The light goes out, but now I'm standing right outside the shed. I reach out and touch the rough planks. The door is ajar. I feel the inside of the wall, cut my hand on something sharp, feel the warm trickle running down to my wrist. Shit. Suddenly I feel a hand on my shoulder. I could throw a punch in the darkness, hit out, ram an elbow into whoever's standing behind me. But I am tired, and my hand hurts. And then the lights come on.

I was expecting you, Hazel says. She does not seem to be wearing much. A very long T-shirt. Flip-flops. Her hair is undone, tousled, the fringe half-covering her face. I was wondering when you'd come, she says. She leads me to a camp bed in the corner of the hut. She closes the door, fastens the bolt. Why, I say. Because, she says. Ouch, she says, when she sees the gash in my wrist. If I didn't know what just happened, she says, I'd say you were looking for a fast way out of the jungle. Squeeze the wound, she says, as tight as you can. She bends down to a trunk next to the bed, rummages, comes up with a first-aid box. I look around the inside of the hut. It's tidier than the main shack across the airstrip. A pair of boots by the door. A large, military-style rucksack up against the wall. An improvised black-out patch over the window. A vase on a make-shift desk. Flowers of a kind I have never seen before, purple with red and yellow patches, tall and jagged as flames, pink fleshy stamens long and erect as pencils. This'll hurt, she says, and she presses a cotton wool pad soaked with a blueish liquid against my wound. It does hurt, like sandpaper, or nettles doused in white spirit and set alight. I look at her naked legs, and the pain is gone. Her skin is smooth and white. She has varnished her toenails. A deep scarlet. There, she says, applying a tight gauze bandage around my wrist. Not sure what your folks back home will make of this, though. She smiles. Do you have any folks back home, she says, or do you stick to Babbon for company. I think of Kaat. Not really, I say. Not exactly.

She gets up, walks over to the desk. She is not wearing a bra. She sits down on a rickety stool, facing me. Do you regret coming here, she says. I don't know, I say. It all depends. I've got a job to finish. That book of yours, she says. Babbon. Yes, I say. You could say that. A job to finish. Like Babbon.

Or maybe it's a bird you're after now, she adds, with a smile. You were talking about birds in your sleep, earlier. Pink cockareens, I say. Does it matter? Hardly, she says. And you, I say. The things I've seen here, she says. Hummingbirds the size of ants. Sloths fixing you with their slow eyes, gripping their branches with fat claws even as you brush past and shake them. Caymans skipping on water, aquaplaning as they dash to catch a capybara for tea. A tropical thunderstorm running amok over the forest, smashing everything back to the first day. After that, everything's just so paltry – dark shapes at the back of a dull mirror – you know?

I don't, but right here, right now, as she speaks, it all makes sense. There's nothing phony here. Nothing's ever been this real. The smile on her face as she looks at me, her head slightly tilted like a quizzical cat, the outline of her breasts against the creases in her T-shirt, her long slim fingers as she paints exuberant figures in the air, radiant like a girl. There's nothing else now. Yes, I say, I know just what you mean. And I've seen shapes in the canopies, she says, frazzled and swaying. I've seen them too, I say. They're birds, I think, she says. But sometimes the light plays tricks in this forest. I know, I say.

I want the moment to last. I'd give anything to stay right here, right now, forever. I'd give the bundle in my bag to stay here in this hut, sitting on this lousy camp bed. Would I? I surprise myself. It's enough to sit here, and to feel this warmth. The pain at the back of my head is gone, the constant throbbing I've felt since Marlow's. Is it a coincidence, I say. What, she says. My landing here, I say. Nothing's a coincidence, she says. You're not angry with me are you, she says. No, I say. Anything but. I've seen what he does to people, she says. Who, I say. Well

Goldhaven of course, she says, surprised. You do know this is all about Goldhaven, don't you. She puts her head over to the other side. I wish she was my cat. What are you trying to do to him, I ask. I don't know, she says. I'd be glad if he's put away, that's for sure. Wouldn't you? I don't know, I say.

I don't know a great deal about Goldhaven. And I've never had strong feelings about these kinds of things. I think of Kaat. Kaat has firm opinions on the matter. You're like a lump of wood, she said. On TV, they were showing lines of bodies by an open ditch, bloodstains on scarves, the wide-eyed horror. Chechnya Georgia Kosovo, I don't remember. Some cold grey hilly place in upheaval. How could it touch me? Kaat was in tears, almost. Here, she said, putting her hand on my chest, what's in there. I don't know, I said. Nothing, Kaat said. The evening did not end well. Kaat left early, things were frosty for a while, then we got back into our rut. Just as well. I don't think Kaat was right, but I have not given it much thought. I don't know, I say. I think of the stone.

It can't be easy, being played for a fool by that man, Hazel says, and she looks at me with something like pity. I don't mind. Maybe, I say. I don't know what I'd do, she says. What's he going to pay you – a million, two? I haven't thought about that, I say. I'm not lying. There are things I have thought about, but I can't tell her. Do they really have their matchmakers with them, their astrologers, as they sit chatting in their clubhouses, running through nephews and cousins and cousins of cousins? I imagine they mix in a little business now and then – the Dubai branch that needs reinforcing – I know Vijay has a niece who would fit the bill nicely – oh that Vijay, you mean New York Vijay – acha, next spring it is then – it'll give us a nice presence in the polished markets for the Gulf – And that's my moment, that's where I will move in. No one will stop me. I will have stepped out of my SL in the driveway in front of the clubhouse, will have parked my Viper there with all the nonchalance of the very rich, will have left my Aston fat and square on the gravel. Parking is for the poor. The likes of me, then, and it won't be long, only step out and leave their keys to some lackey. No one will question me. I will walk up the steps like a third-generation member, I'll be wearing a preppy blazer with my chinos and a white shirt, the top buttons undone. No one will dream of stopping me, they'll think I'm very old Belgian money, rubber and mines, born and raised between Knokke and Villefranche-sur-Mer, a little inbred but very suave. What, what are you doing— the patriarch will start, but I will not let him finish, and I will drop my resignatory epistle on the table.

Thanks for patching me up, I say. It's the least I could do, she says, and the hesitation in her voice could be a giveaway, but I don't mind. There is one thing that bugs me, I say. It's like I'm on a truth-serum, babbling away. I've never been one to babble away. I can't help it now. Her naked legs, her brown eyes, the outline of her breasts under that T-shirt. What, she says. The scar, I say. The story with the crocodile, by the Sankuru river. A story, she says. Just a story. A myth. Another Goldhaven myth.

So, she says, you really haven't thought about the money. It's not quite like that, I say. It's not the most important thing, I say. Really, she says. What is, then. The fact of doing it, I say. I can't imagine what it's like, she says. I've never been on the dark side. It must be so exciting.

I shudder. Is that what you think, I say. The dark side. Oh no don't get me wrong, Hazel says. She gets up, walks over, sits next to me on the camp bed. She smells soft, soapy, baby-duckling downy. Spring-flower fresh. Like a commercial for fabric conditioner. It's right where I want to be. To freeze this frame, to hit pause. She puts her hand on my shoulder. It's not what I meant, she says. It's a fine line, I mean. Between being that horrid man's stooge, and doing the absolutely right thing. It doesn't take much, either way. And it's your call. That must be an amazing call to have to make. Her hand is still on my shoulder. I don't think, I say, I've ever done the absolutely right thing, or the absolutely wrong thing. I think

of Kaat, again. Don't you sometimes think, she said
once, in the middle of the night, that we're just,
like, watching a movie, a really long movie, and then
when the movie's over, the lights don't come on, and
it's all dark, and that's it. Nothing more. Nowhere
to go. Just that darkness, always, forever. It was so
unlike Kaat, I just asked if she had a fever, offered
to get a very strong paracetamol. And it passed, and
I turned over and went back to sleep, and the next
morning she was back to her usual self, off to choose
a gnome, a very special gnome, for her father's
birthday, and rattling off categories and orders of
gnome as if they were thoroughbreds. I didn't understand Kaat, then, but now, with Hazel's hand on my
shoulder, it hits me, sort of. I think I can pull it off,
I say, and look at Hazel. I mean it, here in the calm
white light of the hut, this mellow moment where
everything's in the balance and everything's balanced,
just about. I like Kaat's legs, and more. I like the
feel of Hazel's hand of my shoulder. I want it all.

14

I don't do deals. I'm only an accountant. I do the books once the deal has been closed. The Indians have told me more than once. Don't get ideas now, they say. You can tell the difference between a general and a nominal ledger. You can't tell the difference between a maccle and a feather. So I stay in the back office. And if ever, as has happened once or twice, the Indians need a bum to fill a seat, or to walk a client round the old town, I'm under strict instructions to talk about the weather. Or football. Buy a paper, they will tell me. Memorize the sports pages. Wow them. I don't know a thing about football. But I do as I'm told. On the few occasions that I go to the bourse with the Indians, it's purely for numbers. I stay downstairs, away from the action. I don't talk about deals. But I think the deal I've cut with Hazel is a good deal, as deals go. I wanted to show Hazel the stone, but she was not in the least bit interested. I know, she said. I've seen it, she said. How, I asked. I have my ways, she said. Whatever.

I've got myself a deal, and now I'm on my way back into town. A steamy morning under a blue sky, the ocean in the distance glistening turquoise, almost, behind the sea wall, the sugarcane plantations stretching like a juicy swab of moss all along the river, the shiny estuary, and the stone strapped to my ankle, hard and cold. I have had two curried dumplings for breakfast, and half a bottle of rum to kill the bugs. Up here in the Squirrel, I feel safe and cool and out of reach. The beating of the blades keeping all that organic matter at bay. The cool machinery a talisman against the seething clutching green of the forest. It's a simple deal, really. I give her Goldhaven. No, I don't give her Goldhaven. I tell her where I meet Goldhaven. The time and the place. She will do the rest. I can picture it. Betrayal, Hollywood-style. Tacky and predictable. The hand-over, somewhere in an estaminet down by the docks. A drizzly Sunday morning. A far cry from those glitzy bars with gold-streaked cocktails. Goldhaven sitting at a corner table, smoking. A half-empty glass of lager. Goldhaven sitting with his legs crossed, one black-sleeved arm casually stretched out along the back of the worn bench. His white shirt casually open to the black curls on his chest. Goldhaven has been winking at the waitress, a pretty mulatto with legs like chopsticks. Goldhaven's fine lips curling into an amused smile. Not anticipation; he's been through this too many times, he's too much of a professional. Amusement. It's all a game to him, and he's curious to see if I have the mettle. I'll have a big bulge in the pocket of my cheap leather jacket. I'll walk straight up to him. The estaminet is almost empty at this time. An old lady with a poodle, slurping Kriek into her wrinkles. I will walk up to Goldhaven, take a chair. Well now, Goldhaven will say with a smile. I'll be honest. I didn't think you had what it takes. I'll take the stone from my jacket, wrapped in a J-cloth. But in the end, Goldhaven will say, my first instinct was right. He will take an envelope from his pocket, open it slightly, show me the contents. Want to count, he will say. No, I will say. Didn't think so, Goldhaven will say, and I will hold out the J-cloth with the stone. Things will happen very quickly then. The old lady will sprint over, her wig slipping to reveal a bob of short brown hair, flashing away with a camera, then thrusting a Dictaphone in Goldhaven's face. And then, only then, will the door be thrust open from the outside, and an excited blue scrum will flood in, Politie on the tables, Politie on the bar, Politie barging in through the windows, Politie with loudspeakers, Politie with yapping and snarling Alsatians, a chopper just audible outside. They don't do things by half-measures here.

There will be no surprise on Goldhaven's face, no shock, not even disappointment; at most a hint of weariness. Did you even know, he will have the time to say to me, just, before he's bundled out, did you even know what I was trying to do here, the plans I had? And then he'll be all over the papers, and Hazel will get a Pulitzer, and either way the Antwerp Chamber of Commerce will be mighty pissed, for a month or two, at the bad press. And I'll be PNGed by the Schelde, for a while, but in the end they'll all breathe a big sigh of relief. And who knows. When the thing with Goldhaven is done, in the estaminet by the docks, when the cops have barged in and taken Goldhaven down, the old lady, the one with the wig, who's not so old really, will stay behind, will wipe her make-up and remove her wrinkles. I'll buy you a drink, I'll say. And Hazel will smile and cock her head, like a quizzical cat. Sure, she'll say. Perhaps. And later she'll say, Sorry for that plane thing, it wasn't meant to go quite like that, the bumpy landing and all that. And then she'll ask me, so now you can tell me, what made you think of it, the pink thing? It was all Goldhaven's idea, I'll say. I just tagged along. Pathetic, I know. But the excitement of it—

229

Not the stone, she'll say, silly. The cockareen. Oh, I'll say. And I will tell her about crammed hides and the smell of wet wool and mint cake. And she will laugh, and understand, and maybe she will tell me that she, too, was made to stomp through wet meadows and spiky thorns as a child, in search of Pippo's warbler, or an American snake-eagle, or a Marabou squatting on a smokestack, somewhere between Reading and Slough—

I don't know much about deals, but I think I've got myself a decent enough deal. I give Hazel the time and date. She gets Goldhaven, who'll be getting his just deserts. And I'm getting a chopper ride back to Hopeton. Because Hazel really has her own chopper. She made a call on her Thuraya, and this morning the Squirrel came whacka-whacka-whacka into the old landing strip, hovering above the swamped red soil just long enough for the pilot and myself to hop on. Hazel stayed behind, said she had some loose ends to tie up. What do I know. But before I left her hut, Hazel whispered something in my ear. The stone, she said. Who cares about the stone? It's Goldhaven I want. Who cares if some little pebble gets lost, in the melee. Keep the stone, Hazel said. And that was that.

15

In Hopeton, dropped off by Hazel's chopper, I hitch a ride into town from Willaerts Field on an old Bedford lorry carrying a few dozen vats of rum from the local distillery.

You comin in from the interior, the driver says, a big guy with dreadlocks. You better watch you back, man.

What do you mean, anything up, I ask.

Fayva like the man up to some big op at the airport, he says. Like they're playin' at Armageddon. Tryin to catch some stuff goin' out. What's your game anyway, man, he asks.

I like the solitude of the forest, I say. I'm a bird-watcher.

Birdwatcher, huh, the driver says. Yeah, you send

some o' those bad birds down my way, he says, laughing.

I get out in the centre of town, round the corner from the cathedral, and look for a place to sleep. I have enough cash left, just, for the plane ticket back to Brussels, and a few nights in a hotel. Goldhaven had better make this up to me when I'm back in Antwerp. I find a small hotel, finally, discreet, an old wooden villa with a central patio and bougain-villeas up the façade. I check in, close the shutters, unwrap the bundle. I know nothing about these things, but I am sure it is the biggest stone I have ever seen, the size of a small tangerine, and it shim-mers a deep shade of violet. My hands tremble as I hold it. I put it to my cheek, and it burns like ice. I hold it against the light, the grey glare outside. For a moment I fancy I see something dancing inside, a kind of pale warped fire.

What you see in those things I just don't know, Kaat once said. Kaat prefers simple colourful things made of wood or glass. Mint-green triangles, purple bangles. Yes but, I try to say. If I had the money, I'd buy Kaat a necklace with a big blue stone. To go with your eyes, I'd say, and she'd laugh, her short dry Flemish laugh, and say, what do you know about my eyes, you're practically colour-blind anyway. I am not colour-blind, but there are things I do not see. I never see flowers, normally. I look past them.

Kaat does not mind. Kaat would put the necklace with the big blue stone at the bottom of a drawer and that would be it. I wrap the stone, carefully, and place it on the sink while I have a shower, the first in days. I am worried about what the driver told me, about hassle at the airport.

I wonder what a blue stone would look like on Hazel—

I'm worried. I've been talking to people, on and off, up and down the river. There's not a great many ways to take a stone out of St Andrew's. There's the legal way, the only way if you have any sense. You take it to the offices of the Mining Survey, stand in line and declare your registered trader's number, show your buying sheets, with dates, weight, production area. They will check in their ledgers, counter-check against the production sheets for the area you've declared. Then they will take 25 per cent of the stone's Antwerp value, in cash. You then take the stone to the airport in a sealed envelope, and declare it to the Ministry of Finance. They will check your documentation, make sure the seal has not been tampered with, and take another 15 per cent in return for the definitive export permit. Sensible, but expensive.

Alternatively, assuming that you do not want to lose half the stone's value to the state coffers, you can chance it. If you are not a bona fide dealer, you have no choice. And if you have just come in from the jungle with a clonking big pink stone of very questionable provenance, you most definitely have no choice, unless you want to hand the stone over to the treasury of the state of St Andrew's on a silver platter. I do not.

If you have to chance it, there are not many places to go. The sea is a no-go. The full length of St Andrew's short coastline is capped by a seawall, and the razor-sharp rocks that lie just below the surface make beaching a speedboat a perilous undertaking. And even if you made it out from the shore, chances are you would be picked up by one of the DEA spotterplanes that scour the coastal waters day and night. The DEA might be more interested in crystals of another kind, but if in doubt they will hand you over to the St Andrew's border patrol, and then good luck to you.

You could try the jungle, theoretically. But even if you got a foolhardy pilot at Willaerts Field to risk his life and plane with a flight into the uncharted interior, beyond Cayata, more likely than not a couple of Super Tucanos of the Amazon patrol will challenge you just as you fly over the Brazilian border. Head east, to Guyana, and chances are the local constabulary will pick you up soon as your plane has touched down. Prim and proper puritans in neatly pressed blue uniforms. You don't want to go there. Head west, to Colombia, and chances are some private army or other will pick you out of the sky before you've even found your landing strip. And as for the land route: there is Marlow's, if you even get that far, and beyond that there is nothing. If the mosquitoes don't get you, the ants will. If the ants don't, the caymans will. If the caymans don't, the jaguars will. Well, you don't want to go there.

That leaves the high road. Three flights a week out of Hopeton, to Miami via Panama. Everybody who looks like they're in the industry gets searched, most of the time. If you're unlucky, they lead you off behind a screen and give you the full-over. Considering that you don't have an export permit, you can try one of a number of options. You can try bribing the customs people. Not easy, because there'll be a guy from the Ministry of Finance watching the customs guy. And a guy from the Mining Survey watching the guy from the Ministry of Finance. You can try a false bottom in your cabin-case, but they'll spot that without much bother. Or eat it. Chances are you'll get very sick. Or you can really go rockbottom – wrap the stone in gauze then put it in a condom, then shove it up your arse. And if the stone is of any meaningful size, chances are you won't even get it up your arse.

I go for the high road. I have no choice. I've barely

got enough cash for the ticket back, and I'm through with the jungle. Goldhaven was not much use when he gave me Jocelynho's name and a first fistful of dollars, way back in Antwerp: nobody's going to look at you, kid. You're not on any list, you look like a tourist. You have that harmless look about you. They go for the sharks, like me, not the minnows. No offence kid, but you're a minnow. Just walk on through and smile your harmless smile. Tell them you're a birdwatcher or something.

Yeah, right. My forehead is boiling. I see a jaguar in the corner of my room, ready to pounce. A very large sloth sits on the boxy old TV set, filing down its metre-long claws. You gotta be kidding me, it says, there are no cockareens north of Antwerp. Last one was eaten by Goldhaven around 1927. A black cayman waddles out of the bathroom and places its heavy jaws on my bed. One snap of these, and you're gone, it says. My bundle erupts, just then, the stone growing and growing, sending the cayman and the sloth and the jaguar scampering into the under-growth. I pass out.

I'm woken by a bang. The door, or a window. No, something at the window. I sit up. I'm drenched and my neck hurts. The room see-saws gently, swings slowly into focus. No one. Just another nightmare. I never used to dream. Kaat would mock me, with her simple straightforward suburban Flemish dreams.

236

Brad Pitt come to call for tea, in that house up by the Dutch border. And Mama serving apple pie, like he's just another cousin, Kaat said, and somehow she found it funny. Anything else Brad Pitt did when he came to stay at your place, I asked. Ah, she said, that's not something I can tell, and for some reason she fell into a girlish giggle.

And she'd wake up with a nightmare, once or twice. What, I'd ask, and all she'd say was, I don't know who chooses these nightmares for me. And here I am. I wash down half a dozen aspirins. I know it's pointless, but there's nothing else. It's been ages since I last took my Malarone. I listen. Nothing. I check the bundle under my pillow. The stone's still there, dull and pale. Two o'clock. I check the door. Nothing. I step outside onto the gallery that runs along the first-floor rooms. There is no wind, not a breath. The heat is stifling. Cicadas, somewhere, a few gardens away. I can just about hear the snoring of the guard downstairs, a faint tongue of light extending from the reception into the overgrown patio. And just as I am about to close the door again, I see it. A big ball of black feathers on the worn floorboards below my window. A head with a long curved bill, protruding at an awkward angle. A giant crow. A black curlew. No, an ibis. Its red eyes, unmoving, seem to be looking at me. It must have hit the window, in full flight. I did not know there were ibises in St Andrew's. I did not know there were black ibises. I retch, throw up over the balustrade, run back inside, lock the door. I do not sleep, the rest of the night.

In the morning, my fever has gone down, a little, but the beasties up the Malakuzi river must have had something bad in their gut, and the bump on my head is not going down. It is raining again. The clock says eight. Shit. The flight to Miami is due to leave at eleven. I go outside, check the landing outside my room. The ibis is gone. There is a slight crack in my window.

I go back inside, lock the door, unwrap Jocelynho's bundle. The stone looks at me, heavy and dirty. I hold it up against the light, and see nothing inside. I'm running out of time. I look at *Babbon's St Andrew's and the Maritime Territories*. I look at the stone. I go out, clutching the stone in my pocket. I borrow a sharp knife from the hotel kitchen, and ask the receptionist for some glue. I need to cut a postcard down to size, I say. It's more dificult than I thought. The knife slips and cuts deep into the palm of my hand. But I manage to gouge out a cavity that's just big enough for the stone, leaving a few pages intact at the front and the back of the book. I place the stone in the cut-out, glue it to the boards at the bottom, run a line of glue along the inside of the cut-out pages, put more glue on the remaining pages, shut the boards. I fold Jocelynho's bundle, put it with Babbon's book at the bottom of my holdall. I look at my watch. Better not to arrive too early at the airport; better to wait for the customs people to be busy with the thick of the crowd. I go over to the window, peek out from behind the curtains. Is that a man's shape behind the palm-tree down by the pool? No, just a deckchair, folded. I am losing it. My neck hurts. I lie down.

16

You had a good stay in St Andrew's, the official at passport control asks, without looking at me.

Yes, delightful, I say.

You been here on business or pleasure, the official asks, still without looking at me.

Business, uhm, pleasure, I say.

Pardon, the official says, what is it now, business or pleasure?

Pleasure, definitely pleasure, I say hastily. Bird-watching. Out in the interior.

What birds you see then, the official says, looking at me now, curious.

Harpie eagles, I say. And lots of parrots. Great macaws. Aras, I say.

That all, the official says.

And ibises, I say, nervously. Lots of ibises.

Oh yeah, the official says. What kind of ibis.

Black ibises, I say. Lots of them. Big and black.

Never seen no black ibis in St Andrew's, the official says. He looks at my passport, then places a stamp in it. You have a good flight now.

I move on to the security check. There is a small queue, but things are moving fluidly. No one seems to be getting the full-over. I put my holdall on the conveyor belt of the X-ray machine, step through the metal detector.

Is this your bag, sir? A man in dark blue uniform; sergeant's stripes. St Andrew's constabulary, transport division, his silver badge reads. Empty your bag please, sir.

I put my bag on the search table. Out come dirty socks, dirty underpants, T-shirts stained light red with soil from the interior, dark red with my blood, trousers brown with the mud of the Malakuzi. Jocelynho's leathery bundle. And Babbon's book. The policeman puts on a pair of white gloves, unwraps Jocelynho's bundle, carefully, meticulously examines every fold of it. He goes through my dirty clothes and underwear, looks at the bloodstains on my T-shirts, the gashes on my hands.

What's this, you been in a fight somewhere?

No, I say, er, I got attacked by an eagle up in the interior. A harpie. I bite my tongue.

The sergeant looks at me, calls into his walkie-talkie. Twenty-two, twenty-two, supervisor required at security. Another policeman emerges from an office, a tall man of Indian origin with inspector's pips on his shoulders. He talks to the sergeant; looks at me; scans a piece of paper he has brought with him in a small cardboard file.

You come with us please, sir, the sergeant says, and scoops my belongings back in the holdall.

In an office behind the security check, with half the airport security detail crowding in to get a look, the sergeant empties the contents of my bag onto a large white table. He points the T-shirts out to the inspector, who looks at them with an air of disgust. You go up the Malakuzi, the inspector asks.

Yes, I say. I've been birdwatching.

Birdwatching, where, the inspector asks.

I don't remember, I say. A place called Cayata. A couple of other places, I don't remember. Marlow's.

Marlow's, the inspector says with a frown. That's better left well enough alone. What birds you see there.

I don't remember, I say. I remember the ibis. Black ibises, I say.

Ain't no black ibises in St Andrew's, the inspector says.

The sergeant picks up Babbon's book, tries to take it by one of the covers to shake the pages. Look, he says to the inspector, and forces open the pages. The stone tumbles out, falls to the floor with a light clang.

What's this, the inspector asks, holding the stone in front of me.

I have no idea, I say. Never seen that before.

And the book, I suppose you have never seen that before either.

The book, yes, I say, it's a guidebook I bought before coming to St Andrew's. I last looked at it, er, a couple of days ago, and it was definitely not like this.

A white guy in a Hawaii shirt, crewcut, angular, sunburnt, has come into the room now, and is talking in a low voice to the inspector. The inspector points at me, my bag, its pathetic contents, shrugs his shoulders. The white guy looks disappointed, leaves the room, talking quickly into his mobile phone, yeah, they say it's the one we got the tip on, no, nothing, we'll check him out later.

The inspector and the sergeant whisper, briefly, then the inspector says, I'm arresting you on suspicion of violation of Section Six of the Precious Minerals and Metals (Export Control) Act, 1974. Right, sergeant, take him away.

I am led out past the security check, where people are now being waved past without even the most cursory check, past the passport desk. A man comes walking towards me from passport control, strolling towards security with a big smile. Immaculate white shirt, shiny black jacket, longish black hair. I try to say something, don't know what, just gasp. Goldhaven winks at me, walks right on through security. As I am taken out through the small departures hall and to a police van waiting outside, I see another familiar face at the check-in desk. Hazel, looking shocked. There goes her Pulitzer. I am bundled into the van, the door slammed shut. It was not supposed to end like this.

17

Babbon's just evidence now. Or what's left of him. I don't think there was anything in his book on Maelbroek Gaol. I could write a chapter on it. It would start like this: *When they built Maelbroek Gaol, the forefathers who created St Andrew's from muck and sweat and fevered swamps clung firmly to the Shithole School of Penitentiary Architecture.* Etc. My cell is windowless; but a narrow opening runs along the length of the ceiling, criss-crossed by rusty iron bars; from time to time a guard will walk over the grid and shine a torch into the cell below. The cell is dark but for a vague shimmer of sickly yellow light trickling in through the opening in the ceiling. The walls are rough and wet with sticky goo. I hear an occasional pounding against the wall from what must be the cell next door. I should not be sitting here. Goldhaven should be sitting here.

Hours pass, maybe days, in the darkness. I go from moments of biting cold to burning fever, and back. My head is a washbowl filled with gravel slushing up against its tinny sides. They have taken my passport away. If ever I am let out, I will have to stay in St Andrew's forever. Become a pork-knocker. Trawl the forest, condemned to rummage in the undergrowth, sneak into other people's sluicing operations at night, go through their tailings, steal away at the onslaught of dawn, sleep like a tapir somewhere deep in the foliage, dodging jaguars, mining inspectors, caymans. I will look up at the milky-grey sky and see strange shapes linger in the trees. Part crow, part man, they crouch among the topmost branches on the forest's edge, watching and waiting. I will flee from harpies, will be stalked by Indians and their poisoned arrows. I will become like Old Road, a boatman between this life and the next, merging with the forest. I will live for the glimmer of the hope of finding a big stone one day, a big pink stone, big as a man's fist. I will never see a pink stone. I will scavenge among the huts of Marlow's, dodging the miners' bullets. I will end up floating in the Malakuzi, a hole in my temple, waiting for the piranhas to feed. I will never see Kaat again. I think of Hazel. I think of the Indians, sitting this very moment at their table overlooking the first hole, designing a dynasty. They will come back, again and again, and sit there, their meal undisturbed, no Corvette scrunching the gravel. I should have settled for gnomes; occasional trips to Mallorca; suburban prattle. I sleep, doze, sweat, groan in the heat. Hours flit past in the darkness. My watch has stopped, beads of condensation heavy on the inside of the glass. Animals scuttle across my feet, try to scale my thighs. Four-legged, six-legged, eight-legged. I brush them off, get bitten. There's a clanging noise at the far end of the block. A warder strolling along the gangway above the cells, knocking his nightstick against the iron bars in the ceiling. A key turns noisily in a lock, the door to my cell swings open. Another warder bangs his nightstick against the heavy metal frame. Out out out, he grunts.

18

St Andrew's Customs and Excise. A white weather-boarded building with a tumbling picket fence. Like much of Hopeton it has seen better days; the paint is peeling and planks are falling off all along the front of the building.

I am taken up a rickety staircase, down a creaking corridor, to an interview room somewhere at the back of the compound.

The chief customs inspector is a bit of a jester. Do you want the good news first or the bad news first, he says with a mocking smile.

OK, give me the good news, I say.

The good news is that you are not being charged under Section Six of the Precious Minerals and Metals (Export Control) Act, 1974.

Well, I say, that's good news indeed.

And I don't suppose you want to know why you are not being charged, the customs guy says.

Well, I expect I'm innocent, I say.

The Lord will be the judge of that, the customs guy says. The reason you are not being charged is that you were not seeking to export any valuable mineral classified in Annexe Two to the Act in question.

Oh, I say. Well, that's what I've been saying all along, I say. Somebody planted the damn thing on me.

They really went for the bottom of the class with this one, the chief customs inspector says to his colleagues. He turns back to me. No, we searched your hotel room, and found this. He produces a sealed plastic bag with the scraps of paper I cut from Babbon's book. And that stone of yours is not a stone, he says.

My jaw drops. It's a, sorry, a what, not a stone?

Haha, the chief customs inspector says. When's the good news not the good news? When it's the bad news, actually. He smiles, a broad grin with gold teeth gleaming on both sides.

What do you mean, it's not a stone, I say. I sink into the rickety plastic chair in the interview room. I close my eyes. I see Old Road, Jocelynho, Boss Macquarie and his beast, Hazel, all spinning round the stone. They're thumbing their noses at me. Somewhere in the darkness Goldhaven is saying something. I can't make it out.

It's nothing like a stone, I hear the chief customs inspector's voice, very distant. It's a bloody lump of resin. Didn't take them very long at the lab. Just came apart with a screwdriver and a hammer. I open my eyes. The chief customs inspector produces another bag, containing the dirty blueish-brown fragments of my stone.

Oh no, I say.

Oh yes, he says.

Can I go now, I say. I just want to go home.

Ah, the chief customs inspector says with a glint of his gold teeth. Now for the really bad news. You can't go home. We are charging you. Section Five of the Species (Protection) Act, 1986.

The what, I say. What are you talking about.

This, the chief inspector says, and drops another transparent bag on the table. It contains the leathery bundle in which Jocelynho gave me the stone up in the forest near Marlow's.

Oh that, I say. I got that from some guy in the forest, just a present. It's some old rag, I guess.

That, the inspector says, is the skin of a Korzeniow's olingo.

A what, I say.

I haven't the faintest idea what an olingo is. I'm pretty sure it's not a bird. I would have come across it in *Bodine's Inventory*. And birds don't have skins. Not the kind you can bunch into a rag and wrap up a stone in. A fake stone. The sheer pathetic bloody shame of it. Supposing I had managed to take it out to Antwerp. Supposing I had decided to pull a fast one on Goldhaven. Here I am, in the sea lions' enclosure, punctual for the brother-in-law. He doesn't even need to whip out his loupe. He can tell just from weighing the thing in his hand. He won't even give it back to me, the thing. He'll lob it down and over the barrier into the acquamarine blue of the sea lions' paddling pool. No, nothing so melodramatic. He'll just drop it there, among the old ticket stubs and Cornetto wrappers, and he'll get up and walk off. And later I'll get the enraged phone call, the bollocking from one of the senior partners, a younger brother, maybe: I am bringing the entire trade into disrepute. The family cannot afford the reputational risk it will incur from any further association with me. And I will be read my rights: one bin liner, thirty litres, and everything to be cleared out by 0830 hours the next day. The shame of it.

One of the rarest olingos in the world, the inspector is saying. Native only to St Andrew's. Down to a few hundred individuals in the forests of the Malakuzi. Classification on the Red List, he says with a dramatic pause: critically endangered, and possibly extinct. One of the most docile of our native mammals. And because of people like you, possibly not to be for much longer.

Oh no, I say.

Oh yes, the chief customs inspector says. Take him away, he says, to the attendant policemen.

I am put back in the police van, and my tour of Hopeton continues. I still don't know what an olingo is. A mammal, the inspector said. Docile. I picture something slow and hairy and sloth-like, with rings around its sad eyes and a white goatee. From its hideout by the riverside, it peers out into the dark heart of the forest, and watches all the eating and coupling and killing, and it's so docile, it can't go out and join in, so it just sits there, watching, chewing on the stem of some bamboo-like shrub, and slowly, slowly it drifts into extinction. I should have thought of that. They might have waved me through at the airport. I'm after the only remaining population of Korzeniow's olingos. The Northern Amazonian sub-species, with the rings around its eyes and the silver streak in its goatee. And, and did you see one, they'd ask, all in awe. Maybe, I'll say. It was dark. They're as shy as any creature on earth. You can count confirmed sightings on the fingers of one hand. I'll have a chat about it with the folks at the Natural History Museum when I get back. Oh gosh, they'd say, good luck.

Scratch the Babbon business. Scratch the cockareens. I'm after Korzeniow's olingo. Sheer bloody genius. But it's too late for that now.

19

The cell door opens again the next morning. A bundle of clothes, a T-shirt, a pair of trousers, used but clean, are thrown into the cell. Here, put these on and knock when you're ready, the guard says.

Outside, a police van is waiting. Where are we going, I ask.

Shut up, the driver says. You'll find out soon enough, the man sitting next to him says, a burly constable with a beret, and he drops his Sten gun on the dashboard. The van speeds down the criss-cross street grid of Hopeton's central district, siren wailing, scattering chickens and old BSA motorbikes and autorickshaws, and heads out of town into the plantation land that surrounds the capital. My head starts throbbing again. I feel faint. I bang against the plastic partition that divides me from the driver's cab.

What is this, I ask again. Some kind of disappearance you're planning? I try to open the door from the inside, to no avail.

The van turns into a small mud road leading into a sugarcane plantation. There are ditches on both sides and a gate at the end of the road. I see the last five minutes of my life flitting past in fast-forward. The van will stop at the end of the track, out of sight and out of earshot, away from the bustle of town. There will be bitterns with strange bobbing crests in the sugarcane, and iguanas crawling out of the ditches to watch. There will be no witnesses. The driver will slide open the door. Out, the burly constable will bark, waving his Sten gun. I'll get out, and for a moment he'll look at me, shaking his head. Let's do this, the driver will say. I see your point, about the olingos, I might stammer, but isn't this taking it a bit far? Run, the constable will shout, and I will turn and run down the track, back to the road, and maybe I'll hear the first shot before it's fired, and the bitterns will shriek—

The van stops by the gate. The driver gets out, unlocks a padlock on the gate, gets back in the van and drives on. The mud has given way to tarmac, a vast field of tarmac. The airport building is at the far end. The plane is on the apron; the engines are

254

running. The van stops at the bottom of the steps. Get out, the constable with the Sten gun says. There is another uniform on the tarmac. St Andrew's Immigration Service, his badge reads, and Inspector. He thrusts my passport and a quaintly typed sheet of paper in my hands.

What's this, I stammer. Where's my stuff.

Deportation order, the inspector says. Goodbye and don't come back.

The pilot, who is waiting at the top of the stairs, looks me up and down worriedly, tries to argue with the immigration inspector, does not want me on his flight; but when the inspector declares that either the plane takes me or the plane stays on the tarmac till it has lianas growing over the cockpit, the pilot gives in. The hostesses look at me suspiciously. They do not offer me drinks or food when the plane is in the air. The seat next to me is held free. The passengers further down the row cast furtive glances at me from time to time, cast their eyes down quickly at their in-flight magazines when I look back at them. In Miami, I'm taken straight off the plane and put on the next flight to Europe. DEPORTED, the stamp in my passport says, in screaming red letters, indelibly, by order of the Secretary for Homeland Security. But I'm not going back to the broccoli any time soon, and so much the better.

20

Just over two weeks since I left Mechelen, if the date on my boarding pass is to be believed. It's not even a boarding pass, really. Some kind of passenger manifest thing issued at Miami airport by order of the Secretary of Transportation, who reserves the right to seek full recovery of costs, etc. It could have been months, for all I know, or a couple of days. There was before, and there was after. Something that went splat, out there in the sticks; and something that broke, when they showed me the crumbly remains of the stone that wasn't a stone. Two weeks gone, and all I have to show for it is two letters on my doormat. A letter from the Indians. I am fired. Something about unauthorized leave and unsound accounting practices. They've beaten me to it. Fair enough, I don't blame them. But I'll never know whether they have their astrologers with them, at their clubs. And there's a letter from the white-collar squad inviting me for a friendly chat down the federal police HQ.

There is also a thickset man with eastern European features sitting at my kitchen table. He is wearing combat trousers and a tracksuit top. He has helped himself to a beer from my fridge and is going through a big pile of documents he seems to have ripped from the bookshelf where I keep my personal papers. Bank statements, letters, old Filofax pages. He will skim across a page, then scrunch it up, chuck it on the floor and move on to the next. He has placed a large mallet on the table next to his beer.

Sit, the man says. He has closely cropped fair hair and expressionless eyes the colour of burnished concrete. He has a scar on his face, running down one of his cheeks, a neat straight slash.

Who the fuck are you, I say.

No bad words in presence of Zog Shikzahl, the man says and continues his routine.

I sit down. I am very tired.

Listen, I don't care who you are, I say, or what you're looking for. I don't have it. I don't fucking have anything any more.

Zog Shikzahl is one who decides that, the man says, calmly, and continues his work.

You should be aware that I'm probably under police surveillance, I say feebly, so you'd better watch your step.

No, you not under surveillance. Zog Shikzahl check. Zog Shikzahl know about all surveillance. Now shut mouth.

I sit in silence for half an hour, then Zog Shikzahl sweeps the remaining papers off the table. Now, he says, talk. Where is Goldhaven.

I have no idea, I say. I last saw him in St Andrew's.

No lying, Zog Shikzahl says, and with a single sweep of his mallet has smashed the china in my kitchen cupboard.

I'm not lying, I say. All I know is he was out there same time as me. He doesn't tell me where he goes.

No lying, Zog Shikzahl says, and my stereo is a pile of mangled metal and splintered glass and disjointed plastic.

Where is Goldhaven, Zog Shikzahl says. Goldhaven need bring us big stones. Pink stones. Goldhaven not come back. Goldhaven has broke promise. Zog Shikzahl not leaving country without Goldhaven.

There was no big stone, it was just a big con, I say. The stone was just a shitty lump of brown resin. That's all there is to it.

No lying, Zog Shikzahl is about to say, but then the doorbell rings. Not open, Zog Shikzahl says, but there is an insistent knock. Politie, someone says, and yanks at the doorknob. Militsiya, Zog Shikzahl says, and gets up.

Wait, I say, and rush to the door. I hear a loud crash in the kitchen. When I turn around, I see the kitchen window in shards. Zog Shikzahl is gone.

The Belgian Feds have come to pick me up for my friendly chat. It's pretty haphazard stuff, and they must think me much further in than I am. When did I last see Goldhaven. Was Goldhaven in St Andrew's. What do I know about a place called Likuana. It sounds vaguely familiar, I say, but I can't place it. They show me a pack of black-and-white pictures: Goldhaven talking to people at the bourse; Goldhaven somewhere in Africa, next to a pickup with a very big gun on it; Goldhaven talking to me in Antwerp. Goldhaven handing me an envelope. Goldhaven in desert boots and fatigues, on top of some earthworks with a caterpillar, and some African kids leaning into the picture, making funny faces. Goldhaven wearing shorts and a T-shirt, squatting on a straw mat, under a very fat tree, talking to some African folks in white robes sitting opposite. And pictures of burned huts, roofless, shadows of black smoke etched along the rim of the round walls. The strangest mountains visible in the background, like giant termite spikes rising from the plains. A video still from a surveillance camera, Goldhaven from behind in a hotel lobby with some heavies in black leather jackets. Invoices, wildly scribbled, Accra Durban Dakar. Am I under investigation? No. They may get back to me. I may be called as a witness. Great. A witness for what? We're working on that, the Feds say. Keep in touch. Here's our number.

I walk out of the station, and call Kaat. Her voicemail comes on, in Dutch, Met Kaat etc., and then a beep. I leave no message. I call again a few hours later. Met Kaat, etc. I have nothing. No job, no stone. I drive over to Kaat's place. The top floor of a redbrick townhouse in the stringy outgrowths of Mechelen, between one suburb and another. Pellegrims, scribbled on one of the makeshift tags by the doorbells. It is weeks since I last saw Kaat. I need to feel Kaat. I need to breathe Kaat. I need a shoulder and a chest to cry on. I park in the potholed street outside, go up the narrow staircase, slip my key in the lock. As with everything, Kaat was practical about the key. Don't lose it, she said simply, I won't make another one.

The flat is empty. Kaat's bed is made, neatly. An empty coffee cup in the sink. Kaat's bathrobe on a peg. I pick it up, bury my head in it, smell Kaat's smell. My headache starts up again, and a dull pain in my neck. I drive home in a rush, swallow three aspirins. I should see a doctor. I will not see a doctor. I open a bottle of Chablis, drink with no one. I turn off the lights, hope Zog Shikzahl's not on the prowl, put a couple of chairs up against the door, an empty wine bottle balanced on top. Not that there's any getting away from Zog Shikzahl, if he decides to come back. I turn on the TV. It flickers like a pale fire in the twilight. Perhaps Zog will see its reflection, loitering outside behind a shed or crouched behind a dustbin, doing what Zog does. I don't care. The news comes on. Het Nieuws. Africa, first. Burning huts. Pickups with guns careering through the dust, like something out of Mad Max. Hey, those are the termite hills from that picture the cops showed me. I think. I don't know. The newsreader. Brown hair, medium-long. She looks a bit like Hazel, but she is wearing more than a T-shirt. She has a serious look on her face now. No, puzzled and emphatic, as in, Could you believe, dear viewers, that such a thing could happen in our day and age. Cue a shot from the arrivals hall at Zaventem airport. Tom Van Wyk, reporting. He's gesturing dramatically, Tom Van Wyk, heartthrob in a sheepskin with a very big mike that says VT5, and yet there's nothing to be seen. Tired passengers trickling out through the automatic gates. Wait, here we go. Black-and-white shots in jerky staccato, must be from a surveillance camera in the ceiling. The same place, from above, the same slow-mo trolley traffic weaving about. And something big emerging from the sliding doors now. Much bigger than a trolley. A very large box. No, a crate, astride two trolleys put sideways. You can't see who's pushing it. Now the crate stops, in the middle of the arrivals hall. A figure detaches itself from the back of the crate, strides off out of the frame. Another figure emerges from behind the crate, climbs on top of it. People stop to stare, officials with badges pause and confer. Cue Tom Van Wyk, again, talking excitedly into his mike and pointing. And footage in colour now, doubtless shot by some freelance team, the first to arrive on the scene, before the big networks could get their people in. It's hurried and shaken, but it's in colour. The crate again, filmed at eye level now. It's a rough wooden box, tall as a man and longer still, dirty, streaks of moisture running down the sides, straw sticking out of airholes. From time to time, the crate shudders, jumps on the spot. And then the camera moves up, taking in the figure sitting on the crate. A man in rags, his face a light shade of green. A sudden commotion, the camera jerked around, pointed at the floor, filming a quick jog out of the arrivals hall and to the taxi rank outside. A dirty green van is boxing its way through the waiting line of taxis, coughing and barking, a black plume billowing from its rattling exhaust, and stops sideways up on the pavement. A man gets out, tall, white-haired, commanding. I only caught a brief glimpse of Boss Macquarie in the penumbra of his hut, a fleeting shimmer of his white hair, but I know. Boss Macquarie walks past the gaping sunburnt travellers into the arrivals hall. The camera runs after him, bouncing up and down. Boss Macquarie walks with slow, measured steps, but the cameraman seems to have a tough time keeping up. The green figure in rags jumps off the crate, and with Boss Macquarie carries the crate out and to the van, still followed by the bouncing camera. With a stutter and a spit of black smoke, the van drives off. There's not a cop in sight. Cue Tom Van Wyk, all excited now. I empty my bottle of Chablis. I'm scared, but it doesn't really concern me. Nothing to do with me. But Goldhaven should beware. Serves him right.

When I wake up the next morning, there is a message on the answerphone. Hi, it says, this is Hazel. Don't hang up. There's a pause, then a stutter. I, I thought we could meet up. Please call me back.

I jot down the number. Maybe I will call her, later. Maybe I won't. It doesn't really matter. The miners in my head are back at work, chiselling and drilling and throbbing. I lie down, pass out. Another round. Bloody Falciparum. The parasite's got the upper hand, a big, bad, iron fist in a glove black as insect's guts, comes down to batter my insides to pulp. It's back on the roller coaster, one low after another. It's my liver on the slab down there, lone exhibit in the critters' anatomy lesson. They look and they leer, black-tunicked and white-collared, protozoic slime for faces, multiplying by the second, pairing off, row after row after row, the rafters receding. I have Marlow's inside me, and Joshua Babbon's ghost. I'll be stuck with the critters for ever.

When the attack is over, I do my sums. At this rate, I'll be broke within three months. I could look for a job in the streets around Hoveniersstraat. But no one in their right mind would employ me now. I have Goldhaven's sulphur smell oozing out of my pores. The Indians will make sure no one from the sub-continent touches me. No one trading on one of the bourses will want their membership put at risk by association. At this rate I'll soon be on the ferryboat back to Hull. Assuming the Feds let me go. Would Kaat come with me? I don't know. I don't really know what Kaat thinks. You're all strange, is all she said, once, when I tried to persuade her to come back with me for a weekend. You all say what you don't mean and don't say what you mean. And that was that. And now Kaat's gone. Kaat would not leave like that. Maybe some Tarzan type in a Porsche Cayenne has got to her. A big broad-shouldered hunk with a couple of kilos of gel in his slicked-back hair, all wannabe east coast polo charm, plastered with designer labels, all slobbering womanly lips and wandering hands. Enough to make your dinner and your breakfast come out in a spout. Here they are now, doing 200 in that Cayenne down the Autoroute du Soleil just outside Lyon, big hairy hands wandering all over Kaat's legs.

264

Kaat's amazing legs. Kaat's ivory-pale catwalk legs. Here they go, down past Marseille, into the calanques, Kaat looking out of the window at the sea, aquamarine blue like that big stone I would have given her, that slightly absent smile about her lips. Out they get, wandering off into the bracken on the white rocks, looking for a quiet spot. I break out in a sweat. It's not the malaria, this time. Goldhaven owes me, and he owes me big.

I set off in search of Goldhaven. Goldhaven has made sure his tracks are well covered. I go to Goldhaven's office in one of the grey blocks behind Central Station where dealers huddle together for safety on nondescript floors behind steel doors specified to withstand an RPG. I get as far as the reception, and see the name of Goldhaven's company on one of the aluminium plaques on the wall. Goldline Exploration and Investment BVBA, 4th floor. Do I have an appointment, the receptionist asks. No I don't. Then I can get the hell out of there. Can I at least leave a message for Goldhaven. The receptionist confers with the security man. He shrugs his shoulders, says in Dutch, Hasn't been round here for weeks anyway. No, the receptionist says. Now get the hell out of here.

I stand around the entrance of the bourse, accost the occasional dealer who knows me from before. Sorry, you seen Goldhaven by any chance. Know where I can find him. But no one has seen Goldhaven.

No one wants to know Goldhaven now. Goldhaven's gone, and he hasn't left any redirection forms.

I walk up north past Central Station, past the zoo, shrieking macaws clawing at me from behind the fence, drop in to the public library, head for the shelf with the trade publications. I go back ten, twenty years. There is bound to be a profile somewhere of Goldhaven. Goldhaven as a bright young thing, ready to pluck the glittering prizes from the loins of lady luck. There is. Goldhaven has not changed in twenty-odd years. The same shiny black mane, the same sleazy smile. The scar was not there. Goldhaven has an MBA from a place called Leuven Commercial College.

There are places where a precise English accent and a harmless face still open doors. Leuven is one of them. Goldhaven, Goldhaven the woman in alumni services says. The college has been rebuilt several times over since Goldhaven came here. There's a new lecture theatre, built with brewing money. There's a new assembly hall, built, perhaps, with African money. Goldhaven, I say. A feature. For business week. On outstanding Flemish business schools. Their alumni. A feature.

Goldhaven, she says. How do you spell that. Goldhaven, I say, and helpfully come round behind her desk. G-O-L-D-H-A-V-E-N. Goldegger, Goldhoud. There you are, I say. There's an address, too. An Antwerp address, somewhere out in the docks. And what was it you wanted to know, she asks. Oh, I say, his links with the college. The ethic. Inspiration. Early promise. That sort of thing. She is puzzled, and excited.

On my way up to Antwerp, I stop over at Kaat's place. I have called, again and again. She is not picking up her phone, and not answering her mobile. Met Kaat, again and again. A smudgy grey sky over the suburbs; fizzly rain on the cobbles. Children crying behind curtains. There is a sharp smell in the staircase. A yellow puddle on the second landing. Kaat's door is slightly ajar. I slowly push open the door, hit the lightswitch. There is no one in the living room. I walk on through to the bedroom. There is no one. Kaat's bed, open, undone. Her desk, where she would sit as I lay in, some Sunday mornings, last year, going through some financial control workbook. Why, I said. Because, she said. You mean you like this stuff, I said. No, she said. So why, I said. Because, ja, she would say firmly, and that's as far as it went.

Kaat's wardrobe. Her neat array of khaki tailleurs, the ones she'd wear to work. Two pairs of jeans. Photographs on her dressing table. Her parents, her sister. There is no photograph of me. Kaat's aquarium. A plastic treasure chest by the pump and big lumps of rose quartz. I live with someone, Kaat had said, on one of our earliest dates. Dinner in some mockcastle eatery, on the road out towards Antwerp. Oh, I said, and stared at my oysters. I hate oysters. Perhaps

I was trying to impress Kaat. I don't remember. His name is Bert, Kaat said, looking embarrassed. Oh, I said, and put my oyster down. He's a fish, Kaat said, and laughed out so loud the gel-slicked business-men and their dates around us stared. A framed print on the wall, a couple kissing on a bridge, moonlight. The only art she has, and more art than she will ever care about. Kaat likes shopping, but she does not have a lot of money. Kaat likes travelling, but the furthest she has ever been is Eilat. Kaat likes to dream, but her dreams are simple. Kaat's dressing table. Kaat's hairbrush. Hardwood and enamel. A present from me, I think. I don't remember. Some wisps of brown hair. There is a big scratch on the door of Kaat's wardrobe that I do not remember ever seeing before, a row of long gashes, crescent-shaped. I go to the kitchen. Nothing. Dirty dishes by the sink. Half-empty packs of readymeals for one. A nasty smell. The smell of an unkempt dog. Or a pig, perhaps, or a cat. Kaat does not have a cat. I go out, pull the door shut. I ring the neighbours' bells, but no one is in.

Kaat can't stand cats, breaks out in allergies at the mere sight of one—

Goldhaven's address is in Northern Antwerp, by the harbour, somewhere round Leopolddok. Overgrown tracks, marshalling yards, rusting cranes. The Rotterdam motorway in the background, dull grey water in the dock. The warehouses are disused, but here and there, the backside of a Porsche peers out from an open sliding door. A howl of jet-skis rings over from the neighbouring dock. Goldhaven's place is not easy to find. There is no house number, and no name by the bell. A redbrick shed, built some time during the rubber boom, cathedral-tall. A single steel door at the dead centre of the windowless wall. A ramp, further down, with a garage door. I can make out a long sheet of glass and steel at the top of the building, set back just behind the cornice. Some sort of a penthouse. There is a letterbox by the steel door, letters spilling out. Electricity bills. An envelope with Goldhaven's name on it, printed with the emblem of the local Maserati dealer. I ring the bell, a polished black pyramid emerging from the brickwork. There is no reply. I push the door. It is open. I walk in. A long marble-clad corridor, a lift at the end. There are only two buttons. Zero and PH. I push PH. Upstairs, there is another door. Metal, armoured. There is a hole where the doorknob should be, and a frazzled line right down the edge. The door opens gratingly when I push it. Scraps of metal on the floor, long steel shards, mangled bits of the cylinder, grey filings. Whoever came to pay Goldhaven a visit meant business. Goldhaven's loft is the size of several tennis courts. Polished concrete floors; rough brickwork with arty patches of gold tiling. Industrial lights suspended from the high ceilings. A glass wrapping running all the way around the apartment; a terrace outside, views of Antwerp and the docks. A huge leather sofa, a coffee table made of fake ingots. I asume they are fake. Whoever came before has tossed the sofa cushions on the floor. Papers lie scattered on the carpet. I walk on through the eerie silence. Goldhaven's kitchen, shiny leather-faced cabinets around a central island the size of a bulldozer. Someone has yanked open the drawers and scattered pots and crockery on the black granite tiles. And further down, facing the thin finger of the cathedral and the fat stub of the KBC building across the water, Goldhaven's bedroom. I sit down on the bed, massive with a big red leather headboard. The cupboards are ajar, piles of black jackets and white shirts on the floor. There is a remote control on the bedside table. I hit a random button; the floor-to-ceiling window opposite the bed turns opaque and a TV menu appears. I push another button; the bed starts to wobble under me. I have seen enough. I wander back into the living room. A sideboard with a collection of old pith helmets on it. Huge glossy prints on the walls in expensive frames. They're abstract, I think, green and white blotches. I take a closer look, and the blotches fade into pixels. Rivers, craters, pits. Goldhaven's garden.

Behind the front door, there is a giant mirror, gilt-framed. Someone has scrawled on it, in a child-like hand, sprawling and unsure. Scarlet lipstick. Durak dumbo idyot Il be bak four you, it says. Oh no. Oh yes. The lift door closes. There is a whirring of cables as the lift goes down. A police siren in the distance, coming closer. I panic, run along the windows, trying to find a door, find one at last, fiddle with the handle, open it, slip out. Now what. It's four storeys down, at least. But there are fire stairs. A big drop at the end. I sprain my ankle, I think, but who cares. There is a police van racing along the quayside on the other side of the dock. It'll be here in a couple of minutes. Too many questions. I won't be able to talk myself out of this one. I run back to my car, jump inside, drive. I am worried about Kaat.

I feel faint. My temples throb. My bones are aching again. I drive back into the centre of town. I have the shivers. I'm wearing two sweaters, and I have the shivers. I should see a doctor. The doctor would refer me to a hospital. The hospital would refer me to the Royal Institute for Tropical Medicine, or the like. And they would ask some serious questions. Ask to see tickets and boarding cards. Inform their Ministry. And who knows what some bloody bureaucrat might do. Put a call through to another Ministry. Who'd put a call through to the Feds. So, you again. Why don't you start again, from the beginning. With a cynical copper's smile. I'm not going to see a doctor. I park by the zoo, behind Central Station. Walk for a few blocks till I get to a dodgy pharmacy that Kaat once mentioned, when she needed something she was embarrassed to talk to her doctor about. Ja, the grumpy old man in the pharmacy says, and I can tell he's not comfortable. I shiver. Thick tearlets of sweat run down my forehead and drop on his counter. He understands. He writes a figure on a notepad. He's added a zero to what I'd pay on prescription. OK, I say. He drops two packets of Malarone on the counter and takes my cash. Go, he says, and I go. In the car, I tear open the packaging, stuff a tablet, two, three, four in my mouth, wash them down with Coke.

I drive on to the tennis club where Kaat works, out in the country. I have never been, but I know the place well from Kaat's descriptions. A tall hedge round the perimeter, security cameras. Granite gateposts, a barrier. I honk. Swipe your member's card, a sign says. I leave the car, walk up the driveway. A turn-of-the-century villa, granite-faced, olive trees in terracota pots, a slick modern extension behind. The sound of tennis balls being whacked. I'm looking for Kaat, I say. Who are you, the girl at reception says. I'm her brother, I lie. Kaat hasn't been in for a few days, she says. Is there a guy called Goldhaven who comes here, I say. Hey, she says, what do you know about a Goldhaven. She picks up her phone, looks at me, says something in Dutch. I turn around, sprint down the driveway, get in my car, drive home as fast as I can.

21

A sunny day, for once, in Mechelen. There's a scarecrow standing on the corner of my street. My good solid grey Flemish street, inhabited by car mechanics and life insurance salesmen and railway engineers. The scarecrow is green. Worzel Gummidge in green, and he's come for me. Oh shit. I try to run, but the scarecrow is quick, too quick, he seems to fly, dancing on the low lichen-licked walls that fringe the sad little front gardens. You got what the Boss wants, the scarecrow says. His voice sounds hollow. The wind skimming dry leaves. I've got bugger-all, I say. You want whatever you want, you talk to someone else. I've got nothing.

The Boss got something you want, the scarecrow says. You got something the Boss wants.

A cloud passes. The fleeting Mechelen sun is gone. The scarecrow has pulled out what looks like an envelope woven from brittle old leaves. He hands it to me. It contains a strand of hair, dirty, matted, with bits of soil and all manner of organic detritus stuck to it. Brown, the shade of Kaat's hair. That proves nothing. The envelope also contains a small patch of fabric, dirty and torn. Sky-blue. Kaat's favourite colour. The colour and texture of her favourite coat. The sky has turned a sly metallic grey.

What, I say.

You know what, the scarecrow says. Somebody take something from the forest that ain't for taking. The Boss ain't happy. You give what the Boss wants. The Boss give what you want.

Supposing I had what the Boss wants, I say.

You give it, I take it. You get what you want.

I haven't got it here, I say. It'll take a few days to get.

The scarecrow stands and says nothing. Thursday, the scarecrow says.

Where, I say.

The forest, the scarecrow says, beckoning vaguely, behind him, south and west, and is gone.

They have Kaat, and I have nothing. I told the scarecrow I had the stone, and I don't. There is no stone. When the scarecrow and his Boss find out, Kaat is dead. I am also likely to be dead. I don't

274

even know where I am supposed to find the Boss. The forest, the scarecrow said. I rage for a day, drink a bottle of cheap whisky, pass out. I feel a yearning for Kaat so strong I could tear the cheap wallpaper off my walls and crunch the lightbulbs in my bare hands. I sit in my dark flat, drink, stare. The TV flickers in its corner, silently. Flemish game shows, desert island contests in bikinis. The Caribbean, turquoise-rimmed. What do they know. Newsflashes, oilwells burning, bombs here and bombs there. Faces, car chases. Crimeshows, nationwide appeals. Dial the hotline, now. I wish I could. I wish I could dial some number, call in a SWAT team. I cannot. Don't mess with the Boss. Don't cross the Boss. Pretty blonde presenters, earnest detectives in glasses. Flemish roof tops, tedious high streets, grainy on CCTV. Bank heists, security van jobs.

Here's a funny one. A man walks into a used-car dealer's yard, rows and rows of Fiestas and Golfs and Clios. An uncannily tall man, his white hair blurred to an angry halo, and he strides to the back of the yard. He pauses by some old wreck at the back of the yard now, a van, a dark grey blob of a van, and then he turns to the camera. It's Boss Macquarie standing there at the back of the yard, and he's looking up, up and across the road, as if he was looking into the CCTV, as if he knew I was sitting here, looking at him. I can't tell if he's smiling,

275

but I think he's looking at me. He yanks open the door of the van, and then a figure walks into the picture from the left, a little man, must be the second-hand car dealer, starts waving at Boss Macquarie, tries to tell him something. Boss Macquarie doesn't move, for a while, just looks, taking it all in, and then it all happens so quickly, the resolution too weak to capture the scene, the dealer's no longer visible, and Boss Macquarie calmly gets in the van. A few seconds, Boss Macquarie must be hot-wiring the van now, then it yanks forward, and silently the rows of Fiestas and Golfs and Clios part, and the van ploughs right on through and disappears out of the frame, foreground left. He's just a black-and-white blur there, in that last split second before he's gone, but I'm sure he's looking up, up at the CCTV, at me. One of the blonde presenters, back in the studio, is interviewing one of the earnest detectives. Cue a photo of the van. It's an old Leyland Sherpa van, its leaf-green paint mingling with an almost equal surface of rust, its ugly mug missing one headlight and both indicators. There's a reward. Just call the hotline.

I get another letter in the mail the next morning. I never get letters, and now they're coming in thick as bad news. This one has my name scrawled hastily on it, in awkward handwriting, and a single postage stamp stuck on all awry. There is no sender's name on the back. The letter was posted in some suburb of Antwerp. Inside, there is a scrap of paper torn from an old edition of the *Atlantic Standard & Telegraph*. It has one line scribbled on it: *Knokke, plage Léopold II, 3pm.* It is signed, barely legible, *Jocelynho*.

Goldhaven must be really scared. Probably thinks his e-mail and phone are bugged. He's probably right. Knokke is not somewhere I'd normally go, but a trip to the seaside should look innocuous to whoever is keeping tabs on me. Why on earth Goldhaven would want to see me, I cannot fathom. I look at my watch. I could just make it if I hit the road quickly.

A grey, muggy day over the Belgian coast. The promenade in Knokke is almost empty. The crowds have retreated to the luxury boutiques behind the concrete barrier of apartment blocks facing the sea, a brutal Maginot line of real estate. Just the sort of place Goldhaven would choose for a rendezvous.

Normally, Goldhaven would be hanging out with the high-rollers at the casino, but things have changed. He has chosen one of the sectioned-off private beaches at the western end of town. Business is bad. Hardly any of the parasols are up. A single bored blonde mum plays with her toddlers in the fenced-off playground. I pay my twenty euros entrance fee, kick my shoes off, walk through the neatly raked sand looking for Goldhaven. Goldhaven is nowhere to be found among the deckchairs and parasols, so I walk further out.

There is a single figure down at the water's edge, sitting in the sand, facing the tide. I cannot tell if it is Goldhaven, from behind. The figure is wearing a pith helmet. I walk down to the waterline. It is Goldhaven. He is sitting with his feet in the water, where the sand blends into the pebbles and broken shells and the sea.

Goldhaven does not look up at me, simply says, Get a bucket and spade.

A bucket and spade, I say. What do you mean. I am convinced Goldhaven has lost his marbles.

Bucket. Spade. Kiddies playing in the sand. Get it, Goldhaven says. He is still not looking at me.

I walk back up to the promenade, head for the nearest souvenir shop, buy an overpriced plastic beach bucket and miniature spade. I walk back to Goldhaven.

Sit down, Goldhaven says. I sit down next to Goldhaven. I look at Goldhaven's face. I cannot see his eyes. He is wearing dark glasses, but he looks thin, and he seems to have aged. There are streaks of white in the wisps of jet-black hair that frame his pale face.

So what's with the pith helmet, I ask Goldhaven.

A souvenir, Goldhaven says, looking out at the grey sea. Reminds me of everything I've left behind.

I suppose you've asked me here so you can apologize for all the crap I've had to put up with. Ever done time in Maelbroek Gaol? You should.

I'm sure I should, Goldhaven says.

I presume you have come to apologize.

I haven't, Goldhaven says, and scoops up a handful of sand.

What then, I say. I hope you've at least come to give me the money you owe me.

I don't owe you any money, Goldhaven says. I seem to remember our agreement was that you'd get the balance on giving me the stone in Antwerp.

Very funny, I say. There was no stone. Jocelynho gave me a stupid lump of resin. Jocelynho, I presume that was you.

Goldhaven does not answer. He seems lost in thought, scooping up handfuls of sand and pouring it over the pebbles, washing his hands in the water lapping up around his ankles. The tide is coming in, and Goldhaven's trousers are getting soaked. I shuffle back to where the sand is dry.

Move back down here, Goldhaven says with a startlingly firm voice. I am convinced now that he has gone mad. Something he saw in the forest, perhaps. I shudder. I move forward. The waves are coming in fast. The seat of my trousers is getting wet.

Pass your bucket over, will you, Goldhaven says.

I pass over my bucket. Goldhaven picks up a large pebble and drops it in the bucket.

What are you doing, I ask.

Look after this for me, will you, he says.

I fish the pebble out of the bucket. It is the size of a small mandarin, irregular, roughly pyramid-shaped. I dip it in the water to wash off the sand. It it pink, intensely pink, faintly translucent like a block of quartz.

Shit, I say. You don't mean.

There was only one way of getting it out, Goldhaven says. So, if you want your sorry, sorry you had to be the fall guy. But someone did. Preferably someone as completely clueless as you.

Why are you giving it to me now, I ask.

It's not safe with me, Goldhaven says. Everyone's after me. I've got to lie low, for a while at least. If I haven't come back for the stone within a year, do with it what you want. Though I rather doubt you'll be able to sell it.

Goldhaven gets up, brushes the sand off his trousers, and walks back up the beach.

I look at the stone. It is huge. I drop it back in the bucket. When I turn around, Goldhaven is gone.

I walk back up the beach with my bucket and spade. No one is watching. I get in the car, drive to Kaat's place. Nothing has changed. The yellow puddle on the landing has dried, or seeped into the floor-boards. The dirty dishes in Kaat's sink are still dirty. The fish called Bert looks listless among the plastic weeds. I sprinkle in some fishfood. I take the stone out of my pocket, and drop it in among the lumps of rose quartz at the bottom of the aquarium. Who could tell, now. Bert is not interested.

I steal back to my flat. The TV's still on. It won't go away now, its steady flicker. I'm too tired to do anything about it. Shampoo commercials, shower gel. Nymphs in tropical waterfalls. Jungle pools. No crocs and no river blindness. If only they knew. The news. Tom Van Wyk reporting, again. He is standing in an empty car park in front of a line of trees. Vreedesteinwoud, it says on the screen, under his name. Vreedestein forest. Grey rainclouds above him. He has a serious look on his silly boyish reporter face. He's interviewing a guy in wellies and a green polo shirt. Some sort of a park ranger. Another shot. A dead animal, tufts of fur scattered around its body. A fox, perhaps. An aerial shot of the forest. Tufts of dark green cabbage. What do they know about forests. The ranger again, painting with his hands. Big, he seems to be saying, this big. I can guess what he's saying. I'm getting good at this. At this, if nothing else. Dogs will not venture into this part of the Vreedestein forest, now. Dogs used to frolic all over this part of the Vreedestein. They used to rampage through the undergrowth, sniffing and peeing and yapping and slobbering. No one ventures into this part of the Vreedestein, now. The pang of the beast hangs about it. The joggers do a hare-turn, now, when they approach the dense stand of beech and oak that marks the outer line. The bikers skid and fall in terror as they take the turn into the vale. Since when? Last Monday, approximately, the ranger is saying. Since last Monday, a monster has been stalking the quiet glades of the Vreedestein. Dogs have disappeared, have taken their usual flamboyant loops through the undergrowth and not returned. Howls are heard, at nightfall. Pterodactyls are seen sitting in the trees. Pterodactyls? How can you be so sure? Tom Van Wyk can't believe it. He does it well, his big-eyed incredulous reporter's gasp. But they have these capes around them, and they're no birds. Just like pterodactyls. Anyone knows that. Back to the blonde in the studio. The weather. Miserable, folks, what else.

The next morning, there's a knock on the door. No, not a knock. A thud. The door gives way. Zog Shikzahl stands in my kitchen, sees the empty bottle of whisky, frowns. The first and only time I have seen any semblance of emotion on Zog Shikzahl's face.

Where is he, Zog Shikzahl says. I ask once. I don't ask again.

He has brought a tennis bag, from which he now

produces his mallet. A swift motion, and my micro-wave is an ugly knot of aluminium and cheap plastic. Zog Shikzahl walks up to me.

OK, I say. I don't know where he is. Zog Shikzahl raises his mallet.

Oh shit, I say.

You bad memory, Zog Shikzahl says. No bad words when Zog Shikzahl present.

Wait, I say, I have an idea.

Zog Shikzahl is not interested in ideas, Zog Shikzahl says. You have, I take. Man money guns girls cars. You don't have, Zog Shikzahl not interested. Boumboum, vroumvroum. Zog Shikzahl stands towering over me and swings his mallet. The malarial beasties in my head kick into overdrive. Thud thud thud, they say, quick quick quick—

22

It is Thursday. A dull gunmetal day over the Flemish plains. Crows shrieking on the edge of the Vreedestein forest, leaves turning jaundice-yellow, black puddles in the sodden soil. I stopped over at Kaat's place to fish the stone from her aquarium. The car park just off the road to Leuven is empty. I march alone down a bridlepath into the woods. There are no walkers out, today, no bikers, no riders.

The grey sky blackens to tarnished silver. The trees get denser. Thickets of browning bramble, cat-mint, black-tipped witch-gorse. Still no sign of anyone. I make a detour through the bushes, look about me to make sure no one's watching, stash the bundle with the stone in a bush.

A buzzing, swarming noise further down the

muddy track. I turn a corner, almost throw up. A carcass lies rotting by the side of the path. A very large dog, barely recognizable, a wolfhound, perhaps. Tufts of grey hair scattered over the path, splodges of red and purple jelly. The dog's throat has been bitten through. A large chunk of flesh torn from its belly. I retch, feel dizzy, walk on. A little further down the path, another carcass. A sheep, this time. Its sides have been torn wide open, the ribcage cleaned out, a tangled white crinoline. The throat has been ripped open.

There are two large shapes up in the canopies of the trees ahead. One of them jumps down, hopping from branch to branch, stands before me. It is the scarecrow.

Where's Kaat, I say.

Where's the stone, the scarecrow says with his empty voice.

First Kaat, I say.

You don't mess with the Boss, the scarecrow says, and turns around, disappears in the bushes. There's a rustle in the undergrowth. A man steps out from among the branches. He has white hair; his skin is pale and wrinkled, but he moves with an energy that makes me take a step back.

You got something that belongs to me, he says with a low, dark voice, and a West Indian accent that clashes with his pale skin. I recognize the voice from the hammock in the hut outside Marlow's, and the strange energy with which he moves from the CCTV tapes they showed on TV.

And you've got something that I want, I say.

The man spits on the forest floor.

Show me that she's alive, I say.

The man grunts. We not talking about her life now, he says. We talking about your life.

I shiver. That's not the deal, I say. Your sidekick told me. I give you what you want, you give me what I want.

The man looks through me, bored. I don't negotiate with thieves, he says. Nobody take from the Boss. Everybody give the Boss what he want. And nobody play games with the Boss. What they do in that Nickery job, he asks. He is not talking to me now but to the scarecrow.

They hustle like to be the Boss his men. They dress up to nail the Boss.

Nobody nail the Boss, Boss Macquarie says. He turns back to me. You choose. You give it now, you live. You give it later, you die. He whistles. There is a growl in the bushes behind him. A dark shape, feline, the size of a small car.

I turn around and run. I jump over roots and puddles and scramble through a small ravine, tear my jacket in the thorns. I can hear the feline crashing through the forest behind me. It will crouch, and flex for the kill, and then it will jump from behind and take me down. I think of Kaat. My plan has failed. My ankle still hurts like hell from the fall I took down Goldhaven's fire stairs. I stumble on a root as I sprint up the side of the ravine, fall over, taste the bitter black soil. A shot rings out, echoes through the Vreedestein. I hear a thud behind me, feel the earth shaking. A mass of black fur and claws lies collapsed a few feet away from me. On the other side of the ravine, there is commotion in the bushes. I hear a loud scream of rage, deep as a canyon, and recognize Boss Macquarie's voice. There is another shot. A moment's silence, then the forest breaks into cacophony. Rabbits appear out of nowhere, stripy chipmunks scurry madly through the ravine; a couple of deer raise their heads above a gorse bush and jump; a murder of crows rises from a tree behind me and starts into a fierce chant; a flock of starlings swirls around me at breakneck speed, chirping loudly. And I think I can hear the creatures in the other forest, too, Boss Macquarie's. The pink-winged aras, laying into a mourning cackle. The tapirs, snorting and jumping headlong into the river like lemmings. The caymans, floating and thrashing, jaws chomping at nothing, tails whacking out at the cruel air. The olingos, turning their comical goateed doll-heads. And the jaguars, waking startled and hurt from their digestive slumber, letting out a deafening roar, enough to make the people along the river shudder—

The vision stops as suddenly as it came. Zog Shikzahl steps calmly down into the ravine, cradling a very heavy rifle with a telescopic sight. He prods the dead beast with his boot, briefly, then says, The girl? A shape flits past, in the branches of an oak tree back where I met the scarecrow. Go, Zog Shikzahl says, and we run. Back into the copse of beech and oak. The feline is dead, but every square inch here is impregnated with its pang. Up, Zog Shikzahl says and points. I see the scarecrow flitting from branch to branch. Zog Shikzahl takes aim, then lowers his rifle. No, he says. The scarecrow flits away. Kaat, I say. We have to find Kaat. Zog Shikzahl points up again. The other scarecrow's still there in the highest branches of a beech tree. Zog Shikzahl lifts his rifle, takes aim. The scarecrow calls my name. Zog puts his rifle down again. We clamber up, painfully, branch by branch. Kaat is almost too shocked to speak. You OK, I say. Ja, she says, OK, very tired. They had that cat under the tree all the time. I couldn't come down. Where's that cat. No more cat, I say.

We have deal, Zog Shikzahl says at the bottom of the tree, and suddenly he's got his mallet in his hand again. Of course we do, I say, and lead him to the thicket where I stashed away the bundle with the stone. Zog Shikzahl takes a quick look, doesn't show any emotion as he handles the biggest pink stone in the world. OK, he says, and puts the mallet away. Zog Shikzahl got to finish job, he says. Without another word he is gone.

Where to, I ask Kaat as we sit in the car, shivering. Kaat coughs, opens the door, vomits in the car park. She wipes her mouth, sits breathing heavily for a minute, then almost smiles. It doesn't matter, she says. We drive back to my place. Cup of tea, I ask Kaat, and she nods. I put the kettle on.

I don't know what I'll do now, I say. I've been fired. It doesn't matter, Kaat says, and then there's a very firm knock on the door. Zog, I say. Now what does he want. But it's not Zog. It's the Belgian Feds, and they have a warrant. They're very polite. Désolé de vous déranger. We have information that you are keeping stolen property, the inspector in charge says. We have to carry out detailed search of this property. Une perquisition. Please sign here. And they give me a form to sign. I could try and argue with them, explain: I had it but then I had to take it to the Vreedestein forest because they took Kaat and they had crossed the Atlantic with this massive feline in their hand baggage, etc. By which time the inspector would have cut me off and nicked me for obstructing police business. So I just sign the form and let them get on with it.

There's a whole team of them, with aluminium

cases full of gear. Donc, one of the cops is saying to the inspector, la taille d'une mandarine tu disais? C'est ça, the inspector says, and then they fan out and start very politely taking my apartment to pieces. There's only one person who could have put them on to me. Goldhaven must have been desperate. Ah oui, the inspector says, turning to us, we will also be looking at Miss Pellegrims' apartment. I suggest you stay here for now. Poor Bert, I say, but the cops are not listening.

What was that question you never asked, Kaat asks, suddenly, that time in Normandy. I don't remember. Kaat says the funniest things, sometimes.

My headache is starting up again. I still have Hazel's phone number, I think. I don't know.

Он не любит Новосибирск

Endings

Goldhaven is dead.

Maybe. Or perhaps Goldhaven is sitting in the lobby of the Baltchug Kempinski, his arm wrapped round the palm-like waist of a doe-eyed beauty with a very heavy necklace. He has found his pink stones, an unlimited supply, he has made peace with the Russians. He has a vast apartment overlooking the river by the Pushkin Museum, a gaggle of bodyguards outside his door, a monster truck in his garage, a special pass to use the Zil lanes. Goldhaven has become the Russians' point man for fancies.

Maybe. Or perhaps Goldhaven is sitting handcuffed to a grey steel table in the interrogation tract of the Ministry of Finance police HQ somewhere on the outskirts of Novosibirsk, rattling off dates and places. He has had a dreadful night. Goldhaven has failed to deliver his pink stones. Zog Shikzahl has delivered Goldhaven. The Russians are not happy. The Russians have no sense of humour. If Goldhaven had known that, he would not be sitting here.

Maybe. Or perhaps Goldhaven is lying at the end of a pier on an atoll somewhere in the Indian Ocean, a very tall, very pink cocktail by his side. Goldhaven has cashed in his chips, monetized his secret stash. Whatever they may take from him, he will always have his Zurich accounts. Goldhaven knows he will never have to work again. Goldhaven has changed his name, changed his face, grown a very big moustache. Goldhaven looks ridiculous, but who cares.

Maybe. Or perhaps Goldhaven has been listed by a committee in New York, his assets impounded, his penthouse put up for public auction by the federal department of justice, his name registered in the travel-ban database of every airport in the universe. Goldhaven's trial is about to begin in the Palais de Justice, a few truckfuls of exhibits being carried up the neoclassical steps. Goldhaven, this is your life, the prosecutor will say.

Whatever. Goldhaven sits by the Sankuru river, watching the logs float past, reading his book, thinking about a very, very big pink stone. Goldhaven is the Prince of Prices, the Lord of Last Laughs.

Also published by
JM Originals in 2016

Blind Water Pass
by Anna Metcalfe

Anna Metcalfe's stories are about communication
and miscommunication – between characters and
across cultures. Whether about a blithely entitled
English teacher in a poor Beijing school, an immigrant
female taxi driver in Paris, or a young Chinese girl
spouting made-up Confucian phrases to please tourists,
the stories examine the assumptions we make about
other people, and about ourselves.

Blind Water Pass is an auspicious debut by
a superb young writer.

Also published by
JM Originals in 2016

The Bed Moved
by Rebecca Schiff

A New Yorker, trying not to be jaded, accompanies
a cash-strapped pot grower to a 'Clothing Optional
Resort' in California. A nerdy high schooler has her
first sexual experience at geology camp. On the night
of her father's funeral, a college student watches an old
video of her Bat Mitzvah, hypnotized by the
image of the girl she used to be . . .

Frank and irreverent, the stories in *The Bed Moved* offer
a singular view of growing up (or not) and finding love
(or not) in today's uncertain landscape.